Nate Rabe is an Australian-American writer who was born and educated in India and Pakistan. He has regularly written on South Asian music and photography for *Scroll.in, TheWire.in* and other publications for many years. He lives in Melbourne, Australia.

THE SHAH *of* Chicago

NATE RABE

SPEAKING TIGER

SPEAKING TIGER PUBLISHING PVT. LTD
4381/4, Ansari Road, Daryaganj
New Delhi 110002

First published by Speaking Tiger 2017

ISBN: 978-93-86338-74-7
eISBN: 978-93-86338-75-4

10 9 8 7 6 5 4 3 2 1

Typeset in Adobe Jenson Pro by SÜRYA, New Delhi
Printed at Thomson Press India Ltd.

For Deano, wherever you are.

1

Jack King, better known in some circles as Jacob Lord, or just plain Jake, stepped outside for the first time in more than four years. He felt he might float away, he was so happy. His worldly possessions—a tiny green Bic lighter, a Swiss army knife with five blades, seven dollars and eighty-five cents—all jumbled up in his front pocket, were his only ballast. He stared for some time at the recently renovated front entrance of the Pontiac Correctional Center, which looked like your typical suburban ranch house: low-hung roof of artificial tiles, yellow and pink petunias in neatly tended beds tucked up against a lush rectangle of brilliant lawn. The prison guard, glowering back at Jack from behind the plate-glass window, looked like your typical ornery suburban neighbour. Jack held his gaze, savouring the first sweet minutes of his regained freedom. The realization that he was no longer on the other side of the wall slowly soaked into him, like a warm bath into chilly bones. Counting this latest stretch, he had spent a total of ten years, three months and sixteen days behind various bars of the United States Prison Service. Enough was enough. He smiled at the guard and then gave him the finger. Taking a deep breath of the thick May air, Jack promised himself: No more jail time. Never again. Not one night. Not one hour.

The prison's parking lot was packed with vehicles, mostly rust buckets and old model pick-ups. Always was, on release day. Kids played tag among the cars, shrieking with delight at not being in school, while their mothers, dolled up in freshly permed hair and tight jeans, smoked cigarettes and waited anxiously for their men. Jack took a second to survey the parking lot until he spotted a newish Seville with a brushed bronze finish. Inside, gripping the wheel like a rodeo roughrider, sat a short man with hunched shoulders and an anxious brow. 'Thanks for coming,' Jack mumbled as he slid into the front seat.

The man gripping the wheel was his uncle. He started the car and headed towards the freeway but didn't say a word. When Jack had called from prison the week before, Uncle Jalal had said he could stay for a few days, no more than a week. Nasreen, Jack's ex-wife and Uncle Jalal's only child, was in California visiting her cousin until Saturday. And when she got back, she would definitely not want to see Jack around the house.

'Cool,' Jack had said. 'No problemo'.

Jack, or Jacob Lord as most people used to call him, had dealt a bit of coke in the pool halls and bars on Chicago's West Side but after a second short stint in Cook County jail in the mid-1980s, he moved to St Paul and tried to renounce the old ways. It took him a couple of rehab sessions—Uncle Jalal gladly coughed up the dough—but within a year or so Jack had a nice little thing going up in the Twin Cities. A taxi licence and a small shop near the university selling magazines and cigarettes. Jack began warming to the straight life. For a while, anyway. The magazine shop did a steady business when the university was in session and the taxi, on the street twenty-four hours a day, brought in five hundred easy bucks a week.

He gave up the nose candy completely and got his drinking pretty much under control, too. Within a couple more years, Jack was looking at selling his taxi licence to an Egyptian named Mo, and using the proceeds as a down payment on a small superette. He'd been watching the papers; there was one out in Coon Rapids going for a song. But then, life hit the skids again. Winters always got Jack down, and right around the end of January, in the middle of one of those polar mid-western afternoons, he got a call from Chicago. Some guy talking about a piece of fruit so fucking ripe, it was just waiting to fall off the tree. A real easy deal. They stood to make fifteen 'G's a piece, at least.

Apparently a couple of dumbfuck Nicaraguans were looking to offload six kilos of Cali cocaine of the finest grade. Jack, pretending to be an interested buyer, would set up an appointment at a motel on the Midway strip: the Forty Winks Lodge. Just when negotiations were going real good, Jack's partner was to walk in, flash a badge and act like he was leading a genuine, honest-to-God, Yankee drug bust. Thirty thousand dollars for an hour's work. 'How good is that, dude?' There was almost no way the deal could go wrong.

In fact, they had almost pulled it off, but just as Jack's buddy was transferring the coke from the Nicaraguans' gym bag to his case, the real cops busted through the door. The Nicaraguans were deported. During the pre-trial paperwork his partner mysteriously disappeared. By St Paddy's Day, Jack was a guest of the Pontiac Correctional Center.

'What will you do now?' Uncle Jalal broke his silence at last.

The world outside the Seville looked like heaven. Clusters of yellow dandelions danced in the over-grown strips of grass by the side of the highway. The sky was wider, bluer and bigger than Jack had ever remembered. The spring sun hurt his squinting eyes. 'Steer clear of prison, one thing's for sure,' he said.

'I'll believe that when I see it.' Uncle Jalal may have been talking but he was in no mood to look at his nephew. Jack had betrayed the family honour too many times for Uncle

Jalal to offer sympathy. A ride back to the city and five nights in the spare bed was the limit of 'family understanding'.

Unlike his previous stints in prison, Jack had pretty much kept to himself in Pontiac. Of course, the 'Brothers' protected him, but for the most part, Jack had been a loner. The Lone Ranger. Another name added to all the others he'd used since coming to America. So many names, sometimes it was hard to remember exactly who he was. 'Jacob' when he first arrived. Then 'Jake' when he began dealing nose candy. After he got busted in Gary trying to offload a garbage bag of Hawaiian weed, the other inmates in Cook County took to calling him 'Five-Oh', as in Hawaii 5-0.

At a time when most brothers were taking names like Raheem and Shakeel, Jack toyed with the idea of using his real name too. He could see the advantage it would bring him while he was inside, but Jack wasn't planning on staying in prison any longer than he had to. The Black Muslim Brothers would probably never see life on the streets again; they needed some sort of identity to cling to. But not Jack. Man, he'd tell himself, that's the whole point you came to this country. To put that stuff behind you. Not be proud of it. So Jack never told anyone his real name. People knew him as that fast-talking baldy guy from Chicago. Jake, Jacob, or Five-Oh. But as his release date from Pontiac came closer he decided he needed a new name for his new life of freedom and, after some thought, settled on 'Jack King'. He liked the ring of that: simple yet majestic.

'I been thinking, Uncle Jalal…' Jack said.

His uncle made an indistinct sound that revealed no curiosity. Jack looked at the old man, then shrugged and started to read the billboards out loud as they flew past the car window.

'Take a Finger Lickin' Break. Left four miles.'

'Troubled? Try prayer. Livingstone Church of Christ. The friendly congregation on I-55.'

Uncle Jalal tapped the radio and covered Jack's voice with an all-news station. For the next dozen miles neither man acknowledged the other, lost in their own thoughts.

Thinking was about all Jack had done in Pontiac. There was no doubt that he had been set up in the Nicaraguan coke deal. How else could you explain his partner's miraculous disappearance? It took months for the rage to stop swirling around inside Jack's gut, but eventually he was able to think straight and come to a few conclusions. For one thing, he realized that even if he got lucky and copped an early release date, he'd be almost forty by the time he got out. Middle age was coming on strong. Second, he had to admit that he'd been hanging out with losers for far too long. For too many years, he had been running other people's scams and what did he have to show for it? Diddly. From now on he was going to be the boss. The time had come to wield the stick, not take another beating. So finally, he promised himself that once he got out of Pontiac he was going to establish himself once and for all as a real player, someone everyone would respect. Jake was going to be the King.

He wasn't going to go straight exactly; there was no way you could sustain the sort of lifestyle Jack enjoyed as a straight arrow. But he certainly was going to find a new set of business associates. And never was he going to spend another night inside. Not one. So during those long, boring days in Pontiac, Jack conducted a survey of all the possible business opportunities he might invest in once he got out. One eye was cocked at the long-term, the other scanned the horizon for mountains of cash. It didn't take very long to see that more than any other, one business stood out above the rest: heroin. Like Chablis wine and wingtip shoes, heroin had always been, and always would be stylish. Forever in demand.

One day in the prison library he had been flipping through a *National Geographic* article on Afghanistan, when the penny dropped. Like a bolt of lightning right down his spine, the idea left him tingling. Most of the world's heroin, the article said, was being processed in factories along the border of Pakistan and Afghanistan. The illicit trade in drugs accounted for more money than the real economy of both countries put together. There was even a beautiful pullout photo of red poppy fields stretching from the edge of the page till kingdom come. For the first time in his life Jack felt like he might have the inside track. *The empire I could build.* Every night, for two years, his sleep was disturbed as he tossed and turned just thinking about it. Jack ripped the photo out of the magazine and taped it to his cell wall, right above his pillow. Every morning and night it reminded him of the beautiful future waiting for him, just on the other side of that wall.

'Like I said,' Jack turned down the volume on the radio. Uncle Jalal shot a quick glance at his nephew as if this was another insult. 'I've been thinking.'

'At least thinking is not illegal.' Uncle Jalal clipped each word; the 'T's as sharp as knives. Thirty years of life in America had done nothing to soften his accent.

'I'll need some money,' Jack said.

'Badtameez!' snapped the older man. 'Have you no manners? Asking for money after all the offers we made to help you, and the thousands of dollars you wasted in your... your filthy life!' Uncle Jalal was close to having a fit.

Jack had expected something like this but persevered nonetheless. 'Things be different now. I was young then.'

'Still you are immature. Nearly forty but what can you show for your life?' he shrieked. 'Bolo! At your age I had the restaurant and grocery plus three apartment buildings!'

Jack liked his uncle, always had, but he wasn't in the mood to listen to the usual you've-shamed-the-family-because-you're-not-a-millionaire speech. 'Not a lot. Just fifteen hundred, maybe two grand if you can afford it.'

'Who can afford to burn his money year after year taking care of a lafanga like you? Tell me? Even fifteen dollars is too much to expect from my side. Those days are over. Completely.' For the first time, he faced his nephew to emphasize that he meant what he said. There would be no more forgiveness. Over the years, as Jack, or Jacob, or whatever he called himself, stumbled from one disaster to another, the older man had always felt it his responsibility to make sure his nephew survived. He had offered his daughter for the boy to marry, found him job after job. He had stopped calculating how many thousands he'd loaned him since he had brought the boy over. It was a question of duty and responsibility to his elder brother, Jack's father. But this latest humiliation was too much, even for the gentle and flexible Jalal to bear. 'You must no longer consider yourself a member of this family.'

'Will you listen to me?' Jack whined as he swung his head around to get a better glimpse of the billboard that sped by.

Eldorado Table Top Dancers. Have fun this weekend. Up Close and Personal.

Jack whistled long and lustily. *Four years been way too long.*

'To what should I listen? More lies? More broken promises?' The Seville was nearly doing ninety. Jack told his uncle to cool it and get in the right lane before the cops forced him to. 'Don't want to see another cop in my life. You dig, right?'

Uncle Jalal had a habit of sweating when stressed. Even though the air conditioner had been on high since leaving the house, he could feel small wet beads tickling his tummy. He slowed down, but his knuckles remained white as he strangled the wheel and tried to calm himself.

'Will you purchase more narcotics? Or waste each cent on wine and beer?'

'I want to go back to Pakistan.'

Jack could see the skyline getting bigger now. Man, no

place like Chicago in the world. The Sears Tower, all those swanky high-rises and yachts along the lakefront. Wrigley Field, the Bulls, Soldier Field.

'That's what I've been thinking.'

'Kya bola?' Uncle Jalal's foot fell off the accelerator altogether; cars tooted and swung around him, flashing their lights. 'What did you say?'

'That's why I need money. To buy me a ticket.'

2

Three weeks later Jack stepped off an ancient jumbo jet at Islamabad International into the heart-stopping heat of a midsummer morning. Inside the terminal, passengers jostled, heaved and elbowed each other on their way towards passport control with the determination and pace of spermatozoa swimming towards the womb. Tempers were short and the ceiling fans were busted.

'Next,' yawned an Immigration Officer with a handlebar moustache and watery canine eyes.

Jack swaggered forward with his head cocked to one side and tossed his passport onto the desk, like a pack of cigarettes onto a bar.

The officer detected a hint of stale alcohol. He stared as Jack rubbed his bloodshot eyes with an open palm and then picked at a food stain on his white cotton shirt that hung out of a pair of stiff new jeans. On top he wore a double-breasted blazer: dark blue with faux brass buttons. His shoes were shiny black wingtips, just out of the box. No socks, the officer noted.

The Immigration man held Jack's passport open with one hand. The photo on the front page matched the face before him now: balding head, medium build, delicate ears with detached lobes. And a smile, floating somewhere between murderous and mischievous. Jack's eyes weren't red in the photo though. They were soft, pale brown...almost see-through. Two muddy whirlpools.

'Your birthplace?' the tired official asked.

'What?' Jack seemed surprised to be addressed.

'In which city you were born, sir?'

'This shithole.' Jack reached up to retrieve his passport but the Immigration man pulled it away.

What's with this dickhead? Just stamp the damn thing and give it back. Got to piss something awful.

'You are American?'

Jack's eyes narrowed. 'Damn tootin'.'

The Immigration man didn't respond; just kept studying the passport, then the man standing before him, slowly flipping through the pages of the document, staring vacantly at each pink and blue page.

'It's the genuine article. Issued in Chicago last week.'

The officer was beginning to piss Jack off. Stress always came to his feet first, making his toes stand up stiff, like the ears on a gazelle suddenly alert to danger. He registered his dislike for people in the toes and over the years he learned to depend on the vibes they sent him.

'This is your passport?' the officer asked, still thumbing through the pages.

'What's that supposed to mean?' Jack's big toe was erect, chafing against the inside of his new shoes. He flared his nostrils at the Immigration man.

Before leaving Chicago, Jack had considered using his old passport but thought better of it in the end. Every federal and state computer, probably every county computer between Chicago and LA, and as far east as Boston, had the name 'Jacob Lord' hidden in one of its databases. In all sorts of columns: possession with intent, grand larceny, attempting to impersonate a police officer, jumping parole. He would have been less visible with an electronic tag around his neck and a Santa Claus hat on his head, than with the old passport. With some of the money Uncle Jalal had given him, he was able to score a fake Social Security Card through an old contact in Calumet. The new passport, made out in his new name, had arrived a week before he was scheduled to depart.

On the plane, Jack had added some more flesh to his plan. He would need two months, three at the most, to tie everything together. Peshawar, up on the Afghan border, was thick with smugglers and heroin factories. Head up there first thing, impress everyone with his foreign ways and sophistication. A deposit would get him the first shipment, which would pay for the second. Three or four shipments of the best smack in the world and Jack would really be King. The King of Chicago. Thirty-five thousand feet over the Persian Gulf, sipping a vodka and orange juice, Jack smiled at the thought. *Sweetness!*

There was a problem though: he only had slightly under fifteen hundred bucks. Uncle Jalal had insisted on buying the ticket—'No loan Jack, it is a gift. I'm so happy you are going home'—and gave him two thousand dollars. More cash than he'd seen in four years but hardly enough for a down payment on a consignment of heroin. As hard as he tried to think of another way, Jack knew that the only place he could locate the kind of money to make his plan a success, was with his family. But getting his hands on even a tiny bit of their millions would not be easy. Uncle Jalal was one thing, Jack knew every one of his buttons; he'd been pushing them for years. But he barely knew the rest of the family.

Jack's half-brother, Shafi, lived in Singapore where he ran the family's Southeast Asian interests. They had never been close and in fact, hadn't seen or talked to each other in more than twenty years. Lina and Mina, the twin sisters, had both married doctors and settled in suburban Toronto. Connection with them had been severed when Jack was locked away for the first time, back in the late 1970s. Jack's mother had died before he'd moved to America and his father, Ali Hassan Shah, adviser to the Prime Minister, multi-millionaire hotel-keeper and all-round industrialist of Pakistan, hated his youngest child with a passion unbound. Jack would have slit his own throat before asking the old man for a penny.

Uncle Jalal may have had a soft spot for Jack but even he wouldn't have agreed to buy Jack's ticket had he known about his nephew's plan. Only Nanima, his mother's mother, might be sympathetic. She had been the only one to cry when Uncle Jalal had taken him to Chicago and every year, without fail, she sent him a garish card to commemorate Eid. The day he was released from Pontiac, Uncle Jalal handed him four of them, wrapped together with a rubber band. His only mail in four years. Before leaving, Jack had tucked one of the envelopes with his grandmother's address into his pocket. She was his only hope.

'It is stated here that your birthplace is this place,' the Immigration officer still wanted to know where Mr Jack King had been born.

'My father is Pakistani, least was, last time I saw him. But me? No way, Jose. Red, white and blue all the way!'

The Immigration man picked up a heavy stamp with a well-worn wooden handle and slammed it down on the first page of the new passport, as if he was killing a snake. He took one last look at the photo, then slowly handed it over.

'Take it!' he snapped. But as Jack reached out, the Immigration man grabbed his wrist and said, 'You have no socks.'

Jack glowered at him, trying to fight the rage that cut through his gut. He yanked his wrist free and pulled away from the desk. Jerk.

'Next,' barked the Immigration man.

Jack dropped his bags onto an airport trolley and shuffled towards the rank of yellow-and-black taxis. Before he got halfway across the road, cabbies were over him like white on rice, pulling his arms, grabbing his luggage, yelling unintelligible things in his face. Despite his protestations, Jack was deposited into the backseat of a new Daewoo. Memories of the Casa del Amour massage parlour back home flooded over him as the driver slammed the door. Cheesy pink plastic roses protruded from the dashboard. Brown velvety curtains on the back and side windows. About as much light as you'd find in a darkroom. But what really clinched it, was the aroma of overly sweet perfume. Jack closed his eyes and, for a second, caught a glimpse of Mitsy, the cute one from Manila—her stockinged legs crossed, pouting teasingly. Beckoning him with a thin index finger crowned with a long pink nail. *Hoo wee!* More than four years without a woman. There in the backseat of the taxi, for just a moment, Mitsy seemed real. But when he opened his eyes, the only person in the taxi was a huge man with pockmarks on his potato nose. He turned the ignition key.

'Hold it,' Jack pulled off his blazer. 'How do you breathe in this heat?'

Slate-coloured clouds were moving in at a steady pace, darkening the early morning sky. The monsoon would break any day now. A fat crow shrieked as it swooped down, right by the taxi's window. Jack jumped. Other taxis were honking, the drivers were yelling for the Daewoo to get a move on.

The driver wiped his wet forehead with his sleeve and squinted, searching his brain for an English word. 'Islamabad?' was all he could come up with.

Jack reached into his blazer pocket and pulled out a packet of Kents, which he handed over to the driver with a nod that he should help himself. 'Hold on. I got it here.' He pulled out a crumpled envelope from his pants, unfolded it and held it up so the driver could read the address. 'Granny's place. Nanima.' Jack stabbed a finger at the address. 'Take me there.'

Twenty years. Twenty-three and a half to be exact. Nearly twenty-five. A quarter of a century! However he counted it, he had been away a long time. Jack pulled back the curtains to check out the countryside. Beyond the black tarmac lay dry fields, low boxy buildings covered with Urdu advertisements and a few scraggly trees, their leaves brown and heavy with dust. Jack had tried to erase Pakistan from his mind ever since leaving all those years ago, so he couldn't say what he expected to find, but the colourless, simmering landscape before him seemed to fit. One big, faded black-and-white movie.

That was the way he always remembered Pakistan: in black-and-white. White was the colour of his mother's favourite daisies in the garden. And of her burial shroud. Before she died, she used to sit in the garden with Jack, giving orders to the gardeners, telling them how far back to trim the rose bushes and how much water to give the elephant-eared plants.

Jack's mother, Tahira Akhtar, had had a plain face with intense almond-coloured eyes. Her frame was slight and her ears pronounced. These three features she had passed on to her son. Jack never tired of gazing at an old, creased black-and-white photo of her, taken in a studio in Rawalpindi. He kept it in his wallet, noting how much he looked like her. But the feature he remembered most fondly, was her voice. In all his years, he had never heard her raise her voice at him, his father or the servants. She spoke Urdu with the grace of a Dilli poet and English with the intonation and accent of the upper class. Each word was exactly right for the sentence, which she delivered with a soft assurance. Whether it was bedtime, when she pulled Enid Blyton off the shelf to read to Jack, or tea time—enchanting her lady friends with Persianized couplets to make her point—Jack found the rhythm and rhyme of her voice intoxicating. He could listen to her for hours. And he never remembered what happened in the Enid Blyton stories about the Seven Friends up a Tree or whatever, because he was far more interested in the music of her voice. It was from his mother that Jack began to understand that speech was both identity and power. When Ali Hassan came home tipsy or began to let his temper fly at the stupidity of a business partner, or later, the temerity of his devilish son, Tahira Akhtar would coax him gently to peace and quiet with her words.

And the magic worked on him, too. Even though she was indulgent when it came to letting him have laddoos from the sweet-maker in Sadr Bazaar or gudhas from the kite-wala on Murree Road, there were times when she refused her son's demands. And when he began to pout or whine she would immediately draw him close and whisper in his ear, 'Beta, now don't be upset. You know one time Mullah Nasruddin was walking in Bokhara and he came across a little donkey braying and crying by the side of the road. The Mullah asked the donkey, because you see, in those days, donkeys were able to speak with humans, "Why all the commotion?"

"The donkey replied, "Until yesterday I was a happy boy going to school with my friends."

"'Well, what happened?" asked Nasruddin.

"'My school is near a sweet-maker's shop. And each morning he makes laddoos that are round and sticky and so sweet. And each morning I steal one or two."'

At this point, Jack would laugh and say 'No. No. I know what you are going to say. That he ate too many laddoos and turned into a donkey.'

'Why a donkey?' his mother smiled, her eyes twinkling.

'Because donkeys are stupid. And to eat so many laddoos every day is also stupid.' Jack nestled into her breast, having forgotten all about the laddoos.

'You're my smart little boy.' Tahira Akhtar hugged her son and gave him a kiss. 'I don't want to take a donkey home. Now come, it is getting late.'

How many times in prison, alone with only his thoughts, had Jack felt like his head was in her soft, comforting lap? He had been her last and slightly unexpected child, and she loved him with a special tenderness. Her scent, warm and clean, came back to him often, as he grew older. If there was one thing he wished for, more than any other, it was that he could see her just one more time. Or maybe just hear her wonderful voice say that she loved him, before she turned out the light.

After she died, Jack's father became twisted and life turned black. The garden, his mother's passion, became a shadowy and frightening place, as did the hallways of the old house. How many times, when the old man was in a bitched-up mood, did his belt—thick and glistening black—slither down his waist and strike? How many times in the blackness of night had Jack been coaxed to sleep by the hate for his father?

Twenty-five years. May as well be 2500.

The taxi veered off the highway into a tiny bazaar. They inched their way through lanes barely wide enough for one car. Local residents went about their morning business oblivious to the steady stream of cars, mini-buses and trucks that choked their streets. Jack positioned himself exactly in the middle of the backseat to get the best view out of both windows, and also, to not be too close to either door. Who knows what these people are capable of? *Stick their hands in and make a grab for my watch, or I might catch something. I mean look there. Guy's throwing up right by that kid who's taking a leak and oh my God!* Jack turned away when he saw a scrawny dog humping another one which had only three legs. Ugliness and ignorance. The very reasons he'd left this country to begin with.

The narrow alleys widened into a street riddled with potholes. 'Where we at?' Jack could hear how bad his Urdu accent was, but who cared? He had already decided that he was going to use only as much Urdu as he needed to get by... like with this cabbie. Otherwise it was English all the way. Not even English. Not the language he learned in Hallbourne Academy all 'wherefore art thou' and 'what a smashing idea!' No, he was going to speak his own language: American. Damn right, buddy. Good old Americanese.

Movement became impossible. Vehicles, traders' carts, animals and masses of the public gummed up the street. The driver turned off the engine and waited. Dripping with sweat, Jack contemplated getting out of the taxi for a breather, but was stopped by a weird sensation. Suddenly, his body felt as light as a feather and his heart took off at a sprint. All the heat, ugliness, chaos and full-throttle noise of the street began closing in on him, pressing him down. Somewhere outside he could hear a policeman yelling at a bus driver: 'Your headlamps are not working. One hundred rupees fine. Pay over there.' Hawkers seemed to be screaming the price of their wares from inside his head. The sounds of the noisy world outside were muffled but in a way that made him feel cold and scared, like something was separating him from it. Everyone was on that side. Over here, he was all alone. The black-and-white movie had turned into a bad acid trip, with a soundtrack cranked up way too loud. A shiver started in his toes and worked its way up through his body. His skin turned clammy and the hairs on his arms stood up. He lay down on the seat and rubbed his eyes. Icicles poked through his skin. The driver's bloodshot eyes glared at him from the rear-view mirror like a hungry octopus. Jack clenched his eyes and breathed hard. He started to pray, but then, just as quickly as it had come, the feeling passed. His head thumped and his ears rang.

What was that? He rubbed his temples and sat up. *Man, this is too weird. I've come back to hell.* If he could have, he would have told the driver to turn around and take him back to the airport. But they were moving forward again, carried against their will. His head, the traffic, the world, everything was out of control.

They entered a leafy neighbourhood right at the foot of the hills. The taxi stopped outside a fat, multi-storeyed house with a marble exterior and a black wrought iron gate at least nine feet tall. The cabbie jumped out and opened the trunk to recover Jack's bags, but Jack couldn't believe his eyes. 'Holy shit,' he muttered.

As Jack got out of the car, a guard with a red turban and starched white uniform strode forward and asked firmly, 'What business?'

'I'm looking for Nanima.' Jack stared at the house. There had to be at least seven or eight bedrooms in that place. *And get a load of that marble!* He walked towards the gate but the guard immediately jumped between him and the house.

'Are you mad? Who do you want to meet?'

'Mrs Wahida Akhtar.' Jack was searching the pockets of his blazer. *Where'd I put those shades?* 'That's some marble. Make the blind see.'

The guard snapped to attention. 'One minute, sir.' He jumped back into his sentry box and after a few seconds stuck his head out. 'What is sir's name?'

'Mr Jack King,' said Jack but added quickly, 'Tell her, her grandson is here. All the way from America!'

Jack still couldn't believe his eyes. A mansion…and just

four weeks ago home had been a nine-by-six cell in Pontiac Correctional Center. *Good thing I kept that envelope.* An old mango tree, spread like a giant umbrella, shadowed the gate. The front lawn was being trimmed by two boys who jumped around on their haunches, tending to rose beds and pots of leafy green plants. A prehistoric push-mower, with its twisted blades gummed up with grass, was propped against the concrete wall bordering the compound.

Another man emerged from inside the mansion and greeted Jack. 'You are Begum Wahida's grandson? From America?' Jack nodded, still taking in the size of the building and expanding the scope of his plan by the second. 'Most welcome, sir. Begum sahiba, your nani, is very pleased you have come.'

'How is she?' Jack asked as he stepped forward, leaving the turbaned guard to deal with the bags.

'She is old and sometimes is becoming ill, especially in rainy season. Arthritis, sahib.'

'Jack to you…Jack King.'

'Excuse me, sir?'

'My name is Jack. Mr Jack King. Don't call me sahib. Understand?'

'As you like, sir. Jacking. Very good name.'

Jack stopped suddenly and shot his arm across the man's chest. 'Let's get this correct from the git go. I'm not jacking,' he made a masturbatory motion with his hand. 'It's Jack King. Two words. Jack. Followed by King.' He lowered his head and glared at the man over the top of his Raybans.

The servant nodded gravely, unsure what sort of creature he was ushering into the house, one who made such nasty gestures in public. 'Jack. King. Of course, sir.' He opened the giant, sculpted wooden doors and stood aside. Jack stepped into a darkened room. Air conditioners hummed in the dimness. The servant closed the door, kicked off his sandals, motioned Jack to sit down, then hurried upstairs to inform the lady of the house that her grandson was waiting.

Jack looked around the grand living room. The chintzy baroque furniture was painted white, gold and a shocking shade of pink. He'd never seen so many lace doilies in his life; on every piece of furniture, under every lamp. The sofa had gilt legs and green-and-white satin upholstery. The chairs had overstuffed seats and stiff backs and looked most uncomfortable. They reminded him of heavily made-up teeny boppers at their first dance. A mirror with an elaborate white and pink frame hung the entire length and breadth of one wall. The lampshades were ornate, oversized and stitched up tight. In the middle of the menagerie, like a bulldog guarding the room, stood a squat coffee table with an onyx top and stout, shiny brass legs.

Absolutely pitiful.

'Beta, is that you?' a thin, frail voice came from the shadows to his right. Startled, Jack turned quickly, nearly giving his grandmother a heart attack. Her face was accordioned with wrinkles and her teeth were nearly all gone. Behind the glasses—lenses as thick as bottle bottoms, heavy black plastic frames—a pair of soft lively eyes blinked up at Jack. *Man, she's got to do something about that beard.* But as soon as his grandmother reached out a creased, shaky hand and touched his face, Jack couldn't stop his tears.

3

'Your journey has exhausted you, hai na?' Nanima spoke a refined dialect of Urdu. Though she would never presume to wear expensive clothes, Nanima's entire demeanour was that of a cultured dowager who only rarely ventured out into the practicalities of life. She passed most of her day in recitation of the Koran and prayer, leaving the running of her palatial house to a handful of servants whom she bombarded with alternating doses of disdain and tenderness. 'Why your father did not inform me, beta?' Nanima set her frail body down into an armchair with a puff of old age. Although she had been schooled in the British colonial educational system, Nanima refused to speak English. She had always considered it distinctly inferior to mellifluous Urdu.

Jack considered for a moment what language he should answer in. 'He doesn't know I'm here,' he said eventually, picking out each Urdu word with care, hoping he was putting them in the right order. The last time he had spoken his native language regularly had been during the first couple of years in America, when he was married to Nasreen. But as their relationship fell apart, more often than not, the only words they had for each other were curses and insults. When he finally moved out of the house, he left most of his things behind in a closet. Just slammed the door on everything. Including Urdu.

'You are surprising him!' Nanima made a wrinkly smile. 'He must be so proud of you. Look,' she gave Jack's cheek a weak tweak, 'so handsome and smart you are, but beta, did someone steal your socks? Thieves will steal anything, hai na? Their blood is that way.'

'Nanima, Father and me...' Jack paused. 'Father does not speak to me. Not a word since 1987.' He said the year in English. He'd completely forgotten how to say numbers that big.

'Tobah!' Nanima grabbed her ears in horror and Jack prepared himself for an onslaught of recrimination, but instead, she said, 'Such a selfish man that Ali Hassan. Greedy as well. His stomach is never full...always gobbling up more and more. And see!' she stopped to catch her breath. 'His very own children are left without adequate clothing.' Jack's sockless feet still held her attention.

Suddenly, he was wrapped up in Nanima's frail but surprisingly firm arms. This time she was the one in tears. Years ago, after his mother had died, she used to do this sort of thing all the time. 'She is gone but she is watching us, beta,' Nanima used to say, stroking his hair until he fell asleep.

'You have made me so happy, beta. So happy you have come to see your old nani,' she sniffled with joy.

Her attitude toward Jack's father came as a pleasant surprise. Jack knew that he was going to need a sympathetic ally if his scheme was going to succeed but to find one so soon...well, he told himself, the plan is just meant to be.

When she recovered, Nanima gushed forth, slipping between Punjabi and Urdu, with the occasional word of English tossed in. She told her grandson about all the marriages, deaths, court cases and mental cases that had hit every branch of the family, most of whom Jack had never heard of. As she spoke, Jack considered how to bring up the reason for his unannounced return to Pakistan. How to get her to shell out the cash. *Does she even have the dough? She's got to...look at this place. The servants and that Land Cruiser in the drive. She's got it but how do I get my hands on some of it?*

Nanima was explaining how a cousin, Shahid, had a house in F7 that was vacant and how he had been meaning to clean it up and sell it. 'But I will make sure he gives it to you, beta. You can live there indefinitely.' She told the houseboy to bring the phone so she could call Shahid right away and tell him the good news. Her grandson had come back from America, so handsome and smart and all.

'Nanima,' Jack coughed. He set his cup on the squat onyx-topped table and adjusted himself in the uncomfortable chair.

'Ji, beta. What is it?'

'I'm happy to stay here with you. Don't bother Shahid. You see I'm back, but not for long.' He cleared his throat. 'Two months only, three at the most.'

'After a lifetime you return for three months! Stay three years, then we can think of releasing you again.' She reached over and pinched his cheeks. 'So sweet you are, beta.'

'I'd love to, really, but you know how it is. The reason I've come…is business.'

She was motioning urgently for the houseboy to bring the phone. 'We are a business-minded family.'

'I've come here to make some contacts. The business will be in Chicago. Where I live in America.'

'But what sort of life are you living there?' Nanima shot yet another glance at Jack's feet. 'Are you married again? Who is looking after you? Tell me beta, eh? There is more to life than making money. That is where your father went wrong, beta. Isn't it? You forget business for some time and just relax here in your homeland. Your associates can manage your affairs while you are here. Shahid is saying the world is all remote control now, push this button from Karachi and the money flies to London. Fsshhh,' she made a hissing sound with her old lips and an unexpectedly lively sweep of her arm. 'No need for walking about, this and that. You stay in Pakistan and do your remote control button, push-push, from here.'

'I'm here to meet some people who can help me expand my business.'

'Who are these people?'

How could he tell her the truth? That his 'associates' were ex-cons, flake dealers and junkies. Big-time losers and scam freaks.

'I have a few names. Some ideas.'

She commanded the houseboy to dial a number then grabbed the phone from him while he was in the midst of doing it. 'Ideas...names...' she muttered. She let loose another galloping string of words to someone on the other end of the line. Shahid, probably. The name didn't ring a bell. *Whose kid is he anyway?* Nanima hung up. 'Shahid will come round just now. He's so happy that you are here again.'

'Who is Shahid?'

'Auntie Hafeeza's eldest, beta. Shahid Malik. He is a big journalist.'

The sketch did nothing for Jack. 'I feel strange to impose on someone I've never met.'

'Families never impose. What nonsense you speak, beta. Go wash now. Shahid will be here soon.' She terminated the conversation with another grand swooping gesture.

Jack hadn't counted on doing the social rounds. The prodigal-son-comes-home drama. *I just need to get the cash, set up the deal and get back to Chicago.* Plus, Jack wondered, how much did this Shahid know about him?

Shahid, twenty-eight years old, editor of the *Capital Crescent* tabloid, feudal scion, single, overweight and bored—wore a light cotton waistcoat over white shalwar-qameez and finely crafted leather sandals. His pudgy cheeks suggested a person accustomed to excessive comfort. His expression reminded Jack of a puppy, eager to please and waiting for a pat of reassurance. Nanima had said Shahid was glad to have Jack back in town, but it was obvious that his cousin had never heard of him until she had called.

The houseboy laid out another round of tea and cakes but Jack didn't touch the stuff. He was thinking it was time for a Bloody Mary or even just a beer. Shahid asked Jack about his business and said that he hoped to visit America himself next year, after he got married. His English was good but you could tell by the way his eyes stopped moving around in his tubby face that he had, at times, found it hard to follow Jack's rapid American. They talked and shared a couple of smokes from a packet of 555s. 'A British brand,' Shahid said with pride. To Jack, the tobacco tasted stale.

'You are most welcome to stay in our house in F7. Only we will need some time to carry out the necessary repairs.'

'I'll be gone by the time the place is ready...don't bother.'

'You must stay for some time with us. Don't disappear so quickly. We are your family.'

Jack knew he wouldn't be able tolerate too many happy conversations with long-lost cousins like Shahid. 'I've come back to take care of business, not for a family reunion. No offence.' Jack picked a tiny piece of dry tobacco from between his teeth and smiled numbly at his cousin.

That was the very reason he'd left this screwed-up excuse of a country in the first place, to get away from people like Shahid. People who tried to act sophisticated but smoked stale English cigarettes. People with absolutely no clue about the world beyond their air-conditioned sitting rooms filled with doily-covered, overstuffed, ghastly furniture. People who liked to invoke the word 'family' so they could get you to act and think like them. What did rich boy Shahid understand about the life Jack lived back in the States? Scrambling, hustling, no back-up, no safety net. No one to lean on. Families don't impose, Nanima had said. Though he respected his granny, Jack's experience had taught him that imposing was exactly the thing families did.

'I'm in and out. Lots of contacts to make, things to sort out. Won't have time to set up house.'

Shahid shook a gold watch that dangled from his wrist, checked the time, and figured he'd almost reached the point where he could get back to work without being too rude. He lit another cigarette and asked, 'What is your business in Chicago?'

'Diversified services,' said Jack, surprising even himself.

'What sort of services?'

'Commodities. Purchasing and distribution. Some logistics. Whole shooting match.'

'Business climate is good in Chicago?'

'Excellent. That's why I can't stay too long here.' Jack was searching the room for a piece of furniture that looked like a liquor cabinet. Nanima had always been a strict Muslim but Nanaji, her husband, had died of a bad liver. Maybe, Nanaji had left some booze behind in some forgotten nook.

'Who are your contacts, may I ask?' Shahid exhaled through his nose then itched the end of it, as if the smoke tickled him.

Jack mumbled that he'd be meeting them soon; Shahid didn't pursue it. He was interested in leaving now; his time was up.

'Okay, Jack, I'm off. Very nice to meet you again. I will contact Nanima about the house. Khuda hafez.'

Jack waved weakly as Shahid closed the door behind him. 'Diversified services. Distribution and procurement. Damn, I'm good!'

The soft but steady monotone of his grandmother reciting her prayers in her room upstairs woke up Jack, who had fallen asleep on the sofa. He shivered. The tears that morning had come from some place inside he didn't even know was sad. But he had felt warm and safe, like a child again, when Nanima hugged him. But now that he'd had a nap and realized where exactly he was, Jack was having second thoughts. *You're a fish out of water here.* For a second, he saw the lakefront in Chicago and his favourite bar, Guido's Italian Saloon, down on Division Street. He was sipping a glass of Chablis and shooting the shit with whoever happened to be hanging out. A depression, as clammy and shadowy as the clouds outside, came over him at the thought of having to spend many long evenings in this strange, boozeless city. *Don't know a goddam soul. How the hell am I going to make it?*

Nanima finished her recitation and came downstairs for dinner but by eight, she was back upstairs in bed. There was nothing on TV except for some Urdu soap opera. The news came on saying that the Prime Minister was on a trip to Singapore and Malaysia accompanied by key advisers. In one of the group shots of the delegation, Jack caught a glimpse of his father, smiling like a hungry fox, standing right behind the Prime Minister. Maybe the Prime Minister's plane will crash and kill every last one of his key advisers. The Pakistan cricket team had lost its second One Day against Australia. The weather report predicted that the monsoon would start within forty-eight hours. When the news was over, a panel of men with serious expressions, in waistcoats, furry hats and thick brush-like beards set about discussing some fine points of Islamic law. Is it Islamic, Jack wondered, for fathers to beat their sons?

The phone rang.

'Hello,' Jack said.

'Is that you, Jack? I am Shahid speaking.'

'No, this is Nanima. Jack can't come to the phone...he's lost his mind already.'

'Haha, right. Of course, a silly question.' Shahid seemed bouncier than this morning. Could he be a bit tipsy?

'What's up?' Jack was glad to talk to someone, even Shahid.

'There's a party going on, at Mads and Nita's place,' Shahid said. 'He's Danish and works for the UN and she's Bengali and does nothing except get stoned all day. Haha. Haha.'

He was tipsy, no doubt about that. 'What you waiting for, my man? Let's party.'

'I'll come pick you up soon. Cheerio. Haha.'

4

Jack was impressed. Real impressed. The last car he had owned was a rust bucket Gremlin with a dented right side panel. 'Could get used to this,' he said as he made himself comfortable in the grey, soft leather front seat of Shahid's silver SLX 230. By the time they arrived, just after eleven, the party was in full swing. A deep, ballistic thud of music speckled with high-pitched giggles and shrieks welcomed the sleek Merc into the dark end of the street.

At the front door a gangly red-faced Scandinavian was slapping guests on the back. 'Shahid baby! Welcome. Nice to meet you, Jack. The bar is open and dinner is on the table soon.' He pushed the new arrivals into the crowded living room like sheep into a railcar. On the dance floor Jack could make out shadowy figures jerking irrhythmically. An old Gipsy Kings tune was blasting through a pair of over-taxed speakers.

Jack looked at Shahid and mouthed, 'Dinner?'

'Welcome to Islamabad,' Shahid nodded enthusiastically, scanning the room for familiar faces. 'Drink till you collapse, eat till you vomit. Haha!'

In a far corner of the big room, behind a linen-draped table stood a man in a white waistcoat who couldn't stop yawning: the bartender. He dispensed drinks like a commando distributing hand grenades. Jack watched as he reached into an iron washtub filled with icy water, grabbed a can of beer, ripped off the tab, chucked it over his shoulder and slammed it into a waiting, open palm. Shahid ordered a vodka and 7UP, Jack took one of the man's alcoholic grenades.

As one tune faded into another the two cousins stood against the wall, sipping their drinks, taking in the scene. Shahid was telling Jack something about one of the guests who had just walked in, badly drunk, but the music was too loud. In a few minutes Shahid's knees bent and buckled and his shoulders twitched as he tried to locate the music's groove. Jack pretended not to notice. *What if someone sees me with this loser?*

In Chicago, Jack's drinking was done at Guido's Italian Saloon, or if he had wheels, at a franchised watering hole in some suburban mall where the junior college girls wore short skirts, drank too many Rusty Nails and threw up in their handbags. He hadn't been to a private party like this for years. Seemed like ages ago. Before the nose candy had fucked up his head. 'Thought this country was a booze-free zone,' Jack was nearly yelling to be heard.

'Officially, Jack, only officially,' Shahid shouted back. 'There is official Pakistan,' he jerked his hands to one side by way of explanation, 'and hidden Pakistan.' Another ambiguous gesture. 'Without hidden Pakistan no one could survive official Pakistan. Haha.'

'Hypocrites,' Jack hissed but Shahid had moved away to talk to someone else.

Jack downed his beer, crumpled the can and let out a deep, cracking burp right onto the lithe neck of a woman wearing dangling pearl earrings and a pair of tight jeans on her finely formed backside. 'Ooh, mama,' Jack moaned as he moved towards the bar for another round. The lady turned and screwed up her nose before whispering something to the man standing next to her. He reached down and gave her bottom a reassuring squeeze. Jack asked the bartender whether he had any tequila. A few seconds later, after slamming down two shots, Jack reoccupied his position against the wall. Shahid was still talking to someone in a dark corner. Mixed with the music, the booze was beginning to relax Jack; the depression he had felt earlier in the evening was fading fast. In fact, he felt so relaxed, he reached out and gave the young lady with the tight-fitting pants a friendly little squeeze of his own.

'Arrey, haramzade!' she turned and hissed. 'Bastard!'

The girl's boyfriend turned towards Jack who kept leaning against the wall, one leg bent at the knee as a prop, smirking. The boyfriend told Jack, in Urdu, to watch himself, then added to her that he didn't know how locals ever got into these parties anyway. He pulled the girl further into the crowd.

'What did you say, man?' Jack stepped forward. 'You saying I'm a local? Is that what you're saying'?' He moved forward one or two steps. The man with the girl hadn't expected this. He muttered, 'Cool it, man, take it easy,' but that only fuelled the fire burning up Jack's gut. 'I just stepped off the plane from Chicago this morning, dickhead. You know a village around here by the name of Chicago?' He slipped his hand into the inside pocket of his blazer and swooped out his passport. 'Check this out, man. This strike you as a local passport?' Jack moved his balding head to within centimetres of the other man's face. But just then Bob Marley started singing everyone's favourite, 'Buffalo Soldier,' and the man and his girlfriend slid away, onto the dance floor.

Shahid grabbed Jack by the shoulders and said, 'Cool it, Jack. Come finish your beer. I'll introduce you to someone.'

Back against the wall, Shahid made sure Jack had a fresh beer and said, 'Never mind, she's a randi, sleeps with anyone.' Jack wrenched the flip top off the beer can and swallowed hard. What a rush! Another big gulp. What an asshole!

'Jack,' Shahid was saying again, 'meet Andy. Andy this is my cousin Jack.'

'Nice to meet you, Jack.' Andy, who was short, with a ponytail and goatee, stuck his hand out. Jack took it warily; he didn't trust people with hair on their faces.

Andy smiled but kept his eyes on Jack, like he was drilling for a secret. If someone had stared that way at Jack in prison, he would have punched the guy's lights out without thinking. He sensed his toes stiffening. He looked around for a place to put his beer, so he could get a good swing at Andy, but then he breathed deep and remembered: he wasn't inside any more. Life on the outside, where people did things for no particular reason, still took some getting used to. Inside, this guy would have been squashed like a gnat.

Jack exhaled deeply and said, 'Intense eyes, dude.' Andy nodded slowly. 'Where you from?' Jack asked.

'Richmond. Virginia.' Andy also had a habit of bobbing his head slightly as he stared. 'Originally. You?'

'Greatest city in the whole US of A. Chicago, Illinois.'

'Originally?'

Jack stopped and gave Andy another hard look. But before he had time to get worked up, Andy twirled a thick joint between his fingers and said, 'How about a smoke?' and moved towards the back door.

Andy said he'd come to Pakistan a few years ago as a backpacker but really liked the culture, so stayed on. He lived in Peshawar, where he worked with an aid organization providing services to Afghan refugees displaced by war. When he'd arrived, the camps were pretty much winding up and the aid agencies were moving on to other disasters. But then the mujahideen started fighting amongst themselves, and now it was boom time again. Refugees were coming back for the second time. The money wasn't great but the cost of living was low. 'My dream,' he told Jack, 'is to build a cabin on a piece of land I've been watching for years. In the Blue Ridge Mountains in North Carolina. I've checked the place out already, the land is available, right next to a little river, with a fairly good access road. "Cosy Nook." I've already decided the name.' Andy took a big hit off the joint and was silent for a second or two, then said, 'Only thing wrong with dreams is most of them aren't worth a rat's without money.'

'I hear you,' Jack said, 'loud and clear.'

'What about you? What brings you to Islamabad?'

'Family ties. My granny lives here.' He took the joint from Andy and sucked hard.

'So you are Pakistani, then? Originally.'

Jack hesitated, letting the hot smoke sink deep into his lungs. When he thought he was about to pass out he exhaled, straight up into the dark blue night. 'That's right.' He felt as if he had just confessed to some horrid crime. There was another pause before he added quickly, as if to lessen the gravity of the confession, 'But I never visit. This is the first time in twenty-five years.' Andy's head was bobbing again. 'And with assholes like that in there,' Jack made a gesture with his thumb towards the house, 'once I'm gone I won't ever be back.'

'How long you here for?'

'Two months. Three maximum. Quicker the deal's done, the better for everyone concerned.'

'I thought you said family ties?'

Jack didn't respond but looked up at the sky, which had cleared to reveal a swathe of twinkling stars. You could see all the way to China from this very spot. So clear and so clean.

'What's your other name,' Jack asked. 'Andy what?'

'Gunnar. Gunnar Andersen.' Jack looked at Andy in disbelief. 'My family's Norwegian. They came to the States in the '40s. So that explains that.'

'Gunnar.' Jack made a pistol with his thumb and forefinger

and said, 'Bang bang!' Andy had obviously seen that before; he didn't even smile.

'Wanna know my real name? I mean, it's Jack here in my passport.' He pulled out the thin crisp booklet but realized it was too dark to read, so stuffed it back into his blazer. 'Jack King. 6456 Artesian. Chicago. My official name. That's me. But wanna know my original name?'

Andy shrugged and said, 'Sure, why not...'

'Yaqub Ali Hassan Shah. See I changed Yaqub, which is Urdu for Jacob, into Jack. Though at one time I was called Jacob or Jake also. Anyhow, Jack is for Yaqub and King, my second name, comes from—'

'Shah. Urdu for emperor. King,' Andy said.

'Hey, you know the lingo. That's great, Andy. Great.' Jack finished off what was left of the joint. 'So that's how I got my name. Jack King.'

There wasn't much more to say. A strange feeling settled over Jack. He felt exposed. Had he given away too much? For a second, he panicked; you never spoke about that kind of stuff in prison. You kept to yourself and revealed nothing to anyone. But suddenly, it had tumbled out before he knew what was happening.

When Andy suggested they go get more drinks, Jack eagerly agreed. But at the table, the embittered bartender said, in Urdu, that there was no more tequila. Jack pretended he couldn't understand and kept repeating his order. But when people started looking around at him he settled for a big glass of vodka, which he downed straight. Then he grabbed two more beers, popping one in his blazer for later.

Two women had just walked in, their long dupattas nearly scraping the marble floor. They both lit up cigarettes and one disappeared towards the bar. Gorgeous. The one waiting for a drink had long black hair pulled back tight, almost reaching her waist. Jack had no doubt about the colour of her eyes even in the darkness: green. Like freshly felted pool tables. Her skin was fair, almost milky, but she was definitely not European. She was balanced on the most outrageously sequinned pair of spike heels he'd ever seen. Her purple and gold shalwar-qameez wasn't cut like the dowdy tent-like ones he remembered his aunties wearing. This one followed each curve of the body and seemed to emphasize her long legs and full breasts. Jack knew he was staring, but what the hell! Four years without so much as a whiff of a woman gave him the right. The woman's full lips, painted a deep shade of violet, seemed made for nibbling. And her smile sparkled as brightly as the flash on a camera.

Andy was huddled up in a chair in the corner, talking to someone. Shahid was on the dance floor but Jack pulled him away to the side. 'Who's that?' he said, nodding towards the woman with the green eyes.

'Afroz. Nice, eh?'

'She free? She married?' Jack was looking at her again. Her lips were settling gently onto the rim of a big wine glass.

'Married? Don't pull my leg, yaar.'

'Thanks, cuz. All I need to know.' Jack shoved him back onto the dance floor and moved to the other side of the room to take up a position close to the woman. Three men, in their mid-fifties, had made their way over to the ladies as well. They were chuckling, offering the girls Dunhills and lighting them with big clunky lighters. Jack listened to them speaking English in their heavy Pakistani accents.

'You must be knowing that Arshad here is pukka sharabi.'

'Sharabi kebabi, yaar. All the ladies are mad for him.'

Losers.

Her friend returned the joker's banter but Afroz seemed disinterested. Jack wanted to hear her voice. He was sure she wouldn't have a Paki accent—each sentence creaking under the weight of Urdu and Punjabi slang. He wanted to introduce himself and offer her another drink, but the gross letches weren't moving away. Hours seemed to pass while he waited, but everyone seemed to be enjoying themselves.

Or maybe they weren't. One of the men, the joker, was starting to move in on Afroz. He was tall—huge compared to Jack—with a flat face and big white teeth, the kind you saw in toothpaste ads. His hair was parted down the middle and hung slightly over his ears, giving him the appearance of a thatched cottage. His hands, Jack noticed, were hairy at the knuckles. One of those hands was moving down behind Afroz, getting ready to cop a feel. Jack shuffled out of the shadows towards the group. He caught a whiff of Afroz's perfume as he passed but didn't stop. He pretended he was heading for a point across the room and made sure to clip the jerk with the Colgate smile. The creep immediately lost his balance and fell onto one knee. His friends laughed and the girls squealed in surprise. Jack wheeled around, as if he had been the one knocked down, and stood over the man on the floor. 'Can't get any at home?'

The men's faces turned pale in unison, then maroon, and for a moment all they could do was stare at this guy they'd never seen before at any of Mads's parties. One of them started to say something, when Jack said, 'Take a hike, pecker.' Still, no one moved.

One of the men whispered to his friend, 'Afroz has no brothers, does she?'

'Move it!' Jack hissed again.

The dance floor was still. Andy looked away. Shahid cursed under his breath and made a move towards his cousin but Jack saw him coming and said, 'Piss off, Shahid. This man's an asshole. He's bothering Afroz here.'

'You've had too much to drink, yaar. Please.' Shahid was urging Jack to back down. Afroz and her friend had melted into the dark room.

'I'm fine,' Jack sputtered. 'I'm having a great time, just want this jerk-off to stop bothering Afroz and her friend, that's all.' He turned towards the men, who, having figured out that Jack was not Afroz's brother, decided they wouldn't let the little gandu faggot get away with this. One of them handed his drink to the other and stepped up to Jack.

But they were dealing with Jack King. Ex-con and veteran of the Illinois State Correctional System. 'Waiting for a bus, fuckface?' Jack pushed the newcomer away. 'They don't run this time of night.' Another push sent the second man to the floor as well. The crowd gasped in horror but Jack could hear a few laughs, too.

Shahid helped both men to their feet, then rushed Jack towards the door. 'Are you mad? Do you know who that is?' he fumbled for his car keys as he pulled Jack down the lane.

'Who gives a fuck? He's a loser.' Jack felt euphoric but confused. 'That was good shit Andy had. He's a nice guy, Shahid. A real nice guy.'

'And Mushtaq Gill is a real bastard.'

'Who's Mushtaq Gill?' Jack was sitting with his legs spread out wide in the front seat of the SLX. 'Lots of legroom in these babies.'

'Mushtaq Gill is the Director General of NIA. National Intelligence Agency,' said Shahid, slamming his door. 'He's the one you just pushed to the floor, Jack.' He jammed the Merc into gear and squealed out of the lane towards home.

They whizzed through the dark streets of Islamabad. It was like driving into the centre of the earth, Jack thought. Or outer space, maybe. About ten minutes passed before Jack said, 'Are we in trouble, Shahid?'

'Not me. But you? Of course.'

5

Mushtaq Gill was hunched deep down in his leather swivel chair. He was listening to the cricket commentary on the radio. Pakistan was 123 for seven and set to lose yet another game. The third in a row. 'These Australians,' the commentator was saying, 'just don't know when to let up.' In a fit of disgust, Gill switched the radio off, preferring silence to bad news. Nothing seemed to be going right these days. Pakistan's glory years as the kings of cricket were far in the past. His brother Razaq's bid to be the exclusive distributor of Jaguar cars in Pakistan had stalled, probably because of the scheme of that corrupt sycophant Ali Hassan Shah. And then, to top it off, some ill-mannered freak without any socks, had humiliated him in front of half of Islamabad at the party last night.

Director General Gill had forced himself to laugh about being pushed to the floor. And to demonstrate that the little bastard, whoever he was, couldn't deprive him of having fun, he had been one of the last ones to stumble home. An out-of-focus memory of Afroz and him holding each other tight and swaying the night away kept gnawing him. Was it an accurate reflection of what had actually happened or the latest in a series of daydreams? Ever since he'd first laid eyes on her, nearly a year ago, Gill had filled his mind with Afroz-fantasies. He had first seen her at a late-night dinner party hosted by a retired Brigadier who had been appointed Ambassador to Kenya. Afroz was accompanied by her uncle but spent most of the evening moving from one part of the crowd to the next. Gill had followed her with his eyes, as if she were a shooting star and could make his dreams come true. She wore a delicate gypsy bracelet around her right ankle which tinkled with every move. The rest of the ladies were decorated in glittery gold brocade and garish jewels; their faces discoloured with lipstick and powder. Afroz stood out, however, by her presence, which was as assured as a peacock in full fan. Her open, intelligent eyes neither fell away nor leapt with naked loneliness when a man approached. For months, he had been haunted by those eyes. And of course, the tinkling anklet. Whenever they crossed paths at parties and functions he always made it a point to spend a few minutes chatting with her. Telling her jokes and reciting spicy couplets.

But what chance did he stand with her now? She was a different sort of woman, Afroz was. Recently returned from England, she volunteered at a number of local charities, even managing one for recovering addicts. She was well connected and came from a good family. Though she was a regular of the party circuit she was somewhat aloof. But she was also chaloo—everyone said so. The way she smoked those cigarettes so openly and confidently, blowing the smoke here and there like a dragon. Wah! You knew what she really wanted in her mouth! The image of her holding the slender fag in her fingers and sucking on the filter with those full red lips. 'Turns you on, no?' he said this to himself.

'Would you like me to turn on the air conditioner, sir?' One of the Director General's many deputies had walked in unnoticed, holding a small notebook with a ringed spine in his hands.

Startled and embarrassed, Mushtaq Gill snapped, 'Have you found the information I requested, on a certain newly arrived foreign-influenced gentleman?'

The deputy flipped open his notebook and said, 'His

name is Jack King, sir. American passport, issued last month in Chicago, valid for the usual ten years. Address is Artesian Ave, Chicago, Illnoise, sir.'

'No 'S'.'

'Excuse me, sir?'

'Never mind. American eh? Thought he was pukka desi. A pure local. Browner than a pie-dog's turd.'

'I have only stated the information listed on his passport, sir.' The deputy closed the notebook and took a seat without asking his boss's permission. 'There is other information I have uncovered which upholds your theory.'

DG Gill sat up in his chair, placed his arms on the thick glass top of his desk, and nodded at the deputy to continue. The officer re-opened the notebook and explained that Mr Jack King was in fact, as DG Gill suspected, a Pakistani. He had left the country almost twenty-five years ago. As far as records showed, he had never returned in the intervening years, even for a visit. 'His father,' the deputy cleared his throat as an indication that bad news was approaching, 'is special economic adviser to the Prime Minister. Ali Hassan Shah.'

If his underling had identified Jack King as Osama bin Laden, Gill would not have been more surprised. He gasped for air, leaning back in his creaky swivel chair to steady himself.

For decades, Ali Hassan Shah had used his money and influence to worm his way into the lap of successive Prime Ministers and Presidents. For twenty years he had been the unofficial Minister-Without-Portfolio to every government—military or civilian—that had ruled Pakistan. No matter how many governments collapsed, how many cabinets were reshuffled or how many ministers sacked, Ali Hassan Shah remained. His secret lay in the belief that ultimate power resided with the man who paid the bills. In his years, he had loaned military governments money to buy fighter planes from the USA, and civilian governments huge amounts of cash to rig the election in their favour. Party loyalty and political ideology meant nothing to Ali Hassan Shah. In a country notorious for its instability, his presence in the corridors of power was considered bedrock. Over the decades, Ali Hassan Shah's already considerable wealth had swallowed up nearly every lucrative foreign concession and distributorship—from hotels to telecommunications. He was a one-man monopoly. New operators, like Mushtaq Gill and his brother Razaq, who had been eyeing the Jaguar concession for years, had virtually no chance of landing a major deal.

The Gill brothers, though, were not quitters. Through their company—Dhamaka International—they persisted to bid, year in and year out, for foreign concessions. Though every time they registered their tender, properly researched to undercut the nearest bid by kilometres, Ali Hassan Shah inevitably wound up with the deal. Land Rover and BMW, the best luxury hotel chains and most of the mobile phone networks, were all a part of Shah Enterprises Ltd. Only meagre scraps—mostly Korean and Russian joint ventures—were left for the likes of Dhamaka International to nibble on.

It wasn't that Mushtaq and Razaq Gill didn't have money. What they lacked was power and influence in their otherwise privileged, leisured lives. As Director General of the NIA, Mushtaq Gill was still the puppet of politicians, a well-paid chaprasi, nothing more. He had the power to investigate, arrest and detain but only after word came down from on high. On the other hand, in addition to controlling the best foreign joint ventures, Ali Hassan Shah advised the Prime Minister. Everyone knew that he was the power behind the throne. As such, Mushtaq Gill and his entire whispering army of agents and informers were about as frightening as plastic chess-pieces. As long as the Prime Minister extended his confidence, Ali Hassan Shah was untouchable. Gill hated his rival and it was his life's mission to unseat the fat bastard and appropriate his influence. With that sort of power, Mushtaq Gill was sure, girls like Afroz could never refuse his advances.

The Director General fumed in his swivel chair. Just the mention of Ali Hassan's name upset him. Was there no escape from the creep? Business was one thing, but now he was popping up in personal matters. 'What brings the little bastard back after all this time? Don't tell me he's joining forces with papaji?' The scenario of the father being reinforced by wealth from abroad would certainly spell the end of the Jaguar deal.

'Business, yes. So he claims. He's here to identify investors for business in America.' Mushtaq Gill's broad face flushed with panic.

'Ali Hassan is not yet aware that his son is in the country,' the subordinate continued. 'Neither does the son, as far as our contacts tell us, want him to know. They have not spoken to one another for more than twelve years. Family feud, sir.' The man paused for a second.

'Continue! Who told you to stop?' Mushtaq Gill sensed hope tickling his stomach again. He rapidly wheeled forward in his chair, giving his deputy a momentary fright.

There was a report, the deputy said, that had yet to be confirmed, that Yaqub Shah, alias Jack King, was a criminal element in America. The servant in the family house swears that he heard Mr King's cousin, Shahid Malik, complaining to his Nanima that he did not want to give his house to a man who had spent time in jail.

'How interesting.' DG Gill felt better the longer his minion spoke.

The deputy closed his notebook. He had finished his report and was waiting for his boss to issue further instructions. But DG Gill wanted time to think. He dismissed his junior and spun around to gaze at the car park directly below his office window. This time it looked beautiful. In each spot he saw a shiny new Jaguar. This one red, that one black. A convertible here. One with a sunroof over there. A most wonderful sight. And in the spot where he imagined his very own shimmering, blindingly white Jaguar would be parked, he saw the sign:

RESERVED FOR ADVISER TO THE PRIME MINISTER.

6

As Nanima sucked a piece of bread between her two reddish gums, Jack considered the events of the previous night. Some people you just can't help. The guy was a douchebag.

Jack watched his grandmother in silence. Her wax-textured, sharply creased skin and her head of snow-white hair exuded comfort and dignity. What did it matter that she could hardly see or that she had facial hair? She'd been the only one who ever really cared. After his mother died, it was Nanima who had raised him and shown him affection. Jack wanted to put his arms around her, like she had put hers around him yesterday, as a way of saying thank you; but he didn't.

Unexpectedly, he remembered a trip to Murree when he was ten. His father had to go to Karachi on business and, as usual, he'd left Jack alone in the house with the servants. When Ali Hassan Shah was in the house the servants were meek mice, never raising their voices, or airing their opinions. They swallowed his insults and physical outbursts in silence. But when he was away, they exacted their revenge on the boy. Jack had no choice in what he ate or when. Desserts were banned and the comic books were locked away. If Jack protested, they would inform his father when he returned that he had been a natkhat and misbehaved every day. Jack would then be whipped by Ali Hassan.

Just as Ali Hassan was pulling out of the driveway, Nanima arrived in Nanaji's chauffeur-driven Toyota Corolla. 'What about the little one?' Jack heard her ask his father who laughed, and then nodded at his driver to keep moving. Nanima hurried into the house to find Jack at the breakfast table playing with some cold scrambled eggs. 'Come, beta, come with me. Your father won't be back for three days. Shall we go to Murree?'

'No!' Jack didn't like adults or their suggestions.

'Come, beta, we'll have fun,' Nanima caressed his hair but he pulled away.

'Leave me alone. I have to finish my homework.' Jack pushed his chair back and was going to run upstairs to his room. As he was about to turn away, he noticed that Nanima had signalled for the cook to come out of the kitchen. The man, a tall Pathan with stooped shoulders, came out staring at his feet, but still managing to glare at Jack as he did so.

'Is this breakfast for a young boy?' Nanima asked. Before the man could open his mouth she was telling him to bring toast, butter and lots of jam. 'And don't come out until you have boiled some milk and put two spoons of Bournvita in it. The young raja needs energy and strength, not cold eggs. Do you eat cold eggs in your house?'

The cook shook his head.

'Then why do you think such a young sweet man, the future master of this household should eat such rubbish? Is your tongue made of stone, Ghulam Nabi?'

'No begum sahiba, but...'

'Keep quiet. Who told you to speak? Your tongue is like a lizard's, always slipping out of your mouth. Hurry now! Do as I say or I will be telling Ali Hassan some stories when he returns.'

The cook disappeared. Jack watched this in wonder. Nanima tousled his hair and said, 'In Murree I will arrange for you to ride a horse. What do you say, sweet beta?'

In Murree Jack rode a pony around the hillside for a whole day and in the evening, he went to the cinema with Nanaji to see Mohammad Ali's latest movie. On the other days, he accompanied Nanima to the bazaar and watched her haggle with the Kashmiri nut-sellers and pick out the sweetest plums and ripest tomatoes. Nanaji, though he didn't approve, was forced by Nanima to give Jack five rupees to buy Archie comics at the Central Book Depot. The three days ended, it seemed, just as they were beginning. Jack hated going back to Islamabad and the big empty house and the servants and his father. He knew both the servants and Ali Hassan would be angry that he'd gone away from the prison they had constructed for him. He was sulking as the Toyota Corolla headed down the hill towards Islamabad. Nanima watched him for some time, sensing his sadness. 'Arrey beta, don't pull such a long face. You are my raja. No one will be allowed to mistreat you.' She gave his cheeks a pinch and then squealed as the driver swerved to miss a family of goats that pranced onto the road. Jack laughed.

'Nanima,' Jack said. The houseboy was clearing the table and Jack was anxious that he did not hear what he was about to say. The old woman looked at him through her thick lenses, with eyes magnified several times over, looking like marbles at the bottom of a glass. 'I have to ask you something.'

She nodded, oblivious to the tea spilling over the sides of her cup.

'What you said yesterday. About staying in Pakistan a bit longer than planned. You may be right, this may be a good place to do some business.'

'Your father will be pleased but, of course, he'll never tell you,' she sipped her tea loudly.

'But all my capital is tied up, you see,' Jack started but then stopped. He took a quick deep breath and began again, 'I'll need some help getting started.'

'I already have arranged with Shahid for you to stay in his house.'

'He's a nice boy, Shahid,' Jack nodded. 'I didn't think I remembered him when you mentioned his name yesterday but now I do...he was the only cousin I thought about when I was in Chicago.'

Nanima smiled.

Jack smiled weakly back. 'But I'll need more than a house.'

'Your grandfather's jeep is just sitting there, beta.' She raised an infirm hand, waving it in the direction of the driveway. 'Old age means I don't get outdoors much. Shahid comes here almost daily to check on me. But your father, he's too busy to visit more than once or twice a year. Never calls me to his house for khana or any function. You can have William as well. He's a very careful driver.'

How am I going to bring this up? One hundred thousand dollars was not a thing you could just ask your old granny for, just like that, over breakfast, without her asking a lot of prickly questions.

Two half-chewed pieces of bread lay on Nanima's plate like disembowelled prey. She let loose a victorious, distinctly inelegant burp and beckoned the houseboy from the kitchen. Jack knew he'd have to ask her now, otherwise the moment would be lost and she'd be caught up in prayers all day.

'I need a hundred thousand dollars...to start up my business here. You know...now that I'm going to stay and use your car and live in Shahid's house.' He tried to act casual; tried to capture the tone his father used to employ when he talked to his brothers about their latest scheme.

Ali Hassan Shah arrived in Pakistan after the Partition, as a refugee with no more than three rupees in his pocket. He used to tell Jack about the rivers of blood that ran through the train carriages, and how he and an uncle had to lie face down in the stuff, pretending they were corpses, in order to stay alive. Marauders—Hindus, Sikhs, even Muslims—attacked the refugees, stealing everything they owned, whether it was valuable or not. Near Ambala, Ali Hassan's father had been captured by a gang of Hindu thugs whose leader's teeth had rotted away from chewing paan. He was led away along with other men and never came back. His mother wouldn't stop screaming until a pock-faced Sikh ran her through with an ornamental sword. Ali Hassan and an uncle were left to fend for themselves. The uncle miraculously still had some money. They bribed a railway official, who allowed them to join a silent and petrified group of women in the ladies' compartment. As the train crawled west towards Lahore, Ali Hassan could make out through the slats of the shuttered windows dead bodies, hundreds and thousands of them, stacked up like funeral biers along the road. 'What saved me was uncle's bribe. Without that money you would not be alive today,' Ali Hassan used to remind Jack. 'Listen to what I tell you, boy. Money is not something to be squandered. It has power. It is power.'

And Jack had listened in horror to the stories of Partition; at least until his mother died. The few rupees he got as pocket money he saved, in an old creased envelope stowed in the back of his shoe cupboard. He kept his little stash a secret, determined that should a time of horrific violence come again, he would have enough for his own bribe and maybe save his father's or mother's life. But then his mother died and the old man started belting Jack almost every day. Jack tried to find a pattern to the lashes but there was none. When Ali Hassan had been drinking, the episodes were inevitable but also somehow less intense. His violence would exhaust him quickly and the booze made him unstable on his feet. When Ali Hassan was stone sober but cold with rage he was most terrifying. Grabbing his son by the throat and pinning him to the wall he would growl and moan and heap his complaints upon Jack. So and so had cheated him and 'Why are you so small? Because of your troublemaking your mother left this world to live in peace. You've also deprived me of peace, little Satan.'

Initially, these episodes were rare but as the months passed, they started occurring most nights. The only way Jack felt safe was to run across the road to where Nanima lived. Jack's understanding of his father's Partition tales changed. The world was a madhouse, full of violence and cruelty. His mother was gone and he no longer worried about saving his father.

A year after his mother died, Jack pulled out his envelope and stuffed two years' savings—ninety-five rupees—into his pockets. His first idea was to tag along with Nanima's cook when he went to the bazaar and buy packets of biscuits and bags of candy, stacks of *Archie* and *Billy Bunter* comics, and wind-up racing cars and helicopters with twirling propellers. But how to explain the sudden presence of all his purchases? His father demanded that Jack get his approval before he spent even four annas. So Jack thought up another plan. Every two weeks the maali lit a fire in an open field, behind the back wall, to burn off the trimmings from the rose bushes and household rubbish. Jack sometimes helped the gardener by tossing in wads of paper or old tin cans from the kitchen. On the day of the next fire, Jack waited until the flames had died down and the maali had returned to other chores inside the compound. With his life savings stuffed under his sweater, Jack ran outside, round the back wall. He stood on the edge of the pit. He felt the heat radiate softly onto his face and inhaled the woody smoke, falling into a slight trance as he watched the fire smoulder. A dog barked next door rousing Jack from his trance. He pulled the notes out from under his cardigan and handful by scrunched-up handful, he tossed them into the burning pit.

As he watched his money burn translucent and then opaque, before quickly disintegrating into grey ash, he decided that his father was an asshole, even though he never knew of such a word. He would never again value money in the way his father did or in the way he had been taught.

However, the casual way his father had talked business and large sums of money had made a huge impression on Jack. That was something he was never able to erase. As easily as other boys' fathers talked of cricket or films, all the talk in Jack's home before, during and after dinner was about money. Late at night, when it was too hot to sleep and the crickets and dogs took turns keeping him awake, Jack would listen to Uncle Jaffar and his father talking about buying the Shabistan cinema in Rawalpindi for two hundred thousand rupees, or whether Flashman's Hotel was really worth the one million and a half that Mr So and So was demanding. As if they were talking about peanuts or popcorn.

Jack tried to reproduce that tone now, as Nanima looked up at him in surprise.

'One lakh dollars is what I need to get me started, even though double that would allow me to start expanding right away. My partners in Chicago will wire the amount to your account in the next few months. It's just that my assets are… frozen. But only temporarily.' She seemed surprised by the chilly reference. 'That's the technical word they use, Nanima. Not literally frozen. Not in ice.'

The houseboy had appeared to help the old woman up to her room but Jack shooed him away; he didn't want anyone else around during these sensitive negotiations.

Nanima wearily looked into her grandson's eyes. He wished she wouldn't do that.

'Your father loves money more than he loves his children but I have never understood such thinking. Your Nanaji was a wealthy man but he never abused anyone. All our money comes from the land…'

Nanima has been brought up in a wealthy ashraf landowning family in India. She had never wanted for anything as a child and agreed without complaint to be married into a secular family though she was herself very devout. When she and her husband arrived in Pakistan in 1948, they got off the airplane loaded with suitcases of cash.

'…What is money, beta…' the old woman sighed with a sense of detachment that only the permanently wealthy could manage.

Jack picked up her line of argument. 'A necessary evil, nothing more,' he said truthfully enough. Jack wasn't interested in money for its own sake, like his father. He liked the lifestyle it afforded—coke, booze, ladies, good times—'One lakh dollars is nothing, I know. But it will help me in my business.'

'How much is one lakh, Yaqub beta?' She refused to call her grandson with that stupid English name. Jack was about to tell her that one lakh meant one hundred thousand, when she said, 'What is ten lakhs? Or even one hundred? When your heart is pure, a single sikka is a fortune. If your heart is full of darkness…' she paused, thinking of Jack's father. She still could not forgive herself for marrying her daughter to such a man. 'For blackhearts even ten crores will never satisfy. They will always be hungry for more.' She paused to catch her breath. Her tender, tired eyes held him softly. 'Your Nanaji told me when he was alive that after his death he did not want me to worry for money. He built this house, purchased that jeep—I never sit in it but twice a year to offer prayers at his tomb—and set up a fund.' She seemed to be readying herself for her prayers.

'What sort of fund?'

The old woman seemed to have a form of secret communication with her servants because the houseboy appeared again, as if out of thin air. She told him to bring the kaghazaat, documents, from upstairs. He disappeared for a few minutes then came down with an oval Cadbury's tin which he handed to Nanima, before expertly slipping back into the kitchen. 'Everything is in here. What does money mean?' she shrugged her shoulders and clenched her eyes shut. 'God is great,' she whispered.

Jack reached into the tin and pulled out a handful of folded papers, some stamped and sealed with red wax. Pages and pages of typewritten legalese. 'Begum Wahida Akhtar Zam Zam Trust,' Jack read aloud. Granny nodded. 'What is this, Nanima?'

'Beta, my husband was a good man. Yes, he indulged in sharaab from time to time and I beseeched Allah tallah every day that he would read his prayers but who can know why this request was unanswered? In the last years he did keep the fast, you know. Yes, he was a good man. This fund he decided upon himself. It is to help poor Muslims make the pilgrimage to Mecca and other holy sites, so they may taste the sacred water of the well, the Zam Zam.'

Jack scoured the papers. He had only half heard what his grandmother said. Most of the documents were in English and he was quickly able to make out that the Zam Zam Trust was set to go into operation after Nanima's death. It was administered by the law firm of Rahman, Khan and Ahmadzai Ltd, (Head Office: Peshawar). Jack was reading fast and aloud. One document was dated a couple of years previously, the year Nanaji had died. Jack pulled out some more papers until he found a financial statement issued by Habib Bank valid as of December the year before. 'Total balance...Jesus H. Christ!' Jack did a quick calculation in his head, then re-counted the decimal points, touching each one with a shaking finger to make sure he had got it right: eight million dollars!

'A lot of money in this little box, Nanima.' Jack fumbled with the lid of the chocolate tin. He was telling himself he should have asked for her for half a million. He dropped it to the floor and broke the spell.

Nanima said she was tired now. She said she would talk to Shahid about loaning Jack one hundred thousand dollars for his business start-up.

'What's he got to do with this?' Jack asked. 'I don't want him to be bothered. He's already letting me use his house, I don't want to burden him further.'

Nanima tutted that he shouldn't be so silly, Shahid was a nice boy. 'He always does what I ask.'

'But Nanima, there is so much money in your fund.' Jack had pulled the lid off again and gazed at the papers in amazement. 'Shahid told me his family has got lots of things going on...business-wise, at the moment. He can't spare the cash.'

She looked at him with an expression that said, he told you that?

'And besides I may need more than a hundred thousand... depending on how the investment pays off and...you know...I don't want to bother Shahid over and over again.'

'Okay, beta. Let me call Ahmadzai this afternoon. He must approve it.' She beckoned to the houseboy to help her retire up the endless flight of stairs.

'Now who are you involving? Just give me the cash...the one hundred thousand, and I'll start my business immediately. Who is this Ahmad—whatever?'

'Inayatullah Ahmadzai, beta. He is the manager of Zam Zam Trust. Each month he releases money for my expenses, for the servants and the food. The bijli bill.'

'Well, tell him to release one lakh this month. Your expenses have gone up temporarily.' Jack was aware that he had lost the casual tone of his father. His voice croaked with desperation.

'Read the documents, Yaqub. It is all stipulated there. All the rules. I must take rest now.' She moved slowly towards the stairs, holding on firmly to the houseboy's elbow, and sighed, 'Old age…such a curse.'

Jack took out the papers again, spread them on the table and began to read. His grandfather had made a packet or two over the years and, Jack figured, before he died he must have come down with a serious case of the guilts. He'd never been much of a Muslim himself and so had set up the Trust in his wife's name, to help poor pilgrims fulfil their religious duty as some sort of a spiritual insurance policy.

The 'pund', as Nanima called the Trust, was administered by an agreement made between Jack's grandfather and a law firm in Peshawar: Rahman, Khan and Ahmadzai. The agreement itself was, in the event of the death of Mr Yusuf Mahmood Akhtar—Jack's grandfather—to be administered by Mr Inayatullah Ahmadzai, MA, LLB, who had sole and perpetual power of attorney as Trustee to dispense of the funds in accordance with the agreement. In order to minimize the burden of financial transactions and worries on the Trust's namesake, Mrs Wahida Akhtar, Mr Ahmadzai was the only person permitted to amend the agreement or cancel or suspend any of its clauses.

Jack made a mental note to look up Mr Inayatullah Ahmadzai when he made his trip to Peshawar. He jotted down the law firm's address, stuffed the documents back into the tin and leaned back into the chair. He lit a Kent and inhaled deeply.

Life was just tits.

7

After converting the most recent bank statement into dollars—there was exactly 8,300,702 dollars in the fund—Jack got Andy's number from Shahid and gave him a call.

'When you headin' back to Peshawar?'

'Tomorrow or maybe today...not sure.'

'How 'bout right now, daddy-o?'

'Now?'

'I've got wheels and I've got a driver. You got the smoke. Let's toke!'

Jack was antsy. The plan had been to acclimatize himself in Islamabad, get a feel for the scene—maybe, a couple of weeks—get the cash together, hit Peshawar, cut the deal and get the hell out of Pakistan for all time. But the Trust documents had put a spanner in the works. Now, he would have to go through this lawyer, Ahmadzai. He needed to see him right away, to get his hands on the money and keep his plan rolling. Jack had been revising the amount of cash he'd need upwards, ever since he'd opened the Cadbury tin. After years of blowing most of his chances, Jack was determined not to let this one slip away.

'What's the word, my man? Ready to boogie on down?'

Andy snickered when he heard the phrase, then coughed a short, dry smoker's cough. 'Yeah, I 'spose. I'm at the Margalla Guest House, right on the main road. I'll be ready in an hour.'

The road to Peshawar, the last town before the Afghan border, was narrow, rutted and molten with traffic. Driven by madmen and dope heads, fat tubular buses dominated the tarmac like a clutch of heavyset matrons at a wedding party. Outrageously done up in glittery silver and shimmery metallic hues, they threw their bulk about and honked with a belligerent authority. Every time a bus roared narrowly past, air horn blaring like an express train, anger formed a ball in Jack's stomach, but William, Nanima's driver, just smiled and shifted gears.

Jack had imagined that the trip to Peshawar would be relaxing and fun, like driving up to the Wisconsin Dells on a summer morning, but instead he was gripped by the fear of a sudden and messy death. When William wasn't playing dodge-'em with the buses, he was slamming the brakes to let herds of stiff-legged goats trot across the road, or avoid children racing on to the highway to retrieve their footballs.

Suddenly, a long red and green bus with a large wart of people hanging out of the back door, pulled up next to the Land Cruiser and hesitated, before lurching sideways and forward at the same time. William slammed on the brakes with all his strength. Jack's bald head thudded against the windscreen.

'Sorry, saab,' William said.

'Shit, close one,' Andy exhaled. The joint he had just lit fell from his hand.

'Goddam country,' Jack was rolling the window down furiously. He stuck his head out into the muggy morning and screamed, 'Fuckin' morons!'

'Your country people, saab,' laughed William. 'Too much crazy.'

'Their asses be arrested in the States.'

Andy told Jack about his theory: that the locals were actually better drivers than in the States, where everything was laid out. These guys had to use their minds and generate their opportunities and be creative just to get to their destination.

Jack told Andy that his theory was full of shit.

William restarted the car and bumped back onto the tarmac. For some time, they drove in silence. The sun was high and hot air was flowing into the jeep, but Jack was too angry to roll the window back up. He glowered at the pale, washed-out dustscape around him. They drove through a range of crumbling yellow clay hills. Jack could taste the dust on his tongue. Big men in starched turbans with long tails rode small grey donkeys. Where were they going? Jack couldn't see any sign of human settlement in either direction. The only industry seemed to be brick kilns with tall red chimneys poking up towards the blank sky in groups of three or four.

The more brown faces Jack saw—the lunatic coach drivers, that scumbag cop at the party the other night and even William, who couldn't stop smiling—what the hell was so funny?—the more agitated he became.

He heard a voice inside him say: You're exactly like them.

Not true at all! Another voice yelled back.

'Hey, William. Pull over,' Jack barked. 'Right there,' he was flapping his hand, 'there by that tree.' As soon as William stopped, Jack jumped out and began kicking the tree trunk as if he might knock it over. Andy rolled down the window and together with William, watched him explode with violence. After a few minutes Jack lit a cigarette and sank to the ground with his head in his hands.

Though stoned, the sight of Jack curled up so tight concerned Andy. He hopped out of the jeep and sat down next to him. Stretching out the joint as an offering, he said, 'Your feet must be killing you.'

Jack inhaled deeply and said, 'When I get upset I feel no pain. Like I'm in another world or something, know what I'm sayin'?' He released the smoke from his lungs in a long stream. 'I don't feel too much,' he said tightly, as he took another hit. It hadn't always been that way. He used to feel lots of things before he'd been sent up to prison. Happy, relaxed, even sad. Most of all, he remembered feeling free—not always tense and nervous, waiting for something to go wrong. But these days, the only thing he seemed to feel was anger.

Andy was bobbing his head like he understood but he was curious about something else. 'I was just seeing...you're not wearing any socks. Don't those shoes cut into your feet?'

'I like it that way,' Jack's pale eyes narrowed, telling Andy to back off. He took another deep hit, laid his bald head against the tree and closed his eyes. He grimaced as he held the smoke inside for a minute. Suddenly, popping his eyes open he said, 'I still don't get it, man. Why would anybody choose to come to this sorry excuse of a country?'

Andy grunted vaguely.

'I'm here 'cause this is where I got some family. But why the fuck you would come here? Just because—'

'I suppose I was looking for adventure. Virginia isn't the most exotic part of the world.'

Jack turned towards Andy at last, and though his expression was blank, it looked like he wanted Andy to keep talking.

Andy had been raised in an immigrant home by parents who believed in liberal politics and the glories of capitalism. He had been taught that others, especially those in poor countries, needed help to get rich. But also that wealth was something to grasp and aspire to. 'Our home was full of a weird kind of 1960s idealism and I was encouraged to help others when the time came,' he said. 'I studied anthropology at the university and—'

'What-pology?' Jack interrupted with a sarcastic grin.

'Anthropology. The science of human societies.'

Jack's grin changed to a bitter laugh. He shook his head disapprovingly. 'You tellin' me society is a science? You actually studied that bogus shit?'

Andy gave a weak smile in return. He'd loved college and anthropology and felt an urge to jump to its defence but instead merely nodded, 'Yeah, I know.' He picked up a stone and tossed it across the highway.

'Go on, dude,' Jack laughed again. 'This is rich.'

After graduating from college Andy had worked for local community groups helping homeless kids and some greenie groups. The pay was low but Andy had found working with people and being able to help them the main reward. Money, the other great family value, was something that didn't seem so important. How could you dedicate yourself to getting rich when right in your backyard there were children suffering and dying?

Andy had had a lot of discussions about this with his younger brother, Erik. He believed that it was every man for himself. 'He was one of those people,' he said to Jack, 'who had a goal for everything in life. He made a plan for the week, the month and the year. His life was laid out in a spreadsheet. He didn't do a thing unless it was written in a box and had a date by it. He was determined to be the CEO of some big accounting firm.'

'I can dig that,' Jack perked up. 'I got a big goal myself.'

Andy had put his brother's absolute dedication to attaining great wealth down to immaturity. He kept working with the homeless and whenever he got together with Erik for a drink, would try to persuade him of the ultimate hollowness of the life he was pursuing. It was a duty he took seriously as an older brother and didn't miss a chance to try to convince him to do something more responsible with his life. But Erik didn't listen. He became, in quick succession, the youngest regional manager in his company, bought a BMW and a couple of years later, a house in Fairfax.

In the meantime, Andy was the one who was beginning to feel hollow. The kids and no-hopers he was trying so desperately to help just didn't seem to have the same level of commitment to their wrecked lives as he did. They were ungrateful and lazy. He wondered if maybe they deserved to be on the streets, after all. One of them even stole Andy's new laptop to score a bit of coke.

'I began resenting the people I was trying to help. Erik was the one doing everything right, it seemed. My folks were so happy about his success that they started to preach to me about doing something real and meaningful. As if all that I had been doing was a waste of time.'

'It was,' Jack said emphatically. 'What did them homeless people do for you 'cept kick you up the ass?'

Again, Andy wanted to explain to Jack that it wasn't so simple. There had been a lot—well, a couple of success stories with the kids, but it wasn't about numbers. You calculated success in a different way when you were dealing with human capital. But again, he stopped short. 'Yeah, maybe.'

'So you ran away,' Jack grinned wickedly. 'Man, you got everything backwards. You should be running in the same direction as your brother. Away from the shit, not towards it.'

'I didn't run away,' Andy snapped. A brittle silence settled between them. The only sound came from the rattle of steel and glass as buses roared past on the highway. What the hell did Jack know about him and Erik? Why did everybody think that being rich and driving a BMW was the ultimate definition of success? Why did it always feel as if he was the younger brother and Erik the more mature one?

William, who had been dozing in the front seat, jumped out of the jeep. He smiled and didn't say a thing, but it was clear that he thought it was time to move again.

After a few minutes of silence—Jack smiling to himself and Andy stewing from his put-down—William pulled out an old cassette, without a cover, from the glovebox and pushed it into the machine. A man's melancholy voice filled the jeep. 'You likeit ghazal, saab?' William was asking. 'Ghulam Ali, most popular ghazal singer in Pakistan. Even Indian peoples likeit Ghulam Ali.'

Ghazals, the poems of extinguished hope, separation and mystical lust; the songs of Ghulam Ali, Mehdi Hassan, and Ustad Amanat Ali, the great ghazal singers of the subcontinent were the one part of his Pakistani self that Jack could never let go of. Whenever living behind bars in a concrete shoebox got too much and he felt like the world had abandoned him, every time his wife had wept and called him a bastard, and sometimes early on Sunday mornings after Guido's Italian Saloon closed, Jack would put on a ghazal tape and begin to heal the wounds. The songs absorbed his sadness in the same way his mother's embrace used to absorb his fear. Ghazals were Jack's one sure place of solace and rest.

Though he didn't like it, he had to admit that it was his father who'd got him to appreciate ghazals. Whenever the old man and his brothers finished discussing business, Jack, lying wide awake in bed, wished he could sit on the floor with them. He would hear the tinkle of ice in the glasses, the sighs and farts of contentment, the lips smacking together smartly with the first sips of Scotch. This was the signal for the ghazals to start.

Ali Hassan, usually only interested in money and ways to make more of it, was a limited conversationalist. He interrogated rather than asked and orated rather than discussed. He would cut off even his uncle—the man who had saved his life during the Partition, who had given him his start in business in Pakistan—mid-sentence and crudely instruct him about matters he knew very well. Any room, no matter how spacious, was never big enough for Ali Hassan. But those evening drinking sessions were different. Ali Hassan still talked loudly but he was also silent for long stretches. He would tell the others to keep quiet because this next couplet was one worthy of particular attention. As the men listened in silence to Amanat Ali or Noor Jehan, Ali Hassan would sigh and explain the couplets.

At first, the language of the ghazal puzzled and frightened Jack. One of his father's favourites, which he played at the beginning and end of each drinking session, was by Amanat Ali. He listened to his father repeat the lines loudly:

> What were the sweet flowers of agony?
> And why was love travelling alone in the desert?
> How come flowers were blooming in the evening?

This was a strange world; one that was hopelessly out of reach but which also beckoned to Jack. 'Can you find a better example of a singer whose voice matches the ache of his heart?' Ali Hassan would bellow. And so the next time the ghazal was played on the phonograph, Jack would listen to the singer's voice and sure enough he could feel the loneliness and sorrow. Later, he would go back and try to decipher the lyrics. In this way, over time, by listening to the ghazals selected by his father, he began to find his way through this strange poetic world.

And after just a ghazal or two, halfway through the second one usually, Jack would forget all the bad things his old man had done to him and imagine himself in the places and circumstances of the singer. As he floated off to sleep, Jack would find himself in a landscape of waterfalls, monsoon clouds and rushing streams, tangled in a woman's long tresses, her tears washing over him, and a half-empty jug of wine by a flickering candle...

Ghazals were the soundtrack to Jack's life. They came in

and stirred things up or calmed things down at the right moment. They heightened his enjoyment and released his tension. When he listened to ghazals he seemed to be able to shed his hardened skin and allow desire, longing and sweet betrayal to course through him. And when he sang along, it was the only time he felt like he didn't hate his family, the country of his birth, and his own brown skin.

William flipped the tape and the music started again. Andy called out from the backseat about smoking another one. Jack said, 'Sure. You want some, William?' The driver smiled even wider but shook his head, 'No, saab. I enjoy drinkit not smokeit.'

'Where you get your drinkit?'

William said that as a Christian he was allowed a monthly quota of alcohol and that the government issued him a permit. 'No, shit!' Jack liked this idea. 'So you can buy booze? Legally?' There might be light at the end of this particularly dark tunnel, after all.

'You are Christian, saab?' William seemed unsure.

'Sure as hell ain't no Muslim. Haven't seen the inside of a mosque since I got married.'

'You believeit Jesus Christ, sahib?'

'Look at my passport, Willie.' Jack had pulled it out from his blazer. 'Jack King. That's no Muslim name, now is it?'

'Yes saab, good Christian name.'

'So I can get me a quota of booze every month?' Jack looked expectantly at the driver.

William wasn't sure. According to Andy, who was lighting the joint and seemed to have forgotten Jack's earlier comment, it wasn't worth it. 'The booze you get on the permit is locally produced and tastes like formaldehyde if it is bad, or piss if it is good. Why go through all the hassle of getting a permit when you can get the real stuff just as easily. Talk to Shahid, he'll put you in touch with his bootlegger.'

'Wha—?'

'Booze is a big item in this country.' Andy took another hit and passed it to Jack. 'Bootleggers, the guys with contacts in the airlines, the diplomatic community and customs, they can get you a case of anything from Pernod to Finlandia vodka or fifteen-year-old Scotch within forty-eight hours.'

'How?'

'It's the way things work here.'

'The official and the hidden.'

'That's right. Two parallel worlds that deny the other's existence but depend on each other for survival. This country is in a state of suspended denial.'

'Hypocrisy, my man, is what you're describing,' Jack took a couple of puffs and passed it back to Andy. 'Great shit, dude. How much you pay for it?'

'I don't.' Andy said that he hadn't paid for a joint since he'd come to Peshawar; ever since he met Khan Sahib.

'Who's Khan Sahib?'

'He works in our office. Gets us our permits and licences and buys supplies for the refugee camps. Since I took the job he's made sure I've got more than enough hash to keep me happy. His way of ensuring job security, I guess.' Andy snorted a dry laugh.

Munni Begum was singing an upbeat number. As the end of the song approached, she repeated one line over and over, challenging the frenetic beat of the drums, raising the pitch as well as the excitement of the audience. Jack imagined her singing to him in the mountains, and demanding that the cupbearer bring more wine. The ghazal ended in a frenzy of drumming, wails from the woman and whoops and cheers from the audience. Although the air was hot and tedious, a sense of hope, like an unexpected breeze, wisped through Jack's body and eased, at last, the tension he'd been feeling ever since his arrival back in Pakistan.

They were approaching Peshawar. The highway was now a double carriageway with hundreds of little three-wheeled scooter taxis buzzing in and out of traffic, like mechanical bumblebees. 'This Khan Sahib,' Jack asked, 'can he procure anything?'

'Nothing yet he hasn't been able to get a hold of,' Andy was still, sprawled out on the backseat.

Jack craned his neck around to look at Andy. 'Dude, we gotta talk.'

8

It was the first morning of the monsoon. The skies had groaned all night with thunder, before opening up and transforming the dusty city into a giant slip of mud. Mr Noor Aslam, a lowly NIA Assistant Sub-inspector with a partiality for cream puffs, eclairs and most things soft and squishy, was contemplating the unavoidable necessity of rising from his spongy mattress and preparing himself for another tiresome day. Despite his elongated title, Mr Noor Aslam—shortish, with a midriff as perfectly proportioned as a large hard-boiled egg—believed that he deserved better. There was a time, fifteen years ago, when the Afghan war was at its zenith, that being a spy had had monetary potential. The Americans loved spies and were willing to finance them. Mr Aslam had joined the NIA because it was known to pay good salaries and demanded very little in return. But as soon as the bloody Soviets retreated from Afghanistan, the Americans closed up their wallets and went back to Washington, setting in motion an endless series of budget cuts and austerity measures in all government departments, especially the NIA.

Of course, in the last few years since Osama and the Arab Afghans had been designated public enemies Number One and Two, the Americans were once again running around Peshawar barking orders. The spy business had rejuvenated. But the NIA and the Americans were only interested in fit, youthful men who were willing to spend months in the tribal areas or even in Afghanistan, sniffing out long-bearded fanatics. Such a scenario disgusted Noor Aslam in the most fundamental way. He required his eight hours a night and regular pots of sweet tea and pastries. In Afghanistan, a feast was hard bread and bony kebabs. Sadly, Noor Aslam's time had passed. Now that spies could once again command respect and fear, he found himself twenty kilos overweight, dyeing his whitening hair once a month and counting the days until he would be released into a miserable retirement.

For the past five years, Assistant Sub-inspector Noor Aslam had done little more than run a handful of tired and undisciplined hacks. His main duty was to keep an eye on the activities of the shrinking number of foreigners working in charities for the few remaining Afghan refugees in and around Peshawar. As if to keep up with the general shrinkage, Mr Aslam's superiors in Islamabad had seen to it that his responsibility and remuneration dwindled by annual increments as well.

Although Noor Aslam felt the injustices of advancing age, poor habits and official neglect deeply, the upside was that he was forgotten in the dark woods of bureaucracy. He reported to no one important about anything significant and therefore, nobody cared to look over his shoulder and make enquiries about what he was doing. It was a rare day, when official duties wound up later than 3:15. He passed most afternoons and evenings chatting with whoever showed up at the Galaxy Hotel dining room or shooting caroms at Haji Murad's Taj-o-Takht Games and Video Hall next to the GPO.

The Assistant Sub-inspector's post-sleep reverie was interrupted by a thunderous banging on the door of his tiny, damp room which he rented from a military family in Peshawar's cantonment area. Mr Aslam's meagre salary didn't allow him to rent an entire house, or for his wife and children to live with him. They remained in the family village near Mardan to which he travelled once a month. Mr Aslam rose from his soft bed and opened the door to find the pig-tailed, nine-year-old daughter of the landlord informing him that there was a phone call for him and he should hurry, because whoever was on the line had said it was most urgent.

'Hello?' Mr Noor Aslam gasped into the mouthpiece, still pulling the string belt of his bathrobe around his corpulent midriff.

The caller identified himself as Director General Mushtaq Gill from HQ in Islamabad. Involuntarily, Mr Aslam's weak back straightened itself. Director General Gill was telling the Assistant Sub-inspector that he had been selected for a special assignment.

So accustomed was Mr Noor Aslam to being a forgotten nobody that his immediate response was, 'Me, sir? Is there not a mistake?' People often confused him with Noorul Islam, a young upstart Inspector, who had a large desk and his own computer on the fourth floor. He was in charge of some Task Force that was tracking down links between Indian agents and Baluch militants.

'No mistake, Aslam,' the Director General snapped. 'There is high-level interest in this assignment which demands absolute discretion. Its success requires someone with no profile and visibility.'

Mr Aslam thanked his superior but then flushed at his own humiliation. 'What is the assignment, if I may ask, sir?'

Islamabad wanted intelligence about a certain prominent American businessman, Mr Jack King. He was well connected (Gill made a reference to the loftiest reaches of government) and had left Islamabad for Peshawar yesterday morning. Noor Aslam's assignment was simple: report on everything Mr King did and said; where he was staying, with whom he was meeting, what he was eating and drinking and most importantly, what his plans were. Daily reports delivered by courier were to be on the Director General's desk each morning by 8:30 a.m. Then the line went dead.

Noor Aslam set the receiver down on the hook and looked out into the dark, wet morning. The humidity was high and the room was stuffy and hot. But still, he couldn't stop a shiver going down his spine. How was he supposed to complete this mission? Nothing in his nineteen indentured years of bureaucratic service had prepared him for such an assignment. His present duties demanded little more than receiving photocopied minutes of tedious meetings attended by foreign aid workers, or a few photos of them on a weekend trip with one of their office girls. He routinely passed these on to Islamabad. Most days though, he found it hard to stay awake at his desk, there was so little to do. He had stopped reading the minutes or looking at the snaps years ago: as far as bores went, aid workers were the champs.

Back in his room he dressed himself in a desultory fashion, first one sock, then his white shirt with the worn collar, followed by his only tie (navy blue; no pattern save some faded food stains). He raked through the clutter of his still sleepy mind for a clue that would help him in his task. By the time he pulled on his recently re-soled shoes, he decided he would have to call on the services of Jamshed Khan a.k.a Khan Sahib, the longest serving operative in the Assistant Sub-inspector's coterie of spies.

'See, I got a plan.' Jack was leaning towards Andy like someone might overhear. 'I'm a businessman and I got a business plan.' It was mid-afternoon, between 2:30 and 3; the lunch guests at Osmania's Restaurant on Jamrud Road had departed long ago, leaving Jack and Andy in the company of white-jacketed waiters who silently polished silver or set tables for dinner as they smoked.

'Sure.' Andy was feeling mixed up. He was still wary of Jack but found having someone new to talk with a welcome relief. He was feeling pretty high from the three joints they'd had on the way up, but not as high as he would have liked to have been. He was still feeling a bit hungry, and thinking about maybe ordering another chicken curry. He was not really listening to what Jack had to say. 'What sort of business?' he heard himself mumble. Maybe what he really wanted was a keema naan instead.

'A little of this, a little of that. Different stuff,' Jack replied.

'Care to be a bit more specific?' Andy had decided to skip more food for the time being but told one of the waiters to bring him another lemon soda.

Jack pulled his feet out of his Florsheims and started to explain. He told Andy about the cab and a bit about dealing coke and doing time in Joliet and Cook County, about the magazine shop and his plans to buy the superette in Coon Rapids. Then, he worked backwards and told Andy about the sting that backfired, about getting set up and about his decision to get serious in life and make his mark.

He ended by telling Andy about the *National Geographic* article and that there was money in his family. 'Like a fucking gold mine, man.'

'So what's the plan, Jack?' Andy rarely showed emotion in his voice. He spoke softly and distinctly, which caused Jack some concern. It reinforced the fact of Andy's education. And in his life of petty crime, Jack had been the most educated of all his compadres. He'd worked with some real dipshits in his day, most of them dumber than a box of rocks. But he'd never hooked up with a college boy before. He didn't know how to read Andy yet. Maybe Andy would try to rip him off. He didn't know. On the other hand, maybe he would see some huge hole in the plan that Jack hadn't even thought of. With a smart kid like Andy on board, it stood a real chance of succeeding. Jack had to make sure Andy liked what he heard.

'See, I figure with a little cash and some concentration,

I could make a fortune. We both could. Back in Chi-town, I know people who have...' he hesitated, and looked around at the waiters who were eating their lunch. 'These people see, have a distribution network pretty well laid out. A finely tuned engine. Mostly coke now, but used to have the concession for smack. You know what that is, right, smack?' Andy nodded. 'Yeah, of course you do. You're smart. But see, these days securing a steady supply of Chaos...is fucking hard. Don't ask why...a lot of different factors involved.' Jack was playing with a straw, twisting it about and tying it into ever-larger knots. 'The Latinos, they control the trade in nose candy, see, but they don't want to lose market share to heroin. And the Mob, they usually maintain the flow of smack. But my sources have been tellin' me the pasta boys have become softer in the last few years. They prefer the soft drugs and the women and all that crap. Smack, for some reason they won't, or can't supply. Regular like. See what I'm sayin'?'

A waiter appeared from nowhere and began clearing the plates and stainless steel curry boats from the table. Jack tossed the twisted piece of plastic onto the pile of dirty dishes and waited till the waiter retreated to the kitchen. 'See, I can access those networks, for sure. With their contacts, I'll be able to expand things a bit...you know, up to Wisconsin, down to Tennessee. There's money to be made even in those Corn Belt states like Iowa and Dakota. Can you believe that? Farmers on dope!'

'So you want to establish a pipeline from this end? Am I on the right track?'

Jack smiled, 'Bull's-eye.'

'And of course, you've got people here who are able to supply.'

'Yes and no... That's where you come in.'

'Me?' Andy gave Jack a bemused look and reached around to fiddle with his rat-tail. 'How me?'

'You live here, my man. You're a local, this is your scene. You've got the contacts. That's all I need from you...contacts.'

'I run a refugee assistance programme for a group of Danish churches, Jack. My contacts are either refugees, government officials or overly enthusiastic and very conservative Scandinavian clergy. Not the sort of contacts you're looking for.'

Even though Andy was playing hard to get, Jack could see the sparkle in his eyes. Reading lips was for the movies.

'What about that Khan Sahib?'

'Khan Sahib gets our jeeps diesel when there's a shortage, gets us water when the city supply runs out and gets me a weekly lump or two of hash. But that's nothing. This country is carpeted with hashish.'

'He'd know where to start asking questions, though.'

'He's an old man, Jack. A grandfather for all I know. I wouldn't feel right asking him for something like this.' His eyes were glued to Jack's. That cabin in North Carolina suddenly popped into his mind.

'Leave the talking to me, dude.'

Andy snubbed out his cigarette, coughed, then scratched his goatee. He started to say something but then changed his mind.

'What you say, Andy? You in?' Jack was tapping a spoon against the water jug. Andy just kept up a smile, bemused and considering, on his dry lips, bobbing his head ever so slightly. Jack's tapping was getting irritating. A hundred thousand dollars were suddenly just a couple of weeks, maybe even less, away. Was he misjudging what Jack was laying out? He was pretty high after all. He chugged his lemon soda in an attempt to sober up.

'Say you found your contacts. You've got the money to buy...what did you call it? Chaos?'

'Un-huh.' Jack dropped the spoon, opened a matchbox, took one out and started picking his teeth.

'I'm no expert, but it would seem to me you're going to need a substantial amount of capital if you're counting on becoming the Chaos king of Chicago.'

Jack was suddenly hostile. 'You insinuating I don't have cash? Like brown folks don't have cash and white folks have it all?' He pulled out a wad of dollars, about a thousand bucks—all he had left—and waved it in front of Andy. 'Check it out. Niggers ain't allowed to have cash? That what you tellin' me, man?'

'Jeez, mellow out, man.' Andy whispered then stroked his goatee. 'Just curious, that's all.'

They were silent for a while. Jack studied the orange and red curry stains on the tablecloth and avoided Andy's penetrating gaze. It was time to go; Jack slipped on his wingtips.

'You consider yourself black, Jack?' Andy asked out of the blue.

Jack stopped and then smiled at the way the question came out. 'Good one!'

'Well, do you? You referred to yourself as a nigger.'

Jack kicked off his shoes again and started fiddling with the ashtray and spoon. 'Interesting question, my man.'

Jack's first friends in America had been the 'Brothers'. They drove most of the cabs in those days and by the 1980s, a lot of the licences in Chicago were going to them, too. Jack had always liked their cool attitude. There were reassuring similarities between them and the people he had grown up with, including, a raw language full of cursing and sexual overtones. If Jack was honest, he supposed he did consider himself to be a 'Brother'.

And in Chicago, that only seemed the right thing. The black man got more respect on the street than the white man. Not being white himself, Jack was considered black in most of the population's eyes, anyway. Sand nigger. Camel jockey.

Raghead. How many times had he heard that shit? What really pissed him off though, was the way other Pakistanis around Devon Street—like Nasreen and Uncle Jalal—put him down for hanging with the brothers. The small-minded Lahori shopkeepers were the worst. They whispered 'monkey' behind a black customer's back, and washed their hands after taking their money. Or if they were driving a cab, they refused to stop and pick up a brother flagging on the street. They made fun of the way the blacks talked and walked. Sometimes it seemed that his own people hated the 'Brothers' more than the whiteys did.

While the whole Pakistani community was trying to make themselves as white as possible: buying houses in Oak Park, sending their kids to college and ditching the shalwar-qameez for suits and ties, Jack was zooming in another direction. It wasn't that he had anything against white people, but Jack had always wanted to be cool, and the honkies...well, they were mostly squares. Jack just felt more comfortable with the 'Brothers'. But more than squareness, deep down Jack knew that he was really running away from being a lousy, brown Pakistani. Not black. Not white. Just that ugly, in-between turd colour.

'When I was a kid it seemed everyone in Pakistan was busting to get to America,' Jack said after a few seconds, 'but I remember my old man tellin' my uncles why he would never go. "No one will call me nigger."' Jack smirked, then fished a Kent out of a crumbled packet from his trouser pocket. The cigarette was bent and some of the tobacco dangled from the end. 'So I knew at a very young age that white people considered us Pakistanis to be "niggers".' With the end of a match, he pushed the tobacco back into the cigarette. 'But in Chicago I don't feel that way, at all. Know what I'm sayin'? There, I'm proud to be a "nigger".' The insight seemed to surprise even him, and he smiled. 'Most of my associates and friends have been 'Brothers'. They've been my loyal family. But here, things are different.

'Now that I'm surrounded by dark skin, the last thing I consider myself to be is black. In my head, I'm whiter than a fucking gallon of milk.'

Jack hadn't talked like this to anyone before; only to himself when there was nothing to do, if the TV was busted or something.

'I'm just curious, Jack, you understand.' Andy was fidgeting with his hair again. 'It's just that I...' he didn't finish. Even though he'd known Jack for all of two–three days, Andy realized that beneath his tough guy persona, there was something fragile about him. Maybe, because Jack didn't wear any socks.

'What?' Jack snapped.

'Nothing. I just want to make sure you know what you're doing, that's all.'

'Relax, daddy-o.' Jack picked a bit of tobacco from his teeth.

Jack's way of talking—a bit of black jive, a bit of Elvis meets Disco Inferno—was also interesting. If anyone else had said such ridiculous things like 'boogie on down' or 'daddy-o', Andy would have avoided the loser, but for some reason it suited Jack.

They finished their cigarettes in silence, then Andy said he'd introduce Jack to Khan Sahib on one condition.

'Name it, dude.'

Andy had been contemplating his next move for months now. Since most of the refugees were going home the Danes had decided it was time to move the operation into Afghanistan. Andy definitely didn't want *that* much adventure in his life, but what did he have to show for his time in Pakistan? Erik, the family's star, was high up the corporate ladder with his parents' loving gaze focused firmly on his seemingly never-ending rise. Andy would be a joke if he came home empty-handed.

His father had lived an outdoor life in Norway but had never been able to afford a cabin after moving to the States. A hideaway in the Smoky Mountains remained his unfulfilled dream. Andy knew he could divert some of his parents' attention back to him if he could build a weekender up in the hills, but there was no way a NGO wage was ever going to make that happen.

But now, here was a guy named Jack, who was asking him for a favour.

'It's going to cost.' He'd done his sums and he knew one hundred thousand was a lot of money. 'But hey, dreams don't come cheap.'

Jack rubbed his hands together and beamed, 'Awright! My man!'

9

'Come immediately! Don't be late,' Assistant Sub-inspector Noor Aslam's voice had quivered over the phone line when he ordered Khan Sahib to meet him at the Galaxy Hotel dining room. While they waited for the waiter to return with a second pot of tea, Mr Aslam picked up a single cube of sugar and popped it into his mouth. The gritty sweetness melting into his tongue compensated slightly for the inconvenience of having to conduct business so early in the morning.

'What is the issue?' Khan yawned.

Khan Sahib was a tall, strongly built Waziri Pathan. Though nearly sixty years old, his beard—trimmed close to his chin with a clean-shaven upper lip—was still black. His hair, also cropped short, was starting to grey on the sides. Several strong features had once made his face striking: a long, broad nose; dark brown-green eyes that moved with the ruthless precision of a hawk; and a tight, sunburned neck that resembled the trunk of a cherry tree. But endless years of struggle and worry had taken their toll. Several rings of thin but deep wrinkles besieged his eyes, which rarely shone any more. They had become cloudy and his gaze doubtful; so much hope had been raised and then cruelly dashed in them over the years...

Khan Sahib had come to Peshawar from his dirty hometown of Bannu, nestled along the border of the Tribal Areas to search for work. During the day, he had driven a small Suzuki van delivering building supplies for the booming construction business. Foreign aid agencies were flooding into the city to help the Afghan refugees in the camps that had mushroomed all around the town now that the Russians occupied Afghanistan. All the foreign workers needed houses, offices and warehouses to store their supplies. He was busy from early morning till after dark. In the evening, Khan Sahib had studied English in the firm belief that this foreign language, the tongue of the Americans who were advanced and rich, would in turn, make him the same. He did well and was able, after a few months, to have small, uneven conversations with the foreigners he met in the course of his work. One of them, a fat red-faced man with thousands of freckles, encouraged Khan to learn typing. Apparently, foreign agencies paid well for locals who could speak and write English. So, late into the night, exhausted from a day of loading and unloading building supplies and then two hours of English lessons, Khan Sahib would peck determinedly at the strange mechanical English keyboard in a 'business studio'—a narrow room with three shaky desks, three short plastic stools and one flickering tubelight—buried deep in an alley in Lohar Mandi.

By the time he reached his mid-thirties, his employment as a clerk in a foreign agency was supplemented by the NIA who paid him a token two hundred rupees each month in exchange for passing on certain documents they expressed an interest in. Though it was not a big amount, his more than eight hundred rupees a month allowed him to turn his attention to family. Farroukh, a chubby boy, was born one winter but all further attempts to further the family had failed. So from the day of his birth the young boy became the fountain and garden of the family. Every extra rupee was put aside for his education. 'He will learn English and study the Koran in Arabic,' Khan told his wife. By the age of eight, Farroukh was learning to type.

The war against the Russians in Afghanistan ground on year after year. Americans and aid organizations came and went. Eventually Khan Sahib secured a job in a Danish church agency as 'office manager' where his salary was much higher but still far from sufficient to retire comfortably. The NIA had lost all interest in foreign aid workers and other than providing his superior Mr Noor Aslam with regular updates and the rare report, Khan Sahib's income was only occasionally supplemented by the intelligence agency.

His plan for Faroukh was that he would secure him and his wife in old age. But where in Pakistan was the scope for a clever but unconnected boy to succeed? Government service paid nil and the family had no resources to invest in any business. All that Khan Sahib made as Office Manager went to meet the monthly expenses. For some time, the father thought that he would secure his son a position with the foreign agencies that he now knew so well, but the writing was on the wall. The agencies were leaving in droves and by the time Faroukh reached an employable age, Peshawar would be lucky to have one or two left. What was required was for Faroukh to secure steady employment for many years at a good salary. The only place such a situation could be found was outside Pakistan—in the Gulf. And so, with the same determination that he had exhibited in learning English and typing many years earlier, Khan Sahib applied himself to the huge task of getting his son a foreign berth.

Khan Sahib made enquiries and settled on an employment agent that promised to send his son to Dubai. The 'agent' ran off with his deposit instead. Chastened and desperate Khan at last managed to secure a position for Farroukh in Qatar. But just a few weeks before he was to depart, as part of his medical clearance by the embassy, the doctors discovered cancer in his elbow. Agonizing months passed as Khan and his wife nursed their child and lost all their savings to doctors, tests and medicines. The young man tried to keep his parents' spirits up by reciting the Koran but grew steadily thinner and, on most days, barely opened his eyes.

Since the day of the diagnosis of cancer, the maza, the joy, had evaporated from Khan Sahib's life. Nothing held his interest. Especially this buffoon Noor Aslam, to whom he had been forced to deliver his weekly reports for the past three years. That some people were paid more than him and had titles didn't bother old Khan Sahib; that was the way God had made His world. Where he did fault the Almighty's design however, was that idiots and nikammas, ne'r-do-wells, like Noor Aslam had both the titles and the extra money. Especially at a time when Khan Sahib's very existence was so precarious. Where was the justice of life?

'There is a man who has come, or is about to arrive, though he may have already arrived—who can say?—about whom the HQ people are demanding information and regular reports daily, every day.' Noor Aslam was excited.

Khan Sahib said nothing. He blinked and surveyed the cakes that Aslam had positioned within easy reach of his puffy tentacles; normally he would have liked one but it was too early for sugar.

Aslam did not share this feeling. He twiddled another sugar cube between his fingers and then placed it on his spongy tongue. 'I received the orders this morning from the Director General himself. Mr Gill. Mushtaq Gill, you know him of course, he was the one appointed by the Prime Minister. And his brother, Razaq, is the big industrialist, isn't it?'

As if he were a puppet, Khan Sahib raised one eyebrow

while at the same time pulling up one corner of his closed lips to form a bored smirk.

'You must do as I say, it is your new assignment, yes. You must put aside all other activities, and provide reports on this Mr King who has come to Peshawar. He is powerful and dangerous and I must provide accurate and full information to Director General sahib without delay. Tomorrow I must make the first report, understand Khan?' Aslam's nervousness had made him consume most of the sugar and it was making him more agitated.

'Where is this man staying?' Khan asked.

'Am I a pir, to tell you such things? Why does the government pay you? To ask stupid questions, is that it? "Where does he stay?"' Aslam squeaked his displeasure but then lowered his voice to a shaky whisper, 'You are the jasoos, Khan. Find him and report to me. First report at seven tonight. This very hotel.'

The older man said nothing. He held the cup of tea close to his lips but didn't drink. Not only was there no justice, now there was no time. Khan had promised Mr Andersen that he would have the annual report typed by noon. He hadn't yet begun. Then there was the appointment at eight in the evening, at the Lady Willingdon Hospital with the doctor who had some information about treatment for his son. And now, this oaf Aslam demands that he drop everything to find some man named 'King'. He sighed, like a balloon was deflating deep within him. He stood up and shuffled out of the dining hall.

Jack decided very quickly that he didn't like Peshawar. The city seemed to be crumbling in on itself with age and neglect. Narrow, crowded laneways intersected each other at every possible angle; buildings leaned towards the streets as if they wanted to hear the secrets of the passers-by.

Jack told Andy that the city made him feel on edge. Like you didn't know what was going to happen next. He didn't like this feeling of not being in control.

'That's because the town is right on the border,' Andy said. The Wild West. The Frontier. Things were done differently on the border. 'Ten minutes from this house, Pakistan officially ceases to exist and the tribal territories begin.'

'What begins where?'

'The tribal territories. A sort of no-man's-land. Where you run to if the police are after you,' Andy said. You could buy and sell anything from a ton of hashish to a Stinger missile in the tribal territory. The Pakistani government had representatives in the territories but they served as mere symbols of authority. No one took them seriously. The tribesmen did as they pleased. Andy began to roll another joint.

Jack wanted a beer. He'd seen a few cans of San Miguel in the fridge but hardly enough to last till suppertime.

'What 'bout them bootleggers you were talkin' about? Give 'em a call. Any chance of getting some Chablis?'

Andy said that he didn't have a bootlegger because booze dried you out in this climate, and when you could get hash, where was the fun in wine or vodka? 'But if you're thirsty, I'm sure there's a party happening. I'll make a call or two later.'

Andy smoked most of the joint and didn't talk much. There was too much to think about. Like Jack's plan. And one hundred thousand dollars. He smiled. When he'd finished, he disappeared into another room. Before stepping into the shower he yelled out, 'I found a party. At Aftab and Shirley's place.' But there was no answer. He walked back to the living room to find Jack asleep on the sofa. He was hugging a cushion with gaudy mirror-work, like a boy clutching his favourite birthday present.

Later that night at the party, Jack grabbed Andy's arm and nodded urgently, 'Look, dude. Check it out!'

'What?' Andy couldn't see what had him so excited.

'Her! The banana.'

'Who?'

'Mmm…hmmm… Mama!' Jack said louder than necessary.

'Who?' Andy repeated. 'Where?'

'Sexy laaydeh!' Jack was staring into the shadows by the front door. He sucked hard on his vodka and 7Up. 'Over there,' he nodded his balding head in a vague direction. 'That chick from the party the other night in Islamabad. What she doin' here?'

Andy still couldn't see who Jack was staring at so he turned away to talk to the hostess. Jack shuffled across the room, nudging aside the crowd, swaggering slightly, and without thinking, stuck out his hand for the woman to shake. 'Din't get a chance to introduce myself last time,' he said. 'Jack King from Chicago.'

She was wearing an orange-and-yellow shalwar-qameez, with pale peach lip-gloss. Her hair was pulled back tight. And so far as Jack could make out she had come alone.

'I suppose you expect me to express my gratitude, is that it?' The woman's tone was wary and distant but she hadn't turned and walked away. Jack was encouraged.

'Not at all. Just din't think it was cool for older men to be pervin' on a beautiful woman like you.' Jack spread his legs wider, trying to appear as relaxed as possible.

'I can take care of myself,' she said, looking right past him and into the dark room. She spoke in a smooth English accent. Every word came out perfectly formed, clear and melodious, and made his South Chicago jive talk sound cheap and silly. A momentary flush of self-consciousness burned his face.

'Get you a drink?' Foxy lady, he added to himself.

She ignored the question. 'You're not from around here, then?' Jack detected the faintest of dismissive smiles on her face. 'Let me guess, you're an American.'

When he had first been sent to prison Jack found the language of the black prisoners more fascinating than any foreign tongue. Many of the words seemed to have no connection with English at all and the rhythm of the language was completely unlike anything he had been taught or the way white people spoke it. The language the 'Brothers' spoke seemed more like a code, filled with secret and weird phrases that kept the uninitiated out. And it wasn't very long after he got to prison before Jack understood that if you spoke like the 'Brothers' you stood a better chance of not getting fucked over.

There had been a handful of Asians in prison—a few Vietnamese doing time for smuggling Chinese into the country on a steamship. Jack was the only one from Pakistan or India. How was one dumbass Pakistani expected to survive in a war zone like Joliet State Penitentiary? The black 'Brothers' were cool. After a couple of weeks they offered him a spot in their gang. Not the full-fledged membership but at least the others knew that if you messed around with Jake you were going to have to contend with the rest of the 'Brothers'.

Jack practised hard at learning this new language, the slang: the intonations and the attendant gestures. He paid special attention to get the syncopation just right. Over time the cadence of his voice slowed down and his words began to sway and stretch out like a hammock between two trees. He realized that if he could make the guy holding the knife to his throat believe that he was part of his own tribe, things usually turned out alright.

Jack was proud of his accent and his new vocabulary. He'd learned the black tongue fluently and it, in turn, had served him well. White Man English just couldn't stand up to this new language, until that is, this 'banana' opened her mouth.

'No, I ain't...no...definitely not from these parts,' Jack felt his shoulders and confidence slouch in unison. 'How about that drink?'

'I'll have a wine, thank you, if there is any. White, please. If not, just a mineral water, Mr King.' As he walked towards the bar, Jack couldn't help feeling the sarcastic nip of her words. A few minutes later, back by her side, he handed her a glass of wine and asked her name.

'Afroz,' she replied. But she wasn't looking at him. She was smiling her incredible flashbulb smile around the room, or lifting a gorgeous hand and wiggling her long slender fingers in greeting at someone else.

'That's beautiful,' Jack said. She gave him a dubious look. 'I'm serious. It's a beauty.'

'What's your name, then?' she said as she extended her face towards someone who was brushing by—another foreigner—who greeted her with a peck on the cheek.

'You just said it. Jack King.'

'Oh,' she said, her eyes still moving about the room, acknowledging people. Everyone except Jack. 'I thought that was just a game.'

He was reaching for his passport. 'No foolin'. See I'm American and...'

'Oh, really?' she looked down at him at last. He was conscious of her being taller than him and, for a moment, he felt uncomfortable.

Afroz turned away immediately, wearing a smile of triumph, as if she'd finished him off in three easy rounds. She sipped her wine and accepted a cigarette from someone else who was talking to her now. A Pakistani with small wire-rim glasses and a nice linen jacket. She made no attempt to introduce Jack. He took a step backwards and retired to a dark corner of the room.

This party was the same as the first one. The music was

mostly Pakistani folk disco crap, grating on Jack's ears; the dancers were a mixture of Europeans and rich Pakistanis of all ages. He glanced in the direction where Afroz had been but she had disappeared. He squinted around the dance floor. He saw Andy deep in conversation with some expats and a young boy, no more than three years old, throwing a tantrum at a tired and angry woman servant. He drank a couple more vodkas and a beer, all the while keeping his eyes peeled for Afroz. At last, he grabbed a pack of smokes someone had left at the bar and went outside to get some air.

The night was unsettled. Clouds blew across a frail crescent moon before clearing away again, as if being chased by some unseen force. The branches of the gulmohur trees drooped low and heavy with moisture. The moon dangled from the end of a cloud and reminded Jack of a film song by Rafi that his mother used to sing to him as a boy. As she sang, her voice breaking and coughing from the yet undiagnosed cancer, he had felt tall enough to reach up and touch the stars. Memories that he hadn't allowed to surface for years flooded over him:

The Holy Family Hospital. Little Yaqub leans against Nanima as they stand next to his mother crying quietly; the pain gnawing up her insides, becoming too much to bear. This is the third day that she hasn't been able to speak or open her eyes. He sucks on the collar of his shirt, watching his mother grimace. A nurse, wearing a starchy white hat like a boat, roughly daubs the patient's perspiring brow. Angrily, Nanima steps forward and swats her away, then whispers softly as she takes on the job of soothing her daughter.

Slowly, Little Yaqub moves closer to his sisters who sit on the floor with their backs against the whitewashed wall. He listens to them curse his father: 'His wife is dying and still he will not cancel his trip!' The nauseating smell of disinfectant and pills and sickness cling to the walls. The footfalls of nurses echo through the dark, canyon-like halls. At last, his mother seems more peaceful. She reaches out to touch his face; her fingers feel as light as gauze. Her touch sends a shiver through his legs. All he wants is for her to be well again. She is suffering too much to speak even his name. Her half-closed eyes say, I will always love you, Yaqub. He wants to hear her say it. He wants to hear her melodious, soothing voice. He pulls away from her, retreating to the folds of Nanima's loose, warm clothing. When his mother dies a few days later, he feels paralysed and numb.

Jack's reverie is broken by the sound of an engine starting up. He turns and sees a BMW backing out into the street driven by the Pakistani with the wire-rim glasses and linen jacket. He feels deflated. Afroz was probably with him.

The moon had all but disappeared and Jack feels the first drops of rain on his wrist, but he doesn't want to get back into the party. An overwhelming sense of futility washes over him. The memories of his mother have upset him. He pulls out another cigarette and lights it, almost desperately. He relishes the hot smoke in his lungs and the cool spray of the light rain on his hands. As he turns around he catches a shadowy glimpse of someone else in the garden.

'That you, Afroz?' he asks tentatively, walking towards the indistinct figure. There is no response but he keeps moving, feeling certain that it's her. 'I'm glad to see you're still here,' he said. 'The party's pretty boring otherwise.'

Afroz didn't answer. Had there been more light Jack would have seen the irritation cross her face as he approached. She wanted to be alone. The man who had just driven away was a friendly acquaintance. But in this country, if you were friendly with your acquaintances and you were a woman, you were, it seemed, daring their manhood to rise up and acquit itself.

The conversation they were having had been fascinating. He had been explaining the influence of German philosophy on Iqbal's poetry and political ideas when, out of nowhere, he leaned forward and kissed her. She pulled back and thanked God it was dark, but then he did it again, trying hard with his thin tongue to force her mouth open. She laughed and made some joke but, thwarted and ashamed, he promptly ran out the door and drove off. Afroz had watched him leave and then gone into the garden to collect her thoughts.

And now, here was another freak approaching.

But she was too polite to be rude. Moreover, as he came forward, talking already, she craved a cigarette—her handbag was in the house.

Jack stopped a few feet from her and smiled. Damn, she is beautiful, he thought. Her perfume was different from the other night, he was sure.

For a few awkward seconds they stood close to each other, unsure of what to say. Jack expected her to acknowledge his presence; she hoped he would just leave. At last she said, 'Share a fag?' she held out a hand with her index and second finger slightly apart.

'Who you callin' a fag?' Blood rushed to Jack's head and made him momentarily dizzy. He had come over to make conversation, not to be insulted.

'I'm just looking for a cigarette, Mr King,' her tone was brittle and exasperated. 'Your sexual preferences are of absolutely no interest to me, whatsoever.'

Another elongated moment of silence. Jack fumbled in his blazer, found the pack of smokes and held it out in her direction. She extracted one, grabbed Jack's cigarette from his mouth, lit her's and then placed it back in his fingers. Jack felt as if he'd been hit by a bus. Afroz tossed her head to straighten her hair, lifted her face slightly towards the sky and exhaled a long plume of smoke into the night. She took another drag and made a move towards the house. 'Thanks for the fag, I mean cigarette, Mr King,' she said flatly.

'Why don't you call me Jack?' he managed at last. He turned and followed her. It had been a long time since he'd had a conversation longer than three words with a woman. She kept walking and was about to enter the house.

'Hey, hold on a sec,' Jack called out, skipping up towards her. 'Who are you? What's a sweetheart like you doing in a dump—'

'Oh, really! Honestly, I've had enough of you men for an evening. Thank you very much for the cigarette.' She opened the door and instantly melted into the laughing, dancing crowd.

10

The office was spacious and well lit; several dark-hued Afghan carpets lay on the floor and green leafy plants drooped out of large terracotta pots in the corners. A hidden air conditioner kept the temperature in the law offices of Rahman, Khan and Ahmadzai as cool as a late autumn day along the shore of Lake Michigan. Behind a rosewood desk the size of a river barge sat an attractive young woman with curly black hair wearing a tight silk shalwar-qameez. She gestured to an armchair by a low coffee table covered with old issues of *Herald* and *Newsweek* and asked if Mr King would prefer coffee or tea or perhaps, something cold.

'Gimme a Sprite,' Jack said as he set himself down in a roomy armchair. His left foot, crossed over his right knee, was jumping like it had a mind of its own. The secretary found it hard to concentrate on her typing.

Mr Ahmadzai had refused to see Jack when he called first thing in the morning, so Jack had had to ring Nanima and explain the situation to her. She promised to call Mr Ahmadzai as soon as she finished her next round of prayers. Sure enough, a couple of hours later, Mr Ahmadzai called Jack at Andy's place and said he would be able to spare a half-hour if he came over immediately.

A door on Jack's left burst open, making the secretary jump. Out strode a tall, well-built man with a head of wavy grey hair like a lion's mane. A very slight pinstripe could be detected in his elegantly cut suit and the man's tie had to be at least a forty-dollar number. 'Nice threads,' said Jack quietly.

The man stretched out a hand and introduced himself, 'Inayatullah Ahmadzai. You must be Yaqub, Ali Hassan's son.' His grip was like iron and voice as confident as a crack of thunder. 'Do come in.'

'Jack King,' Jack said.

Mr Ahmadzai hesitated for a moment. 'Sorry?'

'My name is Jack King. I was correcting you, that's all.'

With a quick look up and down, including a slight pause at Jack's feet, Mr Ahmadzai feigned a smile and said, 'I do apologize. Your grandmother did not inform me that you had changed your name. Do come in, Mr King, and make yourself comfortable.'

While Jack was squirming deeper into a grey leather armchair, Ahmadzai asked, 'What can I do for you today, Mr King? I'm sorry about this morning but you realize that ours is one of the busiest practices in the country and at present I am up to my ears in this damn sanctions business. Never ends.' He crossed his legs and looked at Jack as if to say, make it snappy.

Maybe since he's in a hurry, this won't be a big deal, thought Jack. But then, if he's on a first name basis with the old man he's got to be an asshole. 'What sort of sanctions business does your firm deal with?'

'American sanctions. Imposed by Congress after the recent nuclear tests,' Ahmadzai replied.

Being on the side imposing sanctions made Jack feel good. He was starting to relax. He spread his legs wide and occasionally grabbed his crotch until Ahmadzai was forced to look away. At the same time, Jack was nodding ever so slightly, like he could hear a tune that Ahmadzai couldn't.

'Mr King,' said Ahmadzai a second time. 'What compels you to make a visit to our offices today? Your grandmother has never visited this office. I make a point of calling in on her about twice or thrice a year when I visit Islamabad.'

Jack smiled and clicked his teeth. 'What compels me,' Jack liked the way Ahmadzai didn't even attempt to speak Urdu, 'is a small matter concerning the Zam Zam Memorial Trust.'

Jack looked him straight in the eye. Ahmadzai held a practised expression of affected ignorance, like he was hearing the name Zam Zam for the very first time. 'Indeed,' Ahmadzai said after a pause.

Jack went on. 'As you know, I have been settled in the United States for many years.' He was talking whitey English now. 'During the intervening years I have established a number of businesses in the greater Chicago area. With the state of the economy at present,' he couldn't believe his own ears, 'the climate for business expansion is excellent and my associates and I have drawn up plans for the extension of several of our interests into the wider region.' Jack smiled and gave his balls a flip.

'What region would that be, Mr King?'

'Upper Midwest. Wisconsin and on up through Minnesota.'

Ahmadzai enquired about his businesses and got the standard reply from Jack: distribution and services.

'I'm sure your solicitors, or if you prefer, lawyers, have been involved in the drafting of your business plan.'

Was this a question or a statement?

'Naturally,' said Jack and coughed self-consciously.

Ahmadzai waited, expecting Jack to fill in the names of his solicitors. 'Your firm is? I have contacts in Chicago.'

'A small firm,' Jack heard himself saying, 'Lord, Gunnar and Anderson.' Mr Ahmadzai wrote the name down in a small pad. 'Now, to the matter at hand.'

Mr Ahmadzai wore a gold ring on his pinkie finger. It flashed in the morning light as he pulled out a pack of Dunhills. He pulled the red seal firmly then slid the outer plastic layer off, as if he was preparing a lover for bed. He extracted a long white stick, and without offering one to Jack, returned the packet to his inner pocket. All the while, his gaze never left Jack.

'Mr King, tell me, what is your interest in the Zam Zam Memorial Trust?' He punctuated the question with the click of a well-used silver cigarette lighter. 'It has been established as a humanitarian fund, a charity of sorts, to assist less fortunate Muslims of this country in the performance of their religious duties. Specifically, to assist them in the pilgrimage to Mecca.'

'I'm aware of the nature of the Trust, Mr Ahmadzai. However, as you know, my grandmother raised me from quite a young age. And as such, she has always been a strong supporter of my business activities in the United States. It was she who suggested I look at possible ways to extend them, my businesses, to this country and beyond.'

'I thought you said you were expanding into some place known as the Upper Midwest?' Ash was building up at the end of Ahmadzai's cigarette.

'Of course, in the USA that is the region of our attention. But since arriving in Pakistan, Nanima, my grandmother, your client, has been encouraging me to test the waters so to speak, in this country.'

'Am I to understand that you are interested in the Zam Zam Trust as a source of capital for your business activities?'

'You may,' Jack nodded. 'Indeed.'

'And what sort of business are you considering, Mr King, in this country?'

'Well, that depends of course.'

'On?'

'Resources. Can't buy a hotel with a thousand dollars now, can you? Don't need a million to buy a taxi.'

'Which hotel do you have in mind, Mr King?'

'I don't have any hotel in mind, Mr Ahmadzai. I am simply referring to the range of possibilities that I have been thinking of since my return to Pakistan from Chicago.'

'Of course.' Mr Ahmadzai set his cigarette in the ashtray. 'And you would like to access the funds held in the Zam Zam Trust.'

'As I've already indicated, yes.' Jack's toes were standing up stiff.

Someone knocked. Ahmadzai cleared his throat, stood up and walked to the door. He returned with a green bottle of Sprite wrapped in a pink paper napkin. He handed it to Jack and poured himself a glass of water. Jack took a sip of the drink through the straw. Negotiations were going pretty good, he thought. As Ahmadzai sat down behind his desk, Jack nodded at a small framed picture of a young girl on one side of the large desk strewn with papers. 'How old is she?'

Ahmadzai seemed surprised, even momentarily embarrassed. 'Seven,' he said.

'Your granddaughter?'

There was a slight hesitation before Ahmadzai said, 'Now Mr King, if you will excuse me, I am quite pressed for time this morning. Is there any other matter I can assist you with?'

'Well,' said Jack, 'there was only the matter of the Trust. However, I feel we have not come to a satisfactory conclusion. Or have I missed something? My grandmother has specifically asked me to discuss this matter with you.'

'Regretfully, Mr King, your grandmother, Mrs Akhtar, is mistaken. She has never taken interest in financial matters and I fear she is under the impression that the money is in a bank account and that all one needs is a withdrawal slip.' He paused. 'But this is not the case, as I'm sure you yourself understand. The Zam Zam Memorial Trust is administered by a very strict agreement bound by rigid legal conditions. The most basic of those conditions is that the funds are to be used for the sole purpose of assisting poor Muslims with the performance of the Haj. The pilgrimage.'

'Don't tell me what the Haj is.' Jack could barely keep his voice even. 'There can be no condition more basic than Nanima insisting on using an amount of that money for other purposes.' He pulled hard on the straw and nearly emptied the bottle of Sprite. He glared at the man across the desk.

Ahmadzai was scribbling on some document on his desk; apparently he'd already forgotten about Mr Jack King. He looked up for a millisecond and mumbled, 'Huh?' before going over the thick sheaf of papers he'd picked up.

Man, you be jankin' me bad.

As he stared at the lawyer Jack could hear his father talking: 'Boy, you'll learn to do as I say or suffer the consequences.' Or: 'You will learn the value of money, you little dog. Don't think you are so smart.' Like a lot of self-made men, Ali Hassan Shah couldn't bear the thought that his son might entertain ideas of doing the same. Jack was expected to step right into the family business and accept, without questioning, that forty years as a commodity exporter, or electronics distributor, or some other equally boring-ass shit was the ultimate experience of life. Jack had learned not to argue with his father, but he made it clear in other ways that he wasn't the sort of child who was going to accept whatever his father said. And seeing this pinstriped lawyer smirking behind a luxury desk fired him up with that old determination again.

'After all,' Jack put the Sprite bottle down louder than necessary on the glass topped table, 'it is her money. Isn't it? She can do what she wants with it.'

Ahmadzai glanced at Jack. 'Yes and no. It is her money in that her husband has left it to her and that allowance is made for her to subsist on the Trust's income until she departs this life. However, Mrs Akhtar, or anyone for that matter, cannot alter the administering terms and conditions of the agreement which govern the Zam Zam Trust.' He returned to studying the documents on his desk.

'...'cept you.'

Mr Ahmadzai looked Jack fully in the face and beamed with artificial grace. 'If you'll excuse me, Mr King, Mr Olafsson from UNICEF is waiting to see me on some urgent matters. So kind of you to drop in. I'm sorry to be a disappointment to you as regards your business plans but you do understand, I'm sure.' He was pulling Jack towards the door. Jack noticed that on his way around the desk, he had turned the framed photo of the smiling girl over on its face.

Now why did he do that, I wonder?

On his way out Jack stopped by the secretary's desk. She had run into Ahmadzai's office to retrieve the Sprite bottle. Jack picked up one of Ahmadzai's business cards from a small plastic stand. As he was turning away he caught sight of a letter signed by Ahmadzai, which the secretary had been preparing to stuff into an envelope. Jack's instincts told him to act quick. The letter flew into his pocket and as he turned, he nearly bumped into an ugly, bearded man with a new-fangled portable phone. Jack nodded a greeting and made for the door. Just as it was closing he heard Ahmadzai calling out, 'Welcome, Mr Olafsson. So good to see you, again.'

There was a message from Andy when Jack got back to the house. The chowkidar said that 'sahib' was very eager to talk with Mr Jack.

'What's up daddy-o?'

'How'd it go, Jack? Did you find the place all right?' The line was crackling and fading in and out.

'No problemo,' Jack tried to sound light-hearted but

he was still smarting from the failure of his meeting with Ahmadzai. 'The guy's a bit of a jerk-off but we had a good talk.'

'Excellent. I can take a lunch break in about a half-hour and we can talk. We should get started right away. When do you get the money?'

'Slight hassle, dude. Mr A is a little hesitant to release the funds, see. He's pulling some shit 'bout terms and conditions and agreements.'

There was a momentary pause. 'But I thought you said it's your grandmother's money. She can do what she wants with it, right?'

'Yes and no.' Jack's temper was storming up through his gut again.

'So what's gonna happen?' Jack could hear the disappointment in Andy's voice, even with the poor connection.

'Don't worry, dude. Everything's under control. See you in a bit.' He hung up and lit a Kent, saying aloud what he hadn't been able to get out of his mind since his meeting with Ahmadzai: 'Sure was a cute picture there on his desk. Why the hell is he so scared 'bout showin' her off?'

11

'What's plan B?'

'Plan B,' Jack said, pacing the room like a boxer anxious to get into the ring, 'be the same as plan A, my friend. Get me a piece of the action and set myself up as the main man in Chi—ca—go. That is the one and only plan. A to fucking Z.' Jack didn't have to tell Andy to roll a joint; he had walked in to the house with a fat one between his fingers.

Jack took the first long puff. Boom! He felt better instantly. 'Plan hasn't changed. But the modus operandi, see, that's gotta be revised. No longer a matter of simply axin' for the cash.'

Andy bobbed his head, playing with his rat-tail.

'Mr A thinks he's done wit me but I ain't started, see,' Jack said. He was strutting like a barnyard chicken, chest out and head cocked high.

'You have not yet begun to fight, eh,' Andy smirked. Unless Jack did the fighting, his Smoky Mountains cabin was going to be just what it had always been—a fuzzy dream that helped him fall asleep at night.

'That's right. Haven't even begun to fight.' Jack stretched his arms out like a fighter doing his last warm-ups.

Andy wanted to keep Jack moving in the right direction. A deal like this was never going to come along again; even if it did, he doubted whether he'd have the nerve to grab it. In order to keep Jack feeling good and in a fighting mood, Andy poured a big glass of vodka for his partner, who had stopped his Muhammad Ali impression and was finishing off the joint.

'What we need is a Luigi.'

'Huh?' Andy slumped into a rattan armchair and opened a can of beer.

'Luigi, you know. The man they send round when you be owing cash to Shylock. Tosses things around. Makes your house look like the city dump. A badass.' He smacked his lips after taking the first swig of the vodka.

'The tribal territory is right through that wall there,' Andy pointed across the room. 'Wild West, Jack. Remember that. You can find as many Luigis as you want over there.'

Outside, a roar of thunder coincided with the opening up of the rainclouds that had been hanging low all morning. The two men watched the storm. The light outside had turned sickly weak and grey. The wind whipped the lemon trees in Andy's garden into a wild dance. Within a minute the garden was a pool of swirling muddy water.

'Damn tootin'. What we need is a real tribal Luigi and send him round to Mr A's place. Know what I'm sayin'?'

Andy nodded but didn't know why. He was pretty sure what Jack was getting at but it wasn't something he wanted to explore at the moment. He didn't like the sound of this. Tribal Luigi? For a few seconds he contemplated Jack, who was sticking his hand out of the window, exclaiming how hard the rain was. He said that they'd talk more this evening. Right now he had to get back to the office. 'See you around six, Jack.'

'Later, dude.' As Andy was moving towards the door, Jack called out, 'Hold up. Where does Afroz live?'

'I don't know. I don't know her that well. We meet up at parties and dinners but I've never spent time with her. You're interested in her, eh?' Andy winked.

'Well, find out where she's stayin'.'

'I'll see what I can do.'

Jack poured himself another vodka and popped a blues

tape into the mini-stereo. He stretched out on the wicker sofa, flipping through a big coffee-table book on China. Twenty minutes later, the phone rang.

'She's staying with a friend in the cantonment. She's got relatives here but spends most of her time in Islamabad,' Andy said.

Jack grabbed a pencil and scribbled down the address. 'Perfect, daddy-o. Thanks.' Jack hung up and immediately had William bring the car out front.

After a few wrong turns, William pulled up in front of an old colonial-era bungalow set deep in a lush orchard of citrus trees. As soon as Jack hopped out he was met by a tall manservant with a full, bright orange beard and a thick bamboo lathi in his hand. He barked at Jack in Pashto.

'I'm here to see Afroz,' Jack replied, still making towards the front door of the house.

The manservant blocked his way and gently but firmly put an open palm on Jack's chest. 'What business?' He spoke this time in the broken Urdu typical of the Frontier.

Jack said again, still in English, 'Afroz. I've come to see her.'

The man shook his head.

Jack stared at the man's beard in admiration. He relented and said, in Urdu, he wanted to meet Afroz.

'Ms Rukhsana is not present. Gone outside,' the servant replied.

'Who is Ms Rukhsana?'

'She is mistress of the house. She's not here. Please leave your name.' The servant was pushing Jack back towards the car.

Jack held his ground and tried to find a window that he could look into and expose what was most certainly the servant's lie.

From inside the house a young woman, Rukhsana, who had only recently woken up, watched the discussion between the stranger and her servant. After a minute Afroz joined the woman and gasped, 'Oh God! How did he find out I was here?'

'You know him?' Rukhsana asked.

'He's the one from Islamabad, remember? Come on,' she tugged at her friend's arm. 'He might see us.'

Rukhsana put her hand to her mouth and whispered, 'You're right, it's him.' She laughed at the recollection of Mushtaq Gill falling to the floor, and the look of horror in his eyes.

Afroz giggled, too, crouching behind Rukhsana's shoulder.

'Nek Amal!' Rukhsana called out. 'Who is it?'

Afroz gave her friend a silent, wide-eyed look of disbelief. 'Shh!' she pleaded. 'He's too strange, believe me.'

The manservant didn't turn to address his mistress but called out, 'A sahib wants to see Ms Afroz, madam.'

'My name is Jack King. I'm from Chicago. I was talking with Afroz last night at the party and...'

'She's not here,' Rukhsana said in Pashto. 'Tell him to go away.'

The servant started pushing Jack again. Jack stood his ground for a second but then stumbled backwards, bumping into the jeep. William hopped out and opened the door for Jack who stood, unmoving. But the front door closed loudly and the servant indicated to William that he better leave.

12

A grimy plate of cream cakes, from which the pineapple pieces had been removed by the kitchen staff, accompanied the two pots of tea. The cream seemed suspiciously dusty but Noor Aslam was hungry. His stomach had growled all day while he waited for Khan Sahib's phone call. It came, at last, a few minutes after four. They sat in the lobby of the Galaxy Hotel at a table with a starched but torn tablecloth next to a window looking down onto a busy intersection. As soon as Khan Sahib shuffled in and took a seat at the table, he handed Aslam his weekly update on the activities of Mr Gunnar Andersen.

'His meeting with the leaders of the Katchi Gardhi camp was routine. Discussions about the distribution of oil—cooking and heating—and sugar, sir.'

Noor Aslam's mouth was full of cake. 'The refugees are still receiving cooking oil? After fifteen years? They only sell it on the market, everyone knows. Except the UN.' That these bloody Afghans, refugees no less, should be getting handouts after all these years, while his own income was being steadily eroded made Aslam's stomach spasm.

'Inter-agency meeting in the afternoon but Mr Andersen was finding it difficult to concentrate, sir. All telephone and fax messages entirely normal. Three to America—his father is ill—one to Copenhagen headquarters and twenty-three local. No unusual numbers or conversations, sir,' Khan relayed in a monotone.

'You have noted all this in your report, undoubtedly, Khan?' Aslam took a swig of milk tea and indicated with his pudgy balloon fingers that he should get to the real point. 'What of the other matter?' Aslam tugged at his tie and moved his jowls from side to side.

Khan viewed his arrangement with the NIA from a personal perspective. As long as he derived benefits from spying he was agreeable. He didn't consider what he did to be helping a cause or protecting his country. That sort of nonsense was for Aslam maybe, not him. And lately, since Faroukh's illness, the regular reports and trips to the Galaxy Hotel were becoming onerous. His precious time, which could be spent by his son's side was being demanded by this fool of a cream puff. Khan had recently mentioned his wish to cease his NIA duties to his wife, but she had insisted that she could care for Faroukh. 'Even if it is but a few hundred rupees a month, they will help us when you take Faroukh to the hospital in Karachi.' And so, even though his heart and mind were less and less engaged, Khan Sahib carried on spying.

But after meeting with Aslam earlier in the day about this Mr King, Khan Sahib had gone away annoyed and more determined than ever to give up spying. He had to visit the lady doctor tonight. He had no time to make enquiries about this case. He had just finished typing his letter of resignation to Aslam, when he overheard Andy telling one of the office girls that he was going to lunch early as he had a guest, an American man, a Mr something—Khan couldn't make out the name—staying at his house.

Khan's curiosity was piqued. He pulled the letter from the typewriter with a grinding metallic whiz. If that donkey Aslam was to be believed, Islamabad was very anxious about Mr King. Aslam said he was a big businessman. Khan Sahib called the office girl over and demanded that she repeat what Mr Andy had told her. The girl trembled in front of the increasingly short-tempered Office Manager. 'Only that he was going to lunch, Khan Sahib. He has an American guest in his house,' she said staring at the floor.

'What is his guest's name?'

The girl shrugged. She hadn't been paying attention. She waited for his outburst.

'You stupid girl. Why do we keep you if you don't open your ears? Will you be so vague the day I sack you?' This sort of mistake was common for the girls in the office; he didn't expect anything different but he wanted to make an impression. 'What is his guest's name?'

Again the girl shrugged; she struggled to hold back a tear. She knew she should pay more attention to what Mr Andy said but he spoke so fast and her English was not that good yet. 'Forgive me, Khan Sahib. You are right to be angry with me.'

'Of course, I am right,' he paused for effect. The tears were now flowing down both cheeks. 'Was the name King?' Khan asked, gruffly but hopefully.

'Ji, sir. Yes, you're correct. It is King. I think that is what Mr Andy said. King. Yes, I'm sure.' She was elated. Khan ordered her back to her desk and smiled.

He pulled himself upright. The heart of a spy always beats curiously, even in old age. If high levels in Islamabad are curious, then King must be a really big fish. What is Mr Andy's connection? Khan removed his hat and gave his weary head a scratch. His professional nose smelled money. Ilyas Khan Waziri decided he'd stay involved with Aslam just long enough to sort this King case out, but then no more. He tossed the resignation letter into the wastepaper basket.

Assistant Sub-inspector Aslam dusted the crumbs from his fat hands and then from his waistcoat. 'This hashish-loving charsi, Mr Andy, is of no interest at the moment, Khan. Islamabad is searching for Mr Jack King. I told you, have you already forgotten? You are getting old, isn't it? Daily updates, Khan. Islamabad is demanding.'

Khan Sahib watched Noor Aslam become more excited. He reminded him of a frog. The old spy was enjoying withholding information he knew Aslam and DG Mushtaq Gill were after. Khan lifted his teacup and slowly poured the liquid into the saucer. Noor Aslam grimaced at the old man's ill manners.

'I have further information about Mr Andy that I would like to report, sir.'

'Mr Andy, Mr Andy. Always Mr Andy. Are you deaf, man? I want to know of Mr King. Where is he? I instructed you to locate him, not Mr Andy. We know his location all the time. Islamabad is demanding information on Mr King. Urgently.'

'Mr King,' Khan paused and sipped his tea from the saucer, 'is at present located in the residence of Mr Andy in University Town where he is a houseguest.' He put the saucer down and folded his hands across his belly.

Aslam's masticating jowls slowed, then stopped completely as if the batteries had gone dead. A speck of cream had fallen onto his chin. After some time Aslam swallowed and downed a glass of water.

'Khan!' he whispered loudly. 'Are you sure? Can it be so? Are you sure?'

'Unless two Mr Kings have arrived in the last twenty-four hours, I am confident of my information.'

'Khan! Everything Mr Andy says to Mr King, where they attend parties, to whom they are relating and what time they are eating. Tell me everything. King, according to Islamabad—they phoned me again—is here to make contacts. You must ensure that he contacts the right persons.' Aslam was eyeing the old spy like he was a piece of cake.

'What sort of contacts, sir?'

'How do I know? That's why you are there, isn't it? If he wants to contact a taxi driver, he should be our taxi driver. Same if he wants to contact the imam of Mahabat Khan mosque.' Aslam burped silently. 'He is still ours, no?'

Not only him, there wasn't a mosque in the city whose imam did not provide weekly reports to NIA, Khan Sahib reassured his boss.

'Good good. Tomorrow then, Khan. Seven p.m. Here. I expect a full report on King's activities. Understood?'

In a series of slow, deliberate movements Khan Sahib rose from the chair, adjusted his woollen hat, turned towards the door and shuffled out into the evening gloom. Thunder and lightning danced across the city's flat, crumbling skyline. Globs of garbage floated by on the watery streets. Normally, he would have caught a bus but tonight he allowed himself the luxury of an autorickshaw. There was urgent business to attend to.

As William drove back to Andy's house, Jack smoked a Kent and gazed blankly at the cloudy sky. The last thing Jack had expected to come across in this country was a gorgeous, nice-smelling and bold woman like Afroz. In fact, meeting any sort of woman in Pakistan had not entered his mind. After he'd split up with Nasreen there'd been a couple of short-term affairs and there was Mitsy from Manila at the Casa d'Amor Massage Parlour. But with her schedule—working most nights—getting together had been a hassle. Besides, Mitsy couldn't really believe that Jack wanted to be with her. 'You sure, Jake, you really don't mind? I mean with my work and all, you know...' Jack hadn't minded at all. They were almost a regular couple—hanging out and watching TV. Though they mostly just cuddled and talked Jack would always make sure she got her sixty bucks. After he moved to the Twin Cities, he'd visit her from time to time but then he found himself in Pontiac. He hadn't been hugged by a woman in nearly five years.

Getting women had never been a problem for Jack. He knew he could charm the panties off most of them. And the ones he couldn't, he'd just plough straight ahead anyhow until they slapped him or walked away. It wasn't attracting them that was the problem, it was keeping them. After a while they all wanted the same thing: 'Stop the dealing, Jake'; 'Get some real friends, Jake'; 'Why do you have to waste all your money, Jake?' Six months of that crap was about all he could ever handle.

He knew that Afroz had been in the house. As soon as he got back to Andy's, he rang the number that Andy had given him earlier.

The phone rang thrice before it was picked up. 'Asalaam wale kum,' said a woman who Jack took to be Rukhsana.

'Hello, my name is Jack King. I'm from Chicago and I was wondering if I could speak with Afroz, please.'

There followed a long silence. He could hear the woman gasp and then whisper something indistinct to someone else. Afroz!

'Hello,' Jack said again. 'Who am I talking to?'

'My name is Rukhsana. Afroz is not here.'

'Nice to meet you, Rukhsana. You know that your name in English is Roxanne, like the lady in that song by Sting. You should call yourself that, it's much nicer.'

'Yes, I'm aware of that song but I am a Pakistani and I am happy with my name as it is.' She was smiling as she spoke. This Mr King was most unusual. A nice diversion on a monsoon morning. She waited for him to respond and had forgotten about her friend who was standing next to her.

'I'm American,' he said. 'Ever been there? You should come see me in Chicago some day.'

'No, I've not gone. I don't think I'd like it. Too big and expensive, and so much crime, I believe,' Rukhsana giggled slightly. Afroz pinched her arm, making her squeal. Afroz motioned to her to hang up the phone.

'That's what makes America great. It's bigger and better than every other place,' Jack said. 'Now, let me say hello to Afroz.'

Rukhsana was in the mood to keep flirting. But she gave in to Afroz's silent pleading and said, 'She is not here.'

'My gut tells me you ain't tellin' me the truth,' Jack replied quickly. 'I know that she has been staying with you, so why don't you just let me have a word?'

'Excuse me, Mr King, but can I ask how you came to know my address and phone number?' Her voice betrayed a tinge of alarm and anger.

'I made enquiries. Do y'all know Andy?'

'From the Danish office? Yes, I know him.' She knew Andy but not so well and now, she shared Afroz's irritation. What right did he have to give out information about people he barely knew? She scowled into the handset.

'That's right. Did I see you at the party last night, Rukhsana? You have a lovely voice. It's very musical,' Jack replied in his white American accent.

Rukhsana hesitated. 'Really? Thank you,' she said, feeling happy again. But a sharp pinch from Afroz brought her back to reality. 'Sorry, Mr King, your information is not correct. There is no Afroz here. Khuda hafez.' She hung up the phone without waiting for a reply.

'What are you thinking?' Afroz was angry with Rukhsana. She lit a cigarette and sat with her knees against her chest, glaring at her friend. 'I told you I don't want to talk with him and there you are chatting like he's your brother.'

'I didn't tell him you were here,' Rukhsana answered.

'But you were encouraging him. What if he calls again?'

As if on cue the phone emitted two dull rings. 'See! Oh God. He's a freak. Don't answer it,' Afroz said. 'Please, I don't want to ruin my weekend with some ridiculous Mr King from New York.'

'Chicago, he told me,' Rukhsana said as she moved to the phone. She answered it and laughed. 'Yes, just one minute please.' She turned to Afroz and extended the phone. 'For you. It's your uncle,' she whispered.

Afroz jumped up quickly, grabbed the phone and said, 'Good morning Uncle ji. Where are you?'

After a few minutes, she hung up and sat down on the sofa again. She sipped the cup of tea she had made before Jack called. It was Saturday and she hadn't been in Peshawar for months or seen her uncle for weeks, since his last visit to Islamabad. She loved Peshawar, or at least her uncle's house in Hayatabad where she was pampered like a princess. It was a place where she was always welcome. No questions were asked and all of society's restrictions were suspended as soon as she entered the front door. Though he was a teetotaller, there was always gin and tonic in the cupboards and the servants never intruded on her privacy. She liked the irony of the fact that in the wildest city in the country she was able to enjoy a little oasis of calm. She never stayed anywhere else, but this weekend her uncle had builders in for renovations and Rukhsana was delighted to have her company.

'What did he say?' Rukhsana asked, setting down a fresh pot of tea.

'He's in Dubai. He was calling to say that the house will

be ready by the end of the month. But the line was cut before he finished. He's so sweet.'

'Yes, but so are you!' Rukhsana was in a cheeky mood again. When Afroz gave her a quizzical look she said, 'Arrey, men are always chasing you. You are like a honeycomb and the bees are always buzzing around you. Buzz buzz. Buzz buzz,' she giggled.

'Which men?' Afroz poured more tea.

'Big important men, ji! Like Director General Gill sahib.'

Afroz scrunched up her nose.

'And Mr Ustad Jack King.'

Afroz laughed and said, 'Oh please, Rukhsana. He is so weird. And insecure. Repeating "I'm American, I'm American" like a drunken parrot. What is his problem? More importantly, where did he come from?'

'Chicago, my dear. He told me so on the phone.'

'Several times, I'm sure. No, I mean suddenly he's everywhere. We saw him in Islamabad and now he's here. Suddenly popped up like a pimple on the nose. Yuck!'

Rukhsana smiled and recalled the last thing Jack had said to her, about her having a musical voice. 'Weird maybe, but also nice,' she said. Afroz snorted into her cup.

'No, really Afroz. He talks so nicely, really. Like an American. Not all bad.'

Just then the phone rang again. Afroz jumped up, 'It's probably Uncle ji again. Hello!'

'Hey! Afroz. I knew you were there. Roxanne is a terrible liar. This is Jack King. From Chicago.'

'Oh,' Afroz snapped. 'Yes, I'm staying here but please don't bother me any more. I'm trying to enjoy a few days off. Don't call again, Mr King.'

'Hold it! I'm trying to enjoy myself, too. See, I've just come from Chicago and I know nobody in this town, well…except Andy, but he's a man, you know. Why don't we have a drink?

I can come over there now that my driver knows where to go. I can get some wine.'

'I don't think so, no thank you. I really must go. I am waiting for an important call,' Afroz said coldly.

'You know last night you didn't let me finish what I was saying. Let me at least wrap up the conversation, please?'

'I recall asking you for a fag. There was no conversation, Mr King.'

'Call me Jack,' he said, sensing he was gaining ground.

She said nothing, so Jack continued. 'Well I was saying to you, askin' actually, what a beautiful woman like you was doing in a dump like Pakistan. But you interrupted me and left. Not very nice, considering—'

'Considering what?' Afroz was exasperated. Why was she still talking to this guy? She wanted to hang up but he kept jabbering in his idiotic, 'cool' black American voice. She shot a glance at Rukhsana who grinned back at her from the sofa, nodding in an encouraging, teasing way. Afroz scowled and heard Jack saying, 'Considering I gave you a ciga…I mean a fag. Did I turn my back on you? No, I offered you one, just like a friend. That's all.'

Even though she knew he was sounding more hurt than he probably was, Afroz felt a slight stab of guilt.

'I'm sorry,' she said in a softer tone. 'I wasn't in the mood, I suppose.'

'Not in the mood to be told you're a babe? Damn, I'd never get tired of that if I was you.'

'I was just tired.'

'You can make it up by having a drink with me.' His hurt tone had disappeared.

'I'm sorry, not today.'

'I won't bite, girl!' His use of the last word and its assumed intimacy annoyed Afroz. But before she could say no, he spoke again. This time with a hesitance that suggested a genuine sadness. 'Haven't had a chance to talk to a lady for a long time.' He paused briefly then said, almost to himself, 'I'm feelin' lonely.'

Jack sighed, mumbled something else and waited for her to respond. He was feeling defeated again. Like at the party the other night when her cool aloofness had made him feel as if she'd knocked him out in three easy rounds. At last, when she didn't say anything, Jack recovered and said, 'I'll give you a call tomorrow and we'll set up a time. Try not to miss me too much!' He hung up, leaving Afroz holding the phone, unnerved. Though her face flushed with irritation, she was tickled by his unselfconscious openness. She didn't want to have any of these feelings today. All she had wanted to do was pass a rainy day sipping tea, chatting with Rukhsana and napping. 'Bugger!' she exclaimed as she put the phone down.

'You're not saying he's a nice guy, are you?' Afroz was irritable after Jack hung up. Now Rukhsana was getting on her nerves as well. 'Maybe not nice exactly,' said Rukhsana. 'But interesting. So full of energy.'

'Full of himself, don't you mean?'

'Of course, but he's different. So unlike anyone else we know.'

'That's no reason to spend time with him. DG sahib is "different" too.'

Rukhsana made a gagging gesture and scowled. 'Don't even mention that man, yuck! At least Mr King is westernized. Like you are.'

'Oh please, Rukhsana!'

Rukhsana shrugged and made a face as if to say, it's true.

Afroz wished her uncle would call again and she could get her mind off this conversation. She turned towards the window, away from her friend and lit a cigarette. Though

Rukhsana was her closest friend, there was a lot they didn't share. They had been introduced by Afroz's uncle soon after she had arrived in Pakistan a year earlier. Rukhsana had taken her around to all the NGOs in Islamabad until she landed a job as the manager of a drug rehab agency. She had also introduced her to the best tailors and been her companion on Islamabad and Peshawar's expat social circuits. Afroz appreciated Rukhsana's help and advice but found her a bit superficial. And her comment about Jack King and her being somehow compatible because they were 'westernized' just underscored the point.

Afroz had had male friends at university, both English and Asians, but she had always broken things up pretty quick. The British guys, like Tim, a quiet Scottish boy from Aberdeen, seemed to have no grunt. He felt intimidated by her but still liked having an exotic 'dark babe' on his arm when they went out. As for the Pakistanis, well, she had yet to find one who didn't think like his grandfather when it came to women. Anwar, from Bradford was drop dead gorgeous but could talk of nothing but football and Hari, the crazy-smart south Indian, couldn't get it up.

'I've had my fill of "westernized" men,' she snapped. 'All sizzle but no sausage, as the Aussies say.'

Rukhsana stifled a guffaw which made Afroz smile again.

'Still, what's the harm in having coffee with him?'

For her part Rukhsana envied her new friend's European background. But Afroz could be overly serious sometimes. Even a bit moody. 'It's just a bit of fun. What else will you do tomorrow?'

Afroz didn't answer. She watched the cigarette burn itself out.

'What's happened has happened, Afroz. That doesn't mean you have to be unhappy for the rest of *your* life. I'm sure they would want—'

'It's not them. Or that,' Afroz said firmly. 'He's such a caricature. I can't take so-called Mr King seriously. "I'm from Chicago!"'

They both laughed again but after another hour of Rukhsana's arguments, Afroz agreed to meet Jack for a coffee at the Pearl Continental the next day.

Khan Sahib had left Aslam with his cakes and tea at the Galaxy Hotel and hailed an autorickshaw. Mr Andy had asked him to come around to his house after dinner to meet his houseguest, Mr King. He said that Mr King needed to interview someone who would assist him in an important job. When Khan Sahib had nonchalantly enquired about the nature of the job, Mr Andy had refused to say but insisted that the candidate must be strong. He repeated the last word and flexed his arms like he was a muscle man. Khan did not ask further questions. He assured his boss that he knew of a few candidates who might qualify.

Slowly working his way into the backseat of the rickshaw, he said, 'Khyber Bazaar.' The driver nodded and made a U-turn, heading towards the heart of the old city, where goondas, badmaashes, 420s and offenders of all types waited for a job just like Mr King's.

Andy was getting anxious waiting. In the office, during the afternoon, he had found it hard to concentrate on his work. He imagined a hundred thousand dollars in his bank account. Even Eric was unlikely to have such an amount lying about. Andy relished the idea of breaking the news to his younger brother and parents. At last, they would notice him again. But these pleasant thoughts took frantic flight as he imagined himself getting arrested and locked away forever. Jack's sudden insistence on bringing in a 'Luigi' to do some dirty work was not welcome news. Was a hundred thousand dollars really worth this? Smoking cigarette after cigarette, he feared there were too many variables in the plan. When he got home he made it clear to Jack that he was not a criminal.

'And you sayin' I am one?' Jack snapped back.

'Well…' Andy was fidgeting with his goatee but he didn't know how to proceed.

'Shiiit! You don't understand the first thing 'bout criminals even if one came up and bit you on your raggedy white ass. Criminals be professional, full-time—' he hesitated, unable to find the word he wanted, 'baddies. That's right. I'm a businessman. There's a difference.'

Andy's eyes said, convince me. His head looked like it might bob right off onto the floor.

'Man, stop that shit,' snapped Jack. 'I'm no criminal. I conduct business and I got to face impediments like any normal-ass businessman. A criminal lives for killin', and thievin'. Did I come to you and say, "Howdy do, Andy, let's kill somebody's ass." I recall I laid out a business plan for you. Now that business plan has been interrupted and requires other means for completion, see.'

'Sure,' Andy said, 'sure thing.' He was aware of how unsure he sounded.

'Ain't no criminal anywhere near this place,' Jack muttered as he disappeared into the kitchen to fetch a couple more beers.

The man Khan Sahib brought with him must have weighed over 120 kilos, with hands the size of dinner plates. His name was Sher Jan. He came wrapped up in a brown woollen shawl and his baggy shalwar pants were pulled up too high, like he'd just crossed a river. He hadn't shaved for a few days and curls of oily black hair hung over his boxer's ears. He wore a white Chitrali hat like the old man's. Khan Sahib said that Sher Jan spoke only Pashto.

Andy offered the two men some tea, which they both refused. Sher Jan was looking around like he'd never been in a foreigner's house before. His eyes were greyish-green like an Uzbek's. Andy figured he must be from one of Afghanistan's northern districts. He started to talk and Khan Sahib translated everything he said. 'An associate, a business associate of ours,' Andy indicated Jack and himself, 'owes us some money. The sum involved rightly belongs to my friend here, Mr King. However, the man refuses to pay the money and all our efforts to persuade him otherwise have failed.' Sher Jan showed no sign that he was interested in what Andy had to say. He was craning his neck to look into the dining room, smiling at the mini-stereo and then staring, first at Jack and then at Andy. Over and over. 'We need someone, such as yourself, to convince him to repay our money.'

'Call the police. They will make him straight,' Sher Jan said.

The simplicity of the response caught Andy off-guard. It made so much sense. Before he could respond, Khan Sahib asked, 'Who is the man?'

Jack jumped in. 'That ain't important. Is he gonna help us?'

'That depends.'

'What sort of price would you think is appropriate for this sort of activity?' Andy was talking in the measured, educated voice he used at work.

Sher Jan shrugged and said the price would be reasonable and just about right, depending on the situation. Andy nodded and said, of course he understood, but it would help to have a rough figure.

Sher Jan wanted to know how many others would be involved? Andy asked how many others Sher Jan thought might be necessary.

Jack could feel his irritation grow, listening to Andy and Sher Jan lob questions at each other like tennis balls. He pulled a foot out of one of his shoes and began massaging his toes. He waited but it didn't look like they were going to stop dancing around the issue.

'Listen, pussy,' Jack moved to the edge of the sofa about six inches from Sher Jan's unshaven face, 'we need one man shaken down. Understand? Frighten him, make him nervous, convince him to pay up.' Khan Sahib tried to keep up with Jack. 'We don't want nobody dead, but if he's feeling a bit sore after you done with him, that's okay. We tell you where he lives and you get to work. Terms are flat rate. Cash. You call in the troops or you do it alone, that is up to you. Interested?'

Sher Jan face was expressionless but he shrugged in a way that Khan Sahib interpreted as, 'Yes, he is very much interested.'

They agreed to meet again, in a day or two, to talk in more detail after Sher Jan had checked out the compound and reported back on how he planned to shake down Jack's 'associate'. Jack gave Sher Jan the address but didn't mention Ahmadzai. Khan Sahib said that Sher Jan was insisting on a down payment, even though Jack could have sworn the big Uzbek hadn't opened his mouth. He glared at Khan Sahib for a second but then pulled out some hundred dollar bills—one, two, three—and handed them to Sher Jan who, at last, smiled.

13

Jack was already at the hotel coffee shop when she arrived. He jumped up and pulled out a chair for her. Afroz smiled and refused a cigarette.

'So what have you accomplished today then, Mr King?' She was determined to control the conversation and be back at Rukhsana's as quickly as possible.

'Just business. Boring-ass stuff.'

He ordered her a pot of tea and answered her questions as if he was being interviewed. Best behaviour, daddy-o, he kept repeating to himself. But after about fifteen minutes in he burst out with a question that had been bothering him for days.

'What's your other name? Afroz...?'

'Gul.'

'Wha—?'

'Afroz Gul.' She adjusted the deep red velvety tie in her hair.

'Wo! Beautiful!'

'Oh, not again,' she couldn't help but laugh.

'Serious, girl. That's some name. Gul, means flower right?'

She nodded.

'Afroz, well that's pretty and easy to remember, too. Sounds almost English, you know...Afroz. Rose. And now you saying your other name means flower,' he paused to shake his head. 'Too much.'

Afroz gave another little laugh. He was cute.

From now on Jack said, he'd call her 'Rose' because the rose was the queen of all flowers. 'That's what my mother used to tell me. And because a King deserves a queen to keep him company.'

'Why not just call me Afroz? You said it's a lovely name.'

'It is, but...well, just...I don't think much along those lines any more. Least try not to.'

'What lines?'

'You know.' He looked at her, but if she knew she wasn't letting on. 'Urdu and all this other local shit. I put that behind me years ago. My brain is trained to function only in English.'

'What was your name before you trained yourself to forget who you are?'

He told her the same thing that he'd told Andy, that he'd been born Yaqub but that he was like another person now; Yaqub was a character he had heard about but never met.

Afroz sensed her defences coming up. Here was another 'westernized' man full of bluster and attitude with nothing to back it up. But because she was brought up to be polite she asked him if his mother and father lived in Chicago, too.

Jack stopped short. He hadn't expected that question and for a second glared across the table at her. 'No,' he said quickly. 'She died when I was little. He lives here, somewhere.'

Before she could ask more he said, 'What do you do? How does a beautiful woman make a life in a cesspit like this?'

'I work.'

'So...?

'In an NGO that helps addicts get back on their feet. I manage the office, the staff and basically do it all. We are very tiny but one of the few places in this part of the country that addicts can get help.'

'What kind of addicts?'

'Heroin. A few struggle with alcohol.'

She noticed that his eyes flashed uncomfortably around the room and he began to fidget. He changed the subject again. 'You ever been in Chicago?'

'No, what's it like?' she asked without curiosity.

She wanted to leave but Jack ordered a second pot of tea and said, 'Best damn city in America. Ain't no other place like it in the world. Did you know that the Chicago river runs backwards? And that Hugh Hefner started *Playboy* magazine in Chicago?'

He was off to the races. Jack regaled her with stories about Chicago—the gangsters, the first McDonald's in the world, Wrigleys Chewing Gum, the time the Bears won the Super Bowl and he almost crashed his car when they scored the winning touchdown, because he wasn't paying attention and the roads were full of ice—and how great life in America was.

He talked like a comic book character and seemed to have a story for every occasion. Almost against her will, Afroz let herself listen to him and soon he had her bent over laughing. Every so often he'd stop to catch his breath and she saw his energy shift. He would get sheepish and stare at the floor, like he was a boy who had lost something precious. For just a second she would get a glimpse of something vulnerable and unprotected but then he'd light another cigarette and say, 'Did you know the whole city burned down about a hundred years ago?'

Two hours passed before out-of-the-blue he announced he had to get his sorry ass back to business. She surprised herself by saying, 'Maybe we can do this again.'

As he left her at the table, Jack knew he'd reeled her in good. But damn, this wasn't part of the plan.

That night just as he was about to hit the sack, Andy's phone rang. 'It's for you, Jack.'

'It's me,' said Afroz. 'Can I interest you in a little road trip tomorrow?'

Jack had about as much interest in exploring Pakistan as he did in taking a tour of the addicts centre she ran. He was here to execute his plan, not to go sightseeing. But this was Afroz asking.

'Sure. Love to.' He hoped his voice sounded convincing.

'Great. I'll see you then. Goodnight, Mr King.'

The following morning Afroz arrived with her driver in a white Toyota Crown a few minutes before nine. Since the monsoon had begun the rain hadn't let up for two days. Cool winds blew off the rocky Hindu Kush. Even though they were drenched to the bone, everyone in the streets and on the tops of buses was laughing and singing. 'Like the first snow back home,' Jack said to Afroz as they made their way through the city.

They drove up the main highway across a short flatland and through small towns with mud walls for an hour or so, then over the misty Malakand Pass, down into the most beautiful valley Jack had ever seen. The earth before them seemed to be covered with layers of luxurious velvet: green, purple or black, depending on how close you were and at what angle the muted sunlight shone. The silvery corrugated tin roofs of buildings caught the occasional light and sparkled like diamonds on the hillsides. They drove up and down bending mountain roads and in and out of little valleys that lay hidden within the big one. And right through the middle, like a great big zipper holding everything together, gushed the urgent waters of the Swat River.

Afroz was wearing a pale blue cotton shalwar-qameez and a navy blue ribbon in her hair that she'd tied in a long ponytail. Jack noticed that her toenails and fingernails were painted in a deep purple. Even Mitsy had never painted her toenails.

As they headed down into another valley, the skies opened up in a deluge so strong the driver struggled to see the road. Once or twice the dark sky cracked open, exposing a thin gash of light that glowed a deep yellow. A gold necklace against black skin. 'Here we are in the darkness down here but a second ago, up there in the mountains, see there,' Jack was pointing up to a break in the heavy clouds, 'the sun be shining and over there mist is rolling in. Eerie.'

'This is what I love about this country,' Afroz said.

'What?'

'The intensity of life, the seasons, especially the monsoon. In England it rained a lot, but always in a steady drizzle. There was never this kind of unrelenting barrage that we're going to have for the next few weeks.' She reached over and touched Jack's leg unconsciously, as if to say, 'Isn't this great?' Jack didn't know what he was supposed to do but it felt nice. For a second, he debated whether he should put his own hand on top of her's, but then let it slide.

She looked young, no more than twenty-six or twenty-seven. He was about to ask, when two young men on a small Yamaha dirt bike roared past, laughing and shouting. They cut in front of the car and Afroz's driver, an old man with a white untrimmed beard, hit the brakes and cursed. The Yamaha swayed on the wet highway and nearly tossed the passenger off, before the driver regained control and took off even faster.

Afroz gasped but then laughed and clapped her hands. 'What fun!' She looked at Jack who was wishing she would put her hand back on his leg. 'Have you ever ridden a bike like that?'

'Like that Yamaha? Or have I ridden a bike that way... like a jive ass hothead?'

'Both.'

When he was fifteen, Jack had seen *The Great Escape* at the Plaza in Rawalpindi. 'Steve McQueen was my idol,' he told her. The idea of commandeering a bike and escaping from prison just wouldn't let him be. 'Guess because that's where I thought I was in Hallbourne Academy...a Nazi stalag.'

Ali Hassan has made a special deal with Mr Nelson, the vinegar-breathed English headmaster of Hallbourne Academy. 'Discipline is what the blodger needs,' Yaqub hears Mr Nelson telling his father. 'And discipline is what Hallbourne was founded to provide.'

'Anything it takes, Mr Nelson. I won't stand in your way. Make him a man.'

For a year and a half, Yaqub endures the taunts and physical abuse of classmates and Mr Nelson's staff, who run the school like a prison camp. His small size makes him an easy target. The headmaster arranges extra sessions of rigorous study on the weekends and physical workouts with soldiers from the nearby Baluchistan Rifles regimental headquarters. When the boy expresses an interest in electronics, Mr Nelson makes sure he is assigned to the mechanics shed instead, where he is forced to learn how to repair motorcycles. The grease, grit and stench sink deep into his skin and give the older boys another reason to shun and bully him.

The only thrill Yaqub enjoys is test driving the big machines before handing over the keys to the workshop's foreman. In a life dominated by Mr Nelson's cruelty and his father's neglect, these fifteen-minute high-speed spins around the regimental compound are the sole bright spot in the boy's world.

During Eid holidays Yaqub sees The Great Escape, *and can hardly sleep. Back in Abbottabad he spends a whole morning tinkering with a huge BSA. By noon the bike is ready for a test run. Yaqub looks like a creature from the swamp, black and shimmery with grease. He rips around the compound, revving the engine, jamming the brakes, stamping the clutch often and hard. Three or four times around the compound and then, bam, right out the front gate while the guards are doing the paperwork on a lorry of troops that has come back from field training.*

Yaqub tears through the town's main bazaar, up the big hill, swinging left towards the bus stand. In what seems like less than a minute, he is leaning hard into the curves of the mountain road leading down to the Haripur plains. The faster he descends towards the flatland, the more the heat pulls him away from 'Hell-burn' Academy. On a straight-a-way he pushes the bike up to seventy, then eighty, his hand vibrating on the accelerator like he's riding a rocket. Though petrified, for those glorious other-worldly seconds Little Yaqub is Steve McQueen. He knows he can't maintain control of the bike but at the same time he is unable to release the accelerator. He laughs and screams and keeps his thumb on the horn as he rips through a small bazaar, where he nearly clips a fat water-buffalo waddling onto the road. Swerving madly, then gaining control for a few more seconds, he hits a gravel patch on the other side of the village and the bike disappears from under him. When he stops rolling he finds himself in the rain gutter by the side of the road with a sore back, tattered pants and knees all torn to hell; but no real damage. He can't say the same for the bike which lies like a dark green pretzel fifty metres down the hillside.

On Monday Ali Hassan is summoned to collect his 'incorrigible' son.

They were having drink at a little Coca Cola stand near a wide curve in the river. 'That's when you were sent to America?' she asked.

'I wish.' Jack had the feeling she was leaning into him to keep warm because the rain and the altitude had made the day chilly. 'I wanted to go real bad. After seeing *The Great Escape* and knowing Steve McQueen was American and all, I prayed that the old man would send me, but he didn't. The only good thing that came out of my great escape was that the old man was humiliated. Wasn't a school left in Pakistan that would have me and for a while he talked about sending me to Bombay to stay with cousins but Nanima refused and said it was because my mother had died that I was misbehaving. But it wasn't. I just liked to run crazy. It pissed my old man off and made me feel free.'

Afroz's old driver was anxious to keep moving; the sky was as black as lead. As they splashed along the highway Afroz seemed eager to know more about his childhood. 'I ain't used to this,' he said.

'To what?'

'Someone taking an interest in my life...usually it's the cops who grill me.'

She smiled, giving his leg another gentle squeeze and said 'I like your stories.' Jack felt himself getting warm and wanting to hug her. She said that she was dying for a fag and asked the driver to pull off the road by a huge brick mound set about fifty feet off the highway.

'What's that?' Jack was staring up at the crumbling mound of ancient brickwork.

'A stupa.'

'Say wha—?'

'A stupa is a special place for Buddhists. There's an old monastery where Buddhist monks used to live and study way up there on the side of the hill.' She stretched her arm out towards a mountain whose top was covered with cottony mist.

'You shittin' me, Rose? This the land of the Pure and the

Holy, the goddamned Islamic Republic and you telling me them Dalai Lama dudes have a thing going here as well?'

'Used to Jack, centuries ago. There's a lot of old ruins and pre-Islamic culture in this valley. Have you ever been to Taxila?'

Jack shook his head.

'It's an entire city dating back to the ancient Hindu days, even before Buddha. Taxila was one of the great universities of the ancient world.'

'In Pakistan? Give me a break.' Jack moved slowly towards the stupa like he was afraid it might open up and swallow him whole.

'I visited the monastery up there with my brother and father, years ago. It's a long walk and in this weather it would be dangerous. But when the monsoon is over, the view will be brilliant. There's a reason for you to stick around a little longer.'

Jack gave her a funny look then lost his footing on the narrow, raised mud footpath that marked the paddy fields, which lay submerged beneath a foot of water. He leapt towards Afroz, grabbing her with both arms. For a second they held on to each other, teetering on the edge. Her breasts pressed against him; he held on to her a few seconds longer than necessary. She laughed, 'You're going to squeeze all the air out of me, Jack!'

He let go as if he'd been electrified. 'Sorry, Rose. I just didn't want you to fall into the water there…'

'Give us a fag, then,' she said still making sure she held on to his shoulder.

'I wish you'd wouldn't call it that,' he said, making a playfully pained face. She lit the Kent and blew the smoke straight up like she was at a table in Vegas.

'So how about it? Why don't you stay a little longer? When the rains stop I'll take you up to that monastery.'

'Stick around to check out a prehistoric Hellburn Academy?' he made a painful grimace. 'No way, Rose.'

They shared her cigarette and stared at the stupa for a few minutes, in silence. When she dropped the butt into the paddy field, Jack put his arm around Afroz's shoulder and pulled her into him. She didn't say anything. He knew she liked it.

14

Afroz told her driver that she and Mr King had decided that they would go home via Abbottabad. Her Urdu was poor: definitely a second language, Jack noted. Sufi, the old driver, was grumbling and tried to explain that Abbottabad was 'that way'—he indicated vaguely to his left—and Peshawar was straight ahead. He would have to drive hundreds of extra kilometres and they would have to spend the night in Abbottabad as it would be dark in two hours and, what about Ms Rukhsana in Peshawar?

Afroz listened politely until Sufi stopped to inhale and said if she and Mr King had to stay overnight in a hotel, well, they would. 'It is not your concern.'

Jack was surprised by the change in plans. His old stomping ground was the last place he wanted to visit. But at the moment, he was thinking about the sleeping arrangements in the hotel. Was Afroz planning on separate rooms or was she telling him something? He pretended to be engrossed in the scenery but was trying to imagine what she might look like out of Pakistani clothes, in her underwear.

The road was climbing again after curling down the Malakand Pass. A pale tungsten-like light shone weakly onto the wet hills as the silver-grey clouds gathered together again, just below the peaks. Afroz was asking Jack about growing up in a boarding school but he was tired of talking. 'Why don't we turn the tables, Rosie? I'll be the cop, your turn to talk now.'

It was as if she had been waiting for him to ask. 'There was an accident a few of years ago between Oxford and Birmingham. The road isn't a major highway, at least the one they were on wasn't—just a windy country 'A' road in the Midlands. Mum and Dad were coming home from a weekend with friends in Birmingham and Dad thought he'd skip the Monday morning rush on the motorway. So he took off on the back road.'

Jack took the opportunity, as Sufi braked on a sharp bend, to inch closer to her.

'It was incredibly misty that morning. I remember waking up in my dorm in Oxford not knowing what time of day it was. The sun was completely obscured.

'It was a day like this. Visibility was bad. Right around Woodstock my father lost control, or someone behind him did, I'm not sure. In any case, their car slipped into a lorry that had stopped in front of them. Both Mum and Dad were instantly killed. The car behind them was damaged but no one was seriously hurt.'

'Shit, Rose,' Jack whispered. He scooted closer and put his hand on her thigh and squeezed. 'Sorry 'bout that.' She put her hand on his hand and squeezed back. But as he sat there waiting for more words to come to mind, she said that she was all right now; coming back to Pakistan had helped.

'In fact, after they died I knew that I would have to come back here. I had wanted to return ever since we moved to England, but daddy always insisted that Pakistan was no place to bring up a girl.' She laughed quietly.

'Daddy hoped that my brother and I would become English. That we would think like the English and settle down in Britain, get good jobs and eventually forget about Pakistan. He was a friend of Bhutto's and after Zia's coup he went to jail for a year. The day he was released he said there was no more hope for the country now that Bhutto was dead.

"Progress has come to an end," he used to say. "Zia will turn the clocks back." So we packed up and moved to Oxfordshire.'

'My old man never considered moving us outta here,' Jack said.

'Daddy was very different. He wanted us to be exposed to western life and ideas. And for him, there was no better country than Britain for that.' Afroz rolled down the window an inch and breathed in the wet fresh air. 'Ahhh. I just love the smell of the monsoon.'

Jack didn't object to the smell but after a couple of minutes he said, 'Roll that thing up, Rose. It's chilly. Tell me more about your father.'

'He felt that way because his own tradition and country had failed him. They had thrown him in jail and brutalized him for no reason. Mum would have been happier to stay in Pakistan. She found the little village where Dad bought a shop too small and alien. She missed the bazaars and fresh vegetables and the whirring fans in the summer. But even she used to swear that Pakistan was not the same place with that "zalil", as she called Zia, in charge.'

Politics—like Nasreen, Hallbourne and his family—was just another part of the past that Jack had buried and walked away from. Of course, he knew that Bhutto had been hanged but unlike the rest of his countrymen, he had celebrated on that day. 'One less hypocrite in the world,' he'd said in a drunken and altogether too loud toast at a sombre 'mourning party', which his in-laws had arranged soon after the hanging. Uncle Jalal, sweat balling up on his forehead, had shouted at Jack for ten minutes, nearly bursting into tears at his nephew's insult to the great martyr of democracy. The rest of the guests pretended that Jack hadn't really meant what he'd said. But he had. To him, Bhutto's hanging by the army was nothing more than another confirmation of the barbarity and primitiveness of the people he'd left behind. It was another wave that pushed his boat further from the shore and closer to a new, more enlightened world. Another stage in his great escape.

'So we lived in our little village outside Oxford,' Afroz continued. 'Daddy ran the small news agency which he found humiliating but better than licking the boots of the generals. Me and my brother went to school every day and slowly, I started turning myself into a nice little English girl. By the time I was fourteen, I spoke English better than most of my classmates, got better marks and never ever wore a shalwar-qameez. But just when I had convinced myself I was not a foreigner, someone would call out 'Paki' or a customer in Dad's shop would whisper 'curry girl' under her breath, and I would remember who I really was.'

In America, Jack had been called names he didn't like or understand but after getting his ass whooped one too many times for retaliating, he decided to use the abuse. To rid his life of every vestige, every possible trace of Pakistan.

'When I was sixteen, my brother, Ehsan, had been bashed and sent to the hospital. I accepted the fact that I wasn't an English girl. After this, it was inevitable that I would return home. But I was too young to do anything about it. Though, I started wearing shalwaar-qameez and developed a huge crush on Imran Khan,' she giggled.

'By the time I entered university the feeling mellowed. "Paki bashing" wasn't as common as it had been, and Asians were starting to be seen as "cool". As an adult, being surrounded by more sophisticated types in Oxford made England seem not so bad. Then when the accident happened, I felt lost. For years, my parents had represented Pakistan for me, my connection to home. Their deaths made it clear that I would have to return. Without them around, I had nothing to keep me in England. It became like a hotel or a dormitory: a temporary, lifeless place.

'About a year after the accident I called Mum's older

brother in Peshawar and he invited me to stay with him until I decided if I really wanted to settle permanently back in Pakistan. I knew, of course, that I did and within six months I got my Pakistani passport and started Urdu lessons.'

'What you're sayin' is that all those years in England, in the land of plenty, had no effect on you? Is that what you're tellin' me, Rose? I don't believe it.'

'Why?'

'That anyone in their right mind would leave England and come back to this hole. What do you see here?'

Afroz said that he was missing the point. 'We have our roots and we cut them out at our own peril.' Jack had definitely not felt this way. 'They anchor us to the ground and don't allow us to stray too far. I tried my hardest to convince everyone, myself the most, that I wasn't Pakistani, but it didn't work.'

'You give up your English passport?'

'It's not about citizenship.'

'Hey, I know what you sayin', Rose. Believe me. It's all in the heart. And my own heart is the complete opposite of yours. Do some open heart surgery, see, and my heart be the same colour as this here passport.' He patted his breast pocket. 'Bet it even has my name, Jack King, in gold letters, just like on the passport.'

'In the driest part of every immigrant's heart, there is a patch of moist soil from back home. I really believe that, Jack. It takes the smallest thing to make it grow. The smell of frying onions or the heat rising out of the ground before the rains.' She gave him a look that made him uncomfortable and conscious of the silence. He smiled at her but she didn't say anything more.

As they took another bend, they were confronted by a rainbow that seemed to end right in the centre of the road that wound along the side of the mountain. As they drove through it, Jack turned around and watched the colours become dimmer and dimmer.

'What are you thinking, Jack?'

'They say a pot of gold be at the end of the rainbow.'

By the time they got to Abbottabad, the small town was completely dark except for a string of cheap tea halls running along the edge of the tarmac. They found a hotel and before Jack could say anything, Afroz stepped up and said in her best English accent, 'A double room, please, for one night. Mr and Mrs Jack King.' The man behind the counter gawped, first at Jack, then Afroz. He fumbled for the register and said that they would have to sign here and asked if they wanted a wake-up call. 'No. Is room service available?' The manager nodded, and wondered if he could send someone to get their luggage. 'We have none,' said Afroz. The manager's expression was composed of equal parts disbelief, disapproval and prurient curiosity. He nodded slightly and led them down a dark hall stained with huge damp spots, like mildewy maps of strange countries, and showed them into their room.

When the door closed behind them, they both looked at each other and burst into laughter. 'A double room, please. Mr and Mrs Jack King.' Jack was strutting on his tiptoes, trying on Afroz's posh accent.

Afroz flopped onto the bed, undid her blue ribbon and watched him. He had interested her from the first time they had met in Islamabad. Even though he had been obnoxious, his intentions had been noble: to keep that letch Mushtaq Gill's hands off of her. It was so easy to see behind his Americanisms and swagger. Jack's facade was like an amateur brass band in full swing. Loud, brash, colourful and all out of step. But behind it hid someone soft, hurt and a little needy.

He was bending over and taking off his shoes. 'Don't

you ever wear socks?' she asked but he didn't hear. He was hanging his blazer on a hook and putting his passport under his pillow. He tapped the pillow and gave her an impish grin.

Jack was not an exemplary specimen of maleness. He was too short and didn't wear socks, for goodness sake. His balding pate brought back memories of her father which made whatever sexual chemistry she might have felt fade right away. He seemed afraid, and had tensed up when she'd touched him. But then he'd nearly squeezed the life out of her at the stupa. Why was she feeling so soft towards this 'dude'?

Most men on the party circuit offered her one emotion: lust. But Jack was something else, like a planet whirling through space. And when he stopped spinning long enough, he unloaded everything he had: his insecurities as well as his charm, both wrapped up in a manic energy.

'Let's chow down.' Jack had his bare feet on the small low table and held up a stained menu with half the prices crossed out and newer, higher prices written in.

They ordered a keema, a dal, a chicken korma and some rotis, most of which he finished off in less than ten minutes. Afroz wasn't hungry and stayed stretched out on the bed. After dinner, Jack burped and said he needed a smoke. A small, black ball came out of his blazer pocket and within a few minutes the sooty, sweetish smell of hash was hanging heavy in the room. Afroz, who never smoked anything other than tobacco, made him open the window and got under the covers to keep warm.

'When do you pick up your pot of gold, Mr King?'

'A-S-A-P.'

'Can I have some?'

Jack handed her the joint eagerly and coughed but Afroz said, 'No stupid, I meant the gold. Are you going to share?'

Whenever he had thought of Nanima's "pund" in the past day or two, his mind had settled comfortably, like a bird on the topmost branch, on the figure of half a million. It was a nice figure and he tried to imagine what five hundred thousand dollars would look like if laid out on a table. If it were in hundreds it wouldn't be that high a stack, but twenties...well, that was another story. 'Course, Rosie. Half the fun be sharin'.'

'I don't want anything, Jack. Just teasing.' She was dozing off. A few minutes later, she was on her side with a Walkman on her head.

'What you listenin' to?' he shouted.

'Ghazals. Not your type of music, Jack King.'

'You joking, girl? The only type of music.' He jumped up and hopped over to the bed. 'Who's your favourite?'

She removed one of the earphones and told him that she loved Farida Khanum and Iqbal Banu but, 'Keep still, Jack. Ghulam Ali and Asha Bhosle are singing a duet.'

'He's my man!' He reached over, pulled off the headset and put it around his head. 'Ever notice how his voice sounds like he's singing from the bottom of the sea.'

She shook her head, 'I don't think I have.'

'Like he's drowning in sadness, far away from any help. Love him.'

The ghazal finished and Jack returned the headset to Afroz. She was nearly asleep. The lights in the room suddenly surged incredibly bright, then in a big whispered 'pop', everything went dark. The rain was coming down in sheets. It was hard to see Afroz even though they shared the bed. Jack reached out to touch her shoulder. She purred for a quick second and burrowed her head in the pillow.

'You know, Rosie, what you were saying about the smallest thing can make our hearts remember who we are. 'Member that?'

'Umm...' Afroz shifted on to her back.

'For me it's not onions or the heat, it's ghazals. Listen

to them and...whump. Right back home, no matter where I'm at.'

She was asleep. Jack put the headset on and listened to another ghazal, contemplating whether he should climb under the sheet next to her. But something told him, it wasn't time. Not yet.

In the morning after breakfast, they checked out and Afroz instructed the driver to do a quick tour of the town. 'Why you doin' this, Rose?' Jack moaned. He was slouched low in the back like a pop star hiding from his wild, screaming fans.

'Where is Hallbourne Academy? I want to see it. Just that, then we'll leave. Come on Jack, it's not going to bite.'

Nearly thirty years on, he hardly recognized anything. The Baluchistan Rifles had a new signboard announcing their regimental headquarters; he had remembered them being much further out of town. A wide four-lane road swept through the place; buses and little Suzuki vans stuffed with people roared up and down. As Sufi pulled out into the traffic Jack saw the board hanging from a white wall with an arrow pointing down an alley: Hallbourne Academy. Some Latin words underneath. He had never understood what they meant. Afroz had seen the sign too and read aloud, 'Truth. Perseverance. Integrity.'

'Torture. Lies. Horseshit,' muttered Jack.

Why was she doing this to him? 'It hasn't changed one bit...still the same old feeling of being choked and suffocated. Shit, Rose, I got business to take care of. Take me back to Peshawar.'

Sufi, also anxious to get back to Peshawar, ripped through town and started down the hill, taking the corners wide and hardly braking. As the car descended towards the plains and Abbottabad became a cluster of white specks against the mountainside, Jack began to relax a little. 'Hey Rose, this the same way I felt the day I made my great escape.' He was sitting up now—swaying and pretending he had the bike between his legs, leaning into every turn. 'The closer I got to the plains, the faster I wanted to go.' Jack was laughing excitedly. 'Hoo wee! Hey look! Right there. See? That's where I lost control.' He whipped around to look at the bend they had just turned. 'One wrong move, that's all it took. Bam, out she went from under me. My ass was grass. Ha ha!'

'What happened after Hallbourne?'

'The asshole exiled me.' Jack said. 'Left me in the care of a "relative" in some bumfuck village hours away from anywhere. My schooling was over. It was time to learn how to make money.

'Running a shop was worse than Hallbourne. No one visited me from Rawalpindi. Nanima had wanted to come once or twice but the old man threatened to break her arms if she did.'

Jack shook his head silently.

'The thing is, I knew it was over now. My great escape had failed, so I learned how to run a shop. Ghazi spent most of the day in the tobacco fields. It was I who cleaned the place up, put in brighter bulbs, wrote prices down on big, clear signs. The customers liked it. After a while, I turned the business around. Ghazi expanded the shop to sell tyres and cloth as well.'

'You make it sound as if you were happy.'

'I was, till some dickhead friend of the old man's saw what was going on and started pressurizing Ghazi into selling the business to his son.

'Ghazi was completely indebted to the old man. There was no way he could resist. One day, the jerk is haranguing Ghazi, telling him that my father will not be happy if his wishes are ignored blah blah blah. I can see that Ghazi is uncomfortable and nervous, so I told the guy he could suck my dick on his way out. "Nothing's for sale."

'He starts yelling at me, saying I was the one who killed my mother. That made me go absolutely nuts. I chased him out of the shop. Ghazi couldn't stop laughing. A week later I was back in Pindi.

'I walked into the house, the fucking parliament had been convened for a special session. Everyone was there. My father, and all my uncles, male cousins and brothers-in-law, you name it. Only Ghazi wasn't there. Must been nearly forty men. No women. Nanima wasn't allowed to show her face. My father orders me to sit on the floor while everyone around me is standing with their arms crossed or sittin' in big armchairs like they had coconuts up their asses and couldn't move, know what I'm saying?'

Afroz didn't smile.

'The old man begins by informing everyone that though he has tried his utmost to give me the best education in Pakistan, and despite his efforts to be patient and kind-hearted, and giving me more chances than Allah gave the devil, I'm through and through an evil child. His voice keeps rising. No one coughs, or dares to even look at him. The gathering is informed that I have cheated Ghazi, and because of my bad advice and arrogant attitude, Ghazi will now lose his most successful business.

'I wanted to say that it was all horseshit but how was I to argue against all the men in the family? Whether they believed the old man or not, no one was about to contradict him.

'All of a sudden, the fucker takes off his shoes. Then, with the others watching, he takes off his socks and motions me to come forward. I'm shittin' myself by this stage. But I crawl forward. The old man puts his sweaty socks and then his shoes, soles down, right on the top of my head. As I'm sitting there trembling he asks all the uncles and cousins what he should do to me.

'No one speaks for a few minutes. Then someone says, "Give him to me, Ali Hassan. I will take him back to America."

'It was Uncle Jalal. I had never met the man and had no clue that I even had an uncle in America. But Uncle Jalal says, "I'll find something worthwhile for him."

'You cannot believe, Rosie, what was happening in my head while Uncle Jalal was talking. Here was someone actually suggesting that I go to America. I nearly flipped. My father's smelly shoes and socks fell off as I lifted my head to see who this man was. I wanted to hug him and say, "Take me right now," but my father shouted and someone jumped up and put the socks back on my head.

'The old man didn't like the idea, but Uncle Jalal promised him there would no more trouble or scandal. A couple of weeks later I was on a plane to Chicago. I made my great escape, after all!'

15

It was well after ten o'clock on another blowy, damp night when Khan Sahib and Sher Jan returned to meet Jack and Andy for the second time. Their beards dripped heavily from the rain. Both men's clothes were soaked through. They took their seats around a wicker coffee table with a cracked glass top. Khan Sahib happily accepted a cup of green tea. Sher Jan contented himself with a big pinch of smelly green snuff from a small round tin he drew out of an inside vest pocket.

Andy hadn't slept well for three nights. His goatee, which he usually trimmed every morning, was starting to look scraggly. He was having a recurring nightmare in which he was led away to jail in chains.

Jack, on the other hand, was calm. Things were finally starting to roll. Travelling with Afroz had taken him back nearly a quarter of century. Whenever he had thought of Hallbourne before, Jack had always felt torn open, and stripped bare. Sharing his story with Afroz though, had been different. He felt oddly relieved, as if he was ridding himself of the pain.

She had left Peshawar for Islamabad the next day. He tried to recall the last time he felt sad about a woman leaving him. He concluded that this was a first. And now that she was gone he was antsy; he wanted to move the plan along and get the deed done. So he could get back to Islamabad, to her.

'The house is a big one,' Sher Jan poked the pinch of snuff deep into the back of his mouth. 'There are many servants.

According to the chowkidar, your man will visit Karachi on Thursday and return on Sunday evening. He usually works in his office at home until early morning. I will visit him at two a.m.' Sher Jan leaned back with his small tree-trunk arms across his chest.

'What about his wife? Any others in the house?' Jack asked.

'She is in England for treatment. One son is in Dubai and one died when he was two,' Sher Jan spoke as if he knew the family intimately.

'No other family?'

Sher Jan said something to Khan Sahib, who didn't bother to translate.

'What?' Jack asked, 'What'd he say?'

'It is nothing important. sir. Only that the gentleman in question has a young daughter, quite young, but she does not live in the house.'

'Where she at?'

'Rawalpindi, sir.' Khan coughed and stared at the floor. 'St Mary's Convent. She is the product of...' Khan didn't look up, 'an improper union, sir. But her father loves her very much. She is not important to this situation, sir.'

Jack remembered the picture of the young girl on Ahmadzai's desk. The man had an illegitimate child. 'Any guns in the house?'

'Of course,' Sher Jan and Khan Sahib looked bemused.

'I mean, guns gonna be a problem? Everyone's bustin' caps someone's liable to go down. Want to avoid that.'

Khan Sahib said, and Sher Jan nodded, that Allah was the Lord and sometimes such things happened. Jack shot a quick look at Andy but he was pretending to read the small print on a bottle of cognac.

'How you intending to "persuade" the man?'

Sher Jan, Khan Sahib translating, said, 'By way of the

cook, some powder will be slipped into Ahmadzai's Coca Cola or tea.'

Jack nodded, waiting for more details. But Sher Jan was finished. That was the plan. Jack stared first at Sher Jan then Khan Sahib. 'That's it?'

Khan Sahib shrugged and smiled.

'What if he don't drink Coke, or he ain't thirsty?'

Sher Jan seemed to think that that didn't matter. He repeated the formula. Mix the powder with Ahmadzai's drink.

Jack looked at Andy who was still engrossed in the bottle of liquor. He reached over and swatted his knee. Andy looked up blankly. Sher Jan pulled out his snuff tin and began to preen himself in the tiny mirror. Khan Sahib, leaning forward in his chair, held an empty tea cup and saucer and waited for someone to say something that he could translate.

For a few moments, the only sound was that of the rain spitting hard against the windows and the whoosh of the trees being tossed around in the darkness of Andy's garden. Finally, Jack jumped up. 'Fuckin' ridiculous! What happens if the man drinks the Coke and keels over in a coma? Huh? Shitload of good that'll be!' Andy didn't say anything but at last put the Courvoisier down. Khan was whispering into Sher Jan's round ear as he continued grooming himself. 'What I want is go in, like this, see...' Jack picked up a chair and began to shake it. 'Grab the motherfucker and shake him till his eyeballs start rolling around. Then you throw him 'ginst the wall,' the leg snapped as the chair crashed onto the floor. 'Slap him up once or twice, show him who he be dealin' with and tell him to fuckin' sign the piece of paper that needs to be signed.'

Sher Jan glanced at Jack with disinterest. Andy was collecting the broken pieces of the chair. Jack lit a cigarette and fell into a rattan armchair, huffing. 'Stupidest plan I ever heard. Shi...ii...it.'

Sensing that he was on the verge of losing out on something big, Khan Sahib tried to explain: 'The beverage will be poisoned, that's right Mr King, but, Inshallah, the man will only drink it after he has signed the papers you are demanding.'

'D'you think he's that stupid?' Jack was massaging the bottom of his foot with both hands.

'Sher Jan will have a pistol which he will display at the appropriate moment, sir, and force him to sign the necessary documents.' Khan Sahib had not discussed this with Sher Jan but the main purpose of the lie was to convince Mr King that Sher Jan could do what was required. 'Upon making the signature the man will be compelled to drink the liquid which, upon his recovery, will make him ill, sir. A special tribal mixture, very effective for such occasions. When he returns to his senses he will not know which way is Karachi and which way is Kabul sir. Complete brainwash.'

Jack had heard some idiotic plans in his time, even been involved in a couple. But nothing as harebrained as this. He grabbed his other foot and began to massage his toes.

Andy had, at last, poured himself a big glass of Courvoisier which he was now sipping, avoiding any involvement.

Khan Sahib and Sher Jan were conferring in Pashto, nodding their heads and gesticulating with their thick hands.

'Happy horseshit,' muttered Jack. 'Biggest dumbass Paki I've ever met in my life,' he was staring straight at Sher Jan. Khan Sahib sensed he wasn't to translate.

Another silence filled the room. After sometime Sher Jan asked Khan Sahib what the American's decision was. Yes or no? Andy wanted to suggest that maybe, they should forget the plan altogether. But sensing the tension in the room, he didn't dare. This deal was taking a heavy toll on his stomach.

'Only way to guarantee a thing is to handle the job yourself.'

'You're gonna do this thing on your own?'

'You volunteerin'?' Andy shook his head. 'Din't think so,' Jack scowled.

'What are you going to do, Jack?'

'Sure as hell ain't gonna let this fool screw things up.'

'The decision,' Jack said, 'is thanks but no thanks.'

'What about the down payment?' Sher Jan asked nervously.

'Keep it. You saved me a big headache.'

Sher Jan smiled and stood up to leave. Khan Sahib shuffled slowly behind him, disappointed. He bent down to buckle his sandals when he saw Mr King walking towards him. Jack opened the door, pushed Sher Jan through it, then closed it firmly in his face. He turned and addressed the old man.

'Listen, Khanny, ain't your fault. I would have been happier if you hadn't found an idiot like him, but don't sweat it.' Jack beckoned him back into the sitting room.

'Sher Jan is stupid sir, I apologize for his foolishness.' Andy was balled up in a chair. He looked spooked and sick. The glass of Courvoisier was nearly empty.

'Give you another chance, old man. How's that sound?' Jack reached into the inside pocket of his blazer and pulled out a hundred-dollar note.

'What sir?'

'You did your best. Appreciate that.' He held the note in his fingers, like he was shaking a rat by its tail. 'But this time, I want a real partner. See what I'm sayin'?'

'Of course, Mr King, sir. Why not?'

Jack sat down and cleared his throat. 'I need a supplier.'

Andy was staring straight ahead. He wished he had never met Jack.

Khan nodded and blinked in a way that indicated Jack should continue.

'Here's the deal, old man.'

'Who is calling at this hour?' Assistant Sub-inspector Noor Aslam liked to get a full eight hours sleep, but was awakened around midnight.

'It is I, Aslam sir,' Khan Sahib whispered. He was calling from a public call office lit up with bright neon tubes.

'Is that you, Khan?'

'Sorry for disturbance, Aslamji, but Operation Kingpin is proceeding smoothly, sir.'

'I know that Khan. You informed me so already this evening.'

Khan explained that he had just come from a meeting at Mr Andy's house and that Mr Jack King had not liked Sher Jan's plan.

'Is there a science in such matters?' Aslam yawned as he spoke.

'Sher Jan is a stupid man, he has never studied science.'

'So what alternative plan did this Afghan fool propose?' Aslam wanted to hurry Khan along; he could see his toes turning pale against the bare concrete floor.

'None, sir. King does not want the service of Sher Jan and indeed,' Khan paused, 'he will do the necessary activity himself.' He waited for a response from his boss but the phone was silent.

'Sir?' Khan whispered. 'Hello, Aslam sahib?'

'Quickly, Khan, why have you called me?' stammered Noor Aslam. 'It's bloody cold.'

'I must arrange another meeting for Mr King, tomorrow, sir. Seven a.m., sir.'

'So arrange it.' Aslam didn't mind being a spy but it helped if there was a plate of cakes and a comfortable chair involved. 'What sort of meeting?'

'He is requesting to meet a smuggler.' Khan Sahib's information had the desired effect on Aslam.

'Really? King is a smuggler? Fantastic. What is the produce

he will be smuggling?' Aslam hoped it would be gold. All glittery and valuable.

'Safoof,' whispered the old spy. Khan could have sworn he heard his grumpy boss catch his breath.

'Gill will be very very happy, Khan. You must report to me the very moment your meeting is completed.'

'Any further instructions, Aslamji?'

'Don't wake me again, Khan.' Noor Aslam skipped off to bed with feet like blocks of ice. But he was happy. King is a smuggler. And God is great. Perhaps, after this case was through, he could afford to have his own house in Peshawar, and live with his wife and children like a proper man.

When the taxi approached the end of the narrow deserted street called 'Storytellers' Bazaar,' Khan Sahib told the driver to stop. Dropping some notes in the man's hands, he disappeared into an alley that stank of piss. Small donkeys slept next to camels, who could be heard slurping their cud. In just a few hours, this network of alleyways—the unmapped heart of the old town—would be jammed with hawkers, tradesmen and shoppers. But at this time, the neighbourhood of ancient wood-fronted houses was absolutely deserted. As he hurried past one window, Khan Sahib heard a woman's giggle and at another, the faint strain of Afghan music. He moved slower as he worked his way down a small flight of stone steps, slippery from gutter overflow, looking for number 33/12. Down at the end of the lane, a man—unaware of Khan's presence—was speaking to someone in a loud whisper, saying that he didn't care if Mohammad was sorry or not. 'He defiled my sister-in-law, he's got to pay the price.' Khan said a quiet prayer for Mohammad and knocked on the door of 33/12.

A young man, no more than sixteen, opened the door slightly. Khan let himself inside, asking for Yahya Jan. The boy turned and disappeared into another room. Khan waited by the door with his hands folded behind his back. Several minutes later, an electric bulb flickered on. Yahya Jan, a clean-shaven giant with one bad eye that lay on its side, grumbled, 'Sher Jan told me you weren't interested.'

'Not in Sher Jan, that's true. He spoiled everything with his idiotic plan.'

'It worked with Farhat. One sip and he was out cold.'

'Farhat had his throat cut because he refused to drink,' Khan sniffed. 'After he was dead, the drink was poured into his mouth.'

Yahya stared at the old man as if he would never understand. 'It is a good plan but you don't like it. No problem. Why have you come here then?'

'The man will do the job himself but he requires our services for a more important matter.' Yahya rubbed his eyes and nodded. Just then a woman floated silently into the room, her head covered with a shawl and said, 'You'll have tea, Yahya Jan?'

Yahya grunted his assent then turned to Khan Sahib. 'King is a smuggler. He was very eager to purchase several hundred kilos of safoof, which he intends to transport to America.'

'Why tell me this?' Yahya asked as he took a pot of tea and two bowls from the tired woman.

'Because,' the elderly spy said, accepting a bowl from Yahya, 'King will purchase the heroin from you. Your uncle, after all, was once a member of Haji Ayub's gang, was he not?'

Yahya nodded and poured himself some tea from the dented, blue tin teapot. 'But Jamil is in jail in Karachi and I know nothing of heroin.'

'Knowledge is for idiots. It is not necessary. Only your presence with me at Mr King's house this morning at seven is required. You speak no English, King speaks no Pashto. I will speak for you. But you must make Mr King believe that you are a big heroin broker. Agreed?'

'As you wish, Khan Sahib,' Yahya finished his tea, yawned and made to stand up.

'One more thing. Don't mention your fool cousin, Sher Jan. Mr King must not suspect you are of the same family. I will introduce you as Yahya only.'

Yahya rubbed his scratchy eyes and nodded. Khan stood up and stepped towards the door, but stopped. He turned towards Yahya, opened his mouth slightly, then closed it. The rain had started to fall again, hissing against the doors and wood windows of the house. The stone floor was chilly and Yahya shivered. He wanted Khan Sahib to disappear but the old man seemed to be deep in thought. Yahya opened the door in the hope that the air would suck Khan out, leaving him free to turn his attentions to Habiba, who sat quietly waiting for more tea orders.

'One more thing, Yahya.' Khan's shoes were off again and he was making himself comfortable on the carpet. He beckoned for Yahya to join him. The huge man, without trying to disguise his impatience, said, 'Khan Sahib, it is late. I will be at your house as agreed. I must sleep now.'

'Just a moment, only a moment, Yahya.' Khan tugged Yahya's big arm down towards the floor. 'One small point to mention, but we should speak,' he arched his eyebrows towards Habiba, 'alone. No one else.'

Yahya gave a short command to the young woman with the mischievous eyes. She lowered her head, wrapped the shawl around her shoulders and glided away as silently as she had arrived. Immediately, Khan scooted towards Yahya Jan and said, 'God gives opportunities every day. Only those who are wise are able to exploit them, Yahya.'

'Philosophy at this hour?' Yahya was annoyed; his eyes had followed Habiba lustfully.

'For years, I have served God and those bigger than me without complaint. What has been my reward?'

Yahya's only cared for his own reward, waiting in bed for him at this very moment.

'Fifteen years and more, watching and reporting the lives of these goras who come to Peshawar. Who they speak with, what they say, who they call, what their contacts are. I used to enjoy it.... When the CIA was here, every day was filled with adventure, Yahya, believe me.

'But since these Arabs and their talibs have taken over, the world has forgotten about Peshawar. I am left to report to that fat snail Aslam about the smoking habits of people as harmless and dull as Mr Andersen.'

Yahya was nodding off. His dead eye was slightly open but his good eye was completely shut.

'Can you guess my reward for fifteen years of loyal service? In the beginning I was retained for seven hundred rupees a month. Now, I give my wife thirty-five hundred a month. More notes, sure, but less value in each one. I ask you Yahya, how I am able to marry off the children?'

'You steal from your European employers,' Yahya's good eye was open again. Khan Sahib was getting on his nerves now. First philosophy, and now he was complaining about his finances.

Khan Sahib grimaced slightly, protesting that he was approaching retirement, and with more Europeans pulling out each year, soon there would be no more need for his reports.

'Khan Sahib,' Yahya said gently, because he was far younger than Khan, and it was not proper to raise your voice in front of an elder. 'Allah, as you say, is the Merciful and Generous One. He will provide.' He stretched and hoped Khan would take the hint and leave.

'My point exactly.

'What?'

'Mr King. Don't you see?'

Yahya stared blankly at the older man.

'Why should others keep the money?'

'Money?'

'Yes, which Mr King will get from Ahmadzai. Next week he will visit Ahmadzai in Hayatabad, force him to pay a large sum of money, because he will be purchasing, or thinking he will be purchasing a certain amount of powder from you.' Yahya was slightly more interested now. 'Why should he keep the money?'

'Because he took it.'

'Yes. No.' Khan Sahib sputtered. 'Of course, he will take it, because your donkey cousin could think of nothing more than powder in the Coca Cola! Ass!'

'If you do the work you keep the goods.' Yahya still didn't get Khan's point.

Khan wanted to leave now. Explaining his idea to this buffalo was a waste of time.

'King will visit that big advocate, Ahmadzai, next week for what purpose, Yahya? Can you tell me?'

'For money. He will demand money from him so that he may purchase heroin from me.'

'Correct. And how much will you receive?'

'You told me. The usual five hundred rupees.'

'What of the rest?'

'The rest?'

'Yes, King will hand over thousands of dollars to you, Yahya. Who will benefit from that?'

Yahya wasn't sure. 'Assistant Sub-inspector Aslam. No?'

'Exactly. We must pass the money to him because it has been received in an official operation. And me? What about my share?'

Yahya shrugged, scratching his armpit.

'Nothing. This is my duty to Mr Aslam and the big ones there in Islamabad,' Khan said sarcastically. 'While he eats all the cake and sleeps by eight-thirty, I am running about from Kohat to Kandahar to make arrangements with idiots like your cousin and you, free of charge. My reward is their pleasure. That is what Mr Assistant Sub-inspector Aslam is telling me,' Khan snorted.

Yahya now was seeing the light. 'Why must you give the money to Mr Aslam? Does he know how much Mr King will take from Ahmadzai?'

'Of course not,' Khan smiled at the younger man. He paused and let the revelation sink into his sleepy head. 'Tomorrow we will tell Mr King that he should provide no less than a lakh for the powder.'

'One lakh?'

'In dollars, Yahya. I have already made the calculations. I will inform Aslam that Mr King will pay thirty thousand dollars for the heroin. That amount I will pass to him.'

'And the remaining portion, Khan Sahib?' Yahya had forgotten about Habiba waiting in his bed.

'Indeed.' Khan smiled. 'Twenty thousand dollars is better than five hundred rupees, no?'

'For me? Twenty thousand American. How much is that in rupees, uncle?'

Khan told him and the younger man whistled. 'Good plan, Khan Sahib. But tell me, there is still fifty thousand more.'

'Allah is generous,' Khan Sahib smiled at Yahya. For an instant Yahya felt a pinch of injustice, but it passed quickly. Khan Sahib was elder after all, he deserved more.

'Everything is well planned, Khan Sahib,' Yahya said admiringly. 'I will meet you as planned: six-thirty at your house.'

'One final issue, Yahya. Please, just for one minute more.' He moved closer to the huge man. 'If we tell Mr King to bring a hundred thousand dollars, he will do so. I am sure of it.'

Yahya nodded. 'Yes. Why not?'

'But in Ahmadzai's house there must be plenty more than that, no? Am I wrong?'

'Of course not, uncle.'

'If the treasury door is open, why should we limit ourselves to only one golden goblet?'

The question was a good one.

'Mr King is a serious businessman, Yahya. I have a feeling that he will leave Mr Ahmadzai's house with more than a hundred thousand dollars. After all, there will be others to pay off—customs, his friend Mr Andy. And he likes to enjoy life, that is obvious.'

'What are you suggesting, Khan uncle?' Yahya was wide awake now.

'Next Sunday evening, when Mr King exits the house of Mr Ahmadzai with the money, which I am sure he will have with him, he will be "greeted" by some unknown persons who will deprive him of his baggage.'

'Unknown persons?'

'Who better to waylay Mr King than your cousin and you?'

'What about Aslam? He will expect the heroin deal to go through, uncle.'

'He will get his thirty thousand to pass on to Islamabad, but then I'll inform him of the sad news that Mr King is no longer interested in heroin.'

'But King will recognize us, if we waylay him.'

'Of course he will, if you shine torches in your face and introduce yourselves and show him your identity cards.' Khan was standing up now; it was time to go. Dawn was a few hours away. 'Use masks, dress as women, paint yourselves green, do whatever you like, but make sure he does not recognize you, Yahya. Remember, twenty thousand is better than five hundred. Now goodnight. Do not be late. We must meet Mr King promptly, as good businessmen.' The old man winked as he shut the door behind him and stepped into the alley.

16

After Khan Sahib disappeared into the drizzly darkness, Yahya returned to the bedroom. Habiba, his young wife, had left her clothes folded neatly on a chair next to the bed. She purred softly and for a moment Yahya felt the urge to crawl in next to her warm body and fill his large hands with her mango breasts. But there is a hierarchy of pleasures, and the fruits of sweet Habiba would have to wait. Khan Sahib's visit had led Yahya's now fully wakened mind down other paths.

The old man's plan was good. Twenty thousand dollars! The amount was bigger than any Yahya had ever dreamed of.

He touched Habiba's cheek—she had fallen asleep—then returned to the front room. With his back propped up by three overstuffed cushions, Yahya quietly picked his teeth with a bit of straw from the kitchen floor. Yes, it was a good plan. Twenty thousand, whatever the actual number of rupees, was far better than his usual fee of five hundred. Khan Sahib had complained about his small salary, but did he ever stop to recall that he had been paying Yahya and his cousin, Sher Jan, the same rate for five years? Was this justice? Yahya and his cousin were always the ones the conniving old bastard called on when he needed a door knocked down or documents lifted or pressure to be applied. If Khan Sahib was planning to benefit from this American King, then why shouldn't he also profit?

The more Yahya worked the straw between his teeth, the less satisfied he became with Khan Sahib's explanation as to why *he* should keep fifty thousand dollars. Does God give opportunities only to foxes and fools like Khan and Aslam? Yahya looked toward the ceiling as if reminding the Invisible Almighty that he, too, never missed his juma prayers or his fast. His thoughts were a jumble: God, heroin, Khan, Habiba's breasts, King, big dollars. After a few minutes of frustrated contemplation, he got on to his feet in a huff, unlatched the door and stepped out into the rain. He stopped three doors down at his cousin Sher Jan's house.

Within a few moments, he was standing in a large room where Sher Jan lay snoring contentedly on the floor, like a buffalo in a pond.

'Wake up, Sheru,' Yahya tapped his cousin's exposed foot. 'Wake up! I must talk to you.'

Sher Jan opened one eye but didn't stop snoring. Yahya patted his face, then twisted an ear. Sher Jan sat upright like he'd been administered a hundred and fifty volts. 'What is it?' he snorted.

'Khan Sahib has paid a visit,' Yahya said, signalling that his cousin should come out to the front room so as not to wake the others—sleeping soundly, covered from head to toe in white sheets, like bundles of cargo in a warehouse.

'I knew that American would reconsider,' Sher Jan said stretching his huge arms and wrapping his sheet around him to keep warm. 'Poison is the best method in such cases.'

'He isn't reconsidering,' Yahya said. 'Sit down. I'll tell you.'

'Who is this man King coming from America thinking he knows best? The plan worked in Farhat's case and with Dawood as well. Remember how he took just one sip and *barump*,' Sher Jan clicked his fingers, 'he collapsed like a baby goat?'

'There will be other occasions, Sheru.' Yahya's tone was consoling. 'Let me tell you the new plan.' Yahya filled in his cousin on Khan Sahib's plan. 'And Khan is expecting us to waylay King outside Ahmadzai's house to deprive him of whatever he has. Obviously, he is also expecting that we will hand over what we collect from King, to him. Follow me?'

Sher Jan was not following. He was finding it hard to stay awake.

'Khan is right to say that King will come out of Ahmadzai's house with more than one lakh. But even a big smuggler like King cannot exit the house with everything.'

Sher Jan had nodded off. Yahya reached over and gave him a tight slap. His cousin popped his eyes open and said, 'Excellent. You are right, Yahya, why not?'

Yahya continued. 'For the past hour I have been asking myself, if Mr Ahmadzai's house is a treasury, like Khan uncle says, why should we wait for Mr King to enter? True, he may come out with two or three lakh dollars. But who cares about King?'

Sher Jan smiled but Yahya knew his cousin didn't understand what he was getting at.

'Sheru, listen to me. My plan will allow us to forget Khan Sahib forever. In fact, he will come begging us for five-hundred-rupee jobs.'

This seemed to perk Sher Jan up. 'I like that idea. What do we do?'

On Sunday morning, he and Sher Jan would go to Ahmadzai's house—not at two a.m. to wait for Jack King to exit with a hundred thousand American dollars, as Khan Sahib's plan demanded; they would go, instead, at one and enter the house themselves. 'Why wait for this King man to take the gold, when we can walk into the goldmine ourselves?'

'I have been to Ahmadzai's house. The chowkidar who guards the place is friendly with me. We can enter without any difficulty. Wah, Yahya! What an idea!'

The cousins huddled together, working out the details of

their plan. Just as first light was starting to whiten the alley's dark walls, the cousins clapped each other on the shoulders and agreed they'd finally found their fortune. Yahya stood to leave, giggling that he had a heroin deal to conclude.

'And I will bring the poison and Coca Cola. Always good to have a back-up plan.'

Andy, Jack could see, was starting to crumble. He had told him that he could back out if he didn't feel up to it, but Andy said, 'I'm still in, Jack. I'm just not used to this sort of thing.'

'What you got my man, is the virgin jitters,' Jack tried to reassure his partner. 'First time in this business, like when you're with a lady for the first time, always be stressful, daddy-o. Sitting by and watching, see, that gets you all antsy 'cause you just waitin' for somethin' to go wrong. You not a participant. Best remedy for you, my man, is to jump in.'

'What are you saying?'

'You be scared 'cause you not in control. You watching me and Khan do everything. What you need is a job.'

'I've got one. I go to it every morning.'

'I mean with me. I appreciate you putting me in touch with Khan, and don't worry about your share, man, Jack King always pay his partner in full. But in reality, dude, I need a partner willin' to participate. Hear what I'm sayin'?'

'Not if it involves killing. Or guns. No way.' Andy was shaking his head, fondling his rat-tail.

'Relax, dude. What I got in mind be a real treat. No guns. No blood. Swear.' Jack flashed the Scout's salute and grinned.

'Tell me in the morning,' Andy said, going to bed. 'And remember, no deals in the house. I'm serious, Jack.'

Andy was still sleeping when Khan Sahib and Yahya arrived to meet Jack precisely at seven a.m. It was cloudy, the trees were dripping and the garden was muddy. Jack led Khan Sahib and Yahya over to a bed of storm-damaged gladiolas and said to Khan, 'So who we got here?'

'Mr Yahya, sir. He is able to arrange the item you have requested.'

Jack and Yahya shook hands and studied each other with curiosity. Yahya didn't smile or show any emotion. Jack squinted in the early morning light. Yahya's bum eye, lying glass-like on its side, while the other one moved around, struck Jack as appropriate. There was a silence, each man waiting for the other to say something. At last Jack said, 'You been in this trade for a while?'

Khan translated and Yahya, as agreed, kept his mouth shut. He only nodded. Jack asked how long exactly, and Khan Sahib replied, 'Many years, more than ten.'

Jack offered both men a cigarette. They declined. He then asked all the questions he'd been thinking of since he'd bid Khan Sahib farewell the night before. 'How long would it take to get the product?'—'Less than ten kilos, today. More than fifteen, within five days, sir.'

'Was the pipeline secure?'—'No shortage of powder. Yahya's factory is near Kandahar sir, the most important poppy area of Afghanistan.'

'What was the price for the purest powder?'—'In dollars: six thousand, sir.'

'Any other parties involved?'—'Only Yahya and myself, sir.'

'What about the customs?'—'Corrupt, sir. Not to worry for that.' 'Which route would he use?'—'Afghanistan, Uzbekistan, Bulgaria, Holland, sir.'

'How do I trust this man?' Jack was looking at Yahya's dead eye.

'He will provide sample, sir,' Khan said automatically.

He was used to not saying no to those who asked him favours.

'How much?'

'As you like. Fifty grams. Ten kilos. Up to you, sir.'

'Why you doin' all the talkin' Khanny?'

'Yahya only understands Pashto, sir.'

'But you not asking him my questions.'

It was true. Khan Sahib had stopped translating and had been saying whatever seemed appropriate. 'We discussed thoroughly before we came here, sir,' he stammered. The old man grabbed Yahya's shoulder and turned him slightly away from Jack. He knew Jack couldn't understand but spoke quickly in Pashto. 'He is saying you are an ugly buffalo. He does not trust someone with your affliction.' Khan Sahib lowered his head and touched his own eye to indicate the problem. Yahya wheeled around and made his one good eye wide, as if he could pull Jack's tongue out of his mouth. Wringing his hands, Khan Sahib turned towards Jack.

'I am sorry, sir. My Yahya, does not have confidence in your ability to purchase. He is regretful, but he must go now.' Yahya was striding towards the gate. One thing Jack had learned was to not make decisions in a hurry, unless it was absolutely essential. He watched Yahya delicately pull his baggy trousers legs up to avoid a large puddle. Khan Sahib had removed his spectacles and was cleaning the lenses with a purple-and-pink checked hankie he'd extracted from his vest pocket. Yahya was almost on the street, nearly out of sight. So too, realized Jack, was his hope of becoming the Shah of Chicago.

'Where's he going, Khan?' Jack gestured towards Yahya, who had disappeared into the street. 'Call him back. If he's got the product, I've got the money. No problemo. Now hurry, get his overly sensitive ass back in here.'

Khan Sahib shrugged, then in what appeared to Jack to

be ten minutes later, arrived at the gate. He turned right and found Yahya picking his teeth, and leaning against the wall that ran around Andy's house. Khan Sahib winked at Yahya and motioned for him to follow him. 'He is a fool, Yahya. He sends his apologies.'

'I could kill him,' Yahya said, refusing to budge.

'He is a guest, Yahya. In America they are very open about their opinions. He understands that now. He admits he is wrong. Come now, let's finish this business.' The old spy pulled Yahya back into the garden where Jack stood, smoking anxiously.

Not willing to let Yahya slip through his fingers again, Jack took out his dwindling roll of hundreds and put four into Khan Sahib's wrinkled palm. 'One's for you, like I told you. The others for him as good faith deposit. Okay. He'll get the rest after I check out a sample. See, money is no problem.' Jack was smiling at Yahya and pointing at the bills.

Khan Sahib folded the crisp dollars in half and put them into the pocket with his hankie. Yahya said something to the old man out of the side of his mouth, then snarled again at Jack.

'Excuse me sir, Mr Yahya is informing you that minimum supply is fifteen kilos sir.'

'How much that be, then?'

'One hundred thousand. Dollars, sir. American,' Khan replied.

'Tell him, if his stuff is good, I'll take thirty.'

Khan Sahib nodded and begged permission to leave. Jack lit another cigarette and watched the two men amble out of the compound. Just as they reached the road, he saw Yahya put his arm around the old man and pull him close, like a good friend.

'This real coffee?' Jack lifted the plunger top and sniffed. 'Awright!' He poured a big mug, mixed in two spoons of sugar and leaned back in a chair with his legs stretched out. 'Feelin' good!'

Andy was chewing a piece of toast covered with red jam. A few crumbs clung to the edge of his mouth. The way Jack came in and told him that the deal was nearly done came as a relief. All they had to do now, Jack said, was get used to being rich. Of course, they still didn't have the money, but at that moment, relief and excitement made Andy generous. 'So what's this job you got for me?' he said, buttering another toast.

'Remember when Sher Jan mentioned Ahmadzai's little daughter the other day? "Product of an improper union," he said.'

'Yeah.'

'When I visited Ahmadzai's office there was a picture of this little girl on his desk. A real cutie-pie. But when I casually mentioned her, he became all nervous and weird, and turned the frame face down on his desk.'

'So?'

Jack leaned forward on his forearms, with hunched shoulders. 'Mr A's got hisself a bastard child. And he don't want no one to know about it.'

'And you are planning to publicize this fact?'

Jack ignored the question and said that every angle of the plan had been covered, except one. Ahmadzai, he told Andy, would not have cash on him. They'd have to get him to sign over the amount they needed.

'That's a pretty big flaw in the plan,' Andy said, his early morning cheer sinking fast. 'He's not going to sign anything. Even if he did, once you leave all he's going to do is call the bank to stop payment, and call the police to arrest you. Or us.'

Jack smiled. 'Unless he know it be in his interest to sign and keep quiet.'

'From what you've told me about the guy, he's not a dumbass. Like you.'

Normally, Jack would have whumped a person talking like that, but he stayed cool. 'That's where you come in, partner.'

'Me?'

'You gonna ride with me and William back to Islamabad this afternoon. We got some ladies to visit. Rose, she's waiting for me. And Ahmadzai's little one, she be waiting for you.'

Andy didn't say anything for a minute, hoping he had misunderstood Jack. 'I've got to go to work, Jack. I'm late already.'

'Call in sick.'

'I can't.'

'Why not?'

'I'm not sick.'

'How you gonna feel when you don't have your hundred thousand dolleros?'

'You want me to kidnap Ahmadzai's girl?'

'We're partners, right?'

Andy nodded.

'We do this together, then. That's what partnership means, see.' Jack paused to tap the end of his cigarette into a saucer. 'Don't worry, man. I make it worth your while, know what I'm saying? You can build two cabins up there in the woods. How's that sound?'

'But kidnapping? You said it wasn't going to be violent.'

'Do it right, there be no need whatsoever for any violence.' Jack's chair screeched as he stood up. 'Now I'm callin' the office and tellin' 'em Mr Andy, he be sicker than a drunken sailor.' Andy stared in desperation at Jack. 'I'm sure Khan Sahib will back you up.'

Jack's spirits were high as William splashed, honked and swerved his way back towards Islamabad. Andy sat sprawled out in the backseat like last time, but was even less communicative. He looked out at the bruised sky like a prisoner longing to be set free. William on the other hand, was happy to be heading home and in a talkative mood.

'Life very bad for Christian in Pakistan, Mr King. Nobody likeit the Christian. All the time cursing, cursing. Even sometime murderit.'

'Why?' Jack asked out of politeness.

'These people, saab,' William moved his eyes in a big circle, as if to indicate the entire world, 'thinkit Christian is kafir. You understand what is meaning, kafir, saab?'

'Sure. Infidel.'

'Yes saab, even though they calling us ahl-e-kitab.'

'People of the Book.'

William nodded. 'Prophet Mohammad, he was good fellow. Not all things bad but many things he tellit Muslims is bad. For example, killit all kafir. But in Koran, Christian people are special...also Jewish people, saab. We are book people because we believe in Holy Book. Koran. Bible. Torah. All holy books, saab. But Muslim people hateit Yahudi and Christian people, saab. In Pakistan very much hateit.'

'Hey, you be the only ones who get booze in this place. That don't sound like bad treatment to me, Willie.' Maybe with the cash he got from the Zam Zam, he and Rosie could take a trip. The seven wonders: Vegas, Chicago, Hollywood, that wax museum in London.

'No sir. Permit should be free but these Muslim peoples, officials, saab, they demanding sometimes two hundred, three hundred rupees for permit. Who can afford, sir? They cheatit us, always.'

'What about your schools, dude? St Paul's, St Mary's. Every Muslim father in this country wants to send his kids to your schools.'

'Fees costit too much, sir. Only rich Muslim children and some Christian children can afford. But my family,' he shook his head, 'not possible, saab.'

Jack nodded but he was wondering more about what colour lipstick Afroz would be wearing and how she'd smell when he gave her a hug.

Near Attock, where the Kabul River joins the blue Indus and turns south to the sea, they stopped for a cup of tea. Andy said he wasn't thirsty and stayed laid out in the jeep. Seated under a tin-roofed cabana painted green and white, Jack watched the rivers coming together but not mixing; fighting against each other. The dirty, brutish Kabul and the chaste, brilliant Indus, two rivers flowing side by side. But by the time they flowed under the Attock bridge, where Jack and William sat, it was impossible to tell where one ended and the other started. A lot of things, thought Jack, were like that. His feelings for Afroz, especially. He was aware of the way he softened when he was with her. But there was part of him that resisted. He wasn't sure at all which feeling he should trust.

William set the two bottles of Sprite on the table and said, 'Excuse me, Mr King. Don't mindit I talking you something.'

'Go for it, my man.' Jack was desperate for a beer.

'Mr Ahmadzai,' he hesitated and looked at Jack as if he'd taken the Lord's name in vain. Jack looked blankly at the driver. 'Mr Ahmadzai is advocate sir. Famous in Pakistan for many big case he fightit in High Court.' Jack nodded.

William said that Mr Ahmadzai was most famous among the Christian community for prosecuting the first blasphemy case against a Christian, a year ago. Tariq Masih was fourteen and had told a friend on the way home from school that the Koran was just the Bible re-written. His friend, a Muslim, told his father and three days later the boy, Tariq, was arrested, and put in jail. 'Gujranwala Jail, very dirty place, saab. The charge was blasphemy against Allah and Holy Prophet Mohammad.'

Jack sipped his Sprite, nodding at William to keep going.

'But real case, Mr King, saab, was Tariq Masih family. They ownit twenty bighas land. Very good land with plenty fruit trees. Lemon, guava, which Tariq father sellit in Lahore. His neighbour, big Muslim zamindar, saab, he wantit land and trees but Mr Masih, he always refuse to sellit property.'

According to the blasphemy laws, William explained, the accused loses all civil rights. So Tariq Masih's father's neighbour made an offer to buy the land again, but this time at a very reduced price. Tariq Masih's father was compelled to sell to pay for his son's court appearances, which in any case were just a formality. Blasphemers are not permitted to own property; the neighbour would have got the Christian's land anyway.

'Mr Ahmadzai he fightit case against Tariq Masih.'

'You sure about that?'

'Oh definite, saab. He visit Nanima many times. I see him. During court case trial his photo come in paper every day. Ahmadzai is famous. For Muslim he is hero. For Christian he is zero, saab. Very bad man.'

After paying for the drinks, Jack said to himself, 'This Mr A's turning into a bigger asshole by the minute.'

17

Afroz called Jack at Nanima's and told him to meet her at Pappasallis for a pizza. After dinner the rain had stopped, so they walked back through the wet streets to her apartment. A retired Brigadier and his family lived downstairs, but Afroz had a private entrance to her upstairs flat, around the back. As she led him up the stairs to her apartment, she told Jack to keep his voice down. 'We can't have the Brigadier asking questions, can we?' Jack was sure she pinched him as she said that.

The moon was nearly full and its reflection quivered in the pools of water on the roof. Jack had scored some booze from Shahid's bootlegger, Bunty—a couple of bottles of Black Tower wine and one of Absolut Citron. He poured two glasses of the sweet wine and added ice to his. Next, he turned on all the fans to get a breeze up and blow the muggy air out.

The emptiness of the rooms surprised him; Jack expected a woman's place to be packed with things, but except for the table and five chairs and a fridge there was nothing in the dining room. The living room was brightly lit, with a few cushions thrown up against the wall but no pictures, or anything on the walls.

'I'm sure this seems small to you, but this place is too big for just one person. Most of my things are still back in England.' She took a sip of the wine and nodded her head towards the bedroom.

Jack followed her. Above the queen-sized bed hung a stunning red, black and white block-print bedspread, which gave the room the intimacy of a Bedouin tent. A big terracotta lamp with an off-white cloth shade, neatly stacked paperbacks and a small tape player lay on a small table by the bed. A second tall Chinese paper lantern stood in the opposite corner. Two armchairs were covered with clothes. One entire wall was taken up by a polished wood wardrobe bursting with row upon row of silky, cottony and delicately tailored clothes. On one side of the bed, against the wall was a dresser and a round, old mirror with a silver frame. Bottles of perfume, upended seashells overflowing with earrings, thin dark boxes of mascara, bracelets and rings lay in two serious piles on the dresser. At one edge of the dresser was a photo of a scowling man with white hair and a plump woman looking bemusedly at the camera. 'My parents,' Afroz said. He stepped gingerly over scattered shoes and looked for a chair or cushion. 'Sit on the bed, the room is such a mess,' she said as she popped a tape into the player then flopped down beside him.

'*Pakeezah*, right?' Jack recognized the tune immediately.

'Daddy used to watch the film at least once a month in England. Usually, on a Friday. He would sit on the big tartan sofa with a glass of whisky, turn the lights down and threaten to throw out anyone who squeaked a word. Our house was as silent as a mosque when we watched *Pakeezah*. His favourite scene was where Meena Kumari has been dancing for the men all night and singing "chalte, chalte..."'

'And then the morning breaks and the train goes roaring by.... And she be thinking of home but she can't go cause she's a dancing girl,' Jack interrupted.

'Daddy used to say that's how he felt. Even though he would never forgive the Generals for what they did to him, he missed Pakistan a lot. Like Meena Kumari, he felt trapped in a place and situation from which he couldn't escape.'

Jack watched Afroz in the shadowy lamplight. He hadn't remembered that scene for years but what she said about being trapped and loving something at the same time as hating it, made him feel as if she had just summed up his life.

When the song was over Jack fast forwarded the tape to the other side and said, 'Now this here is the perfect song for a night like tonight.'

Lata Mangeshkar began to sing 'Mausam hai aashiqana', about the monsoons and flirting lovers. Outside, thunder had started to rumble.

'Oh, you think so?' The ceiling fan turned slowly. A slight breeze had picked up and rattled one of the windows in the front room. Afroz had taken off her sandals and pulled her painted toe-nailed feet on to the bed.

'This weather made for lovers?' Jack asked. 'Damn tootin'. Don't thunder and lightning make you just want to get under the covers and—' he gulped the rest of his wine and hopped off the bed for a refill.

Afroz closed her eyes and stretched out on the bed. Jack could tell by the way her lips moved ever so slightly, and the occasional smile, that she was lost in the music.

Being around Rosie made Jack feel like there was nothing he had to pretend to be. In the sixteen years since he'd first entered the American correctional system, he hadn't opened up about his life like this with anyone. This sort of connection was something else. *Crazy little thing called love, I guess.*

'Listen, Rosie, let me fix you a vodka lemon,' Jack said. She had barely touched her wine and Jack didn't like drinking alone; unless he was alone.

He ducked into the dining room next door and she called out, 'What did you do when you got to Chicago?'

'You mean the first time?' He walked back in with two big glasses of vodka and a little ice.

'Was it what you expected...Steve McQueen and

motorbikes?' She took the glass and sat up on the bed, shaking her long hair out of her face.

It was, he said, as if he'd woken up in the best dream ever and then discovered it wasn't a dream. 'It was everything I imagined it to be but new and much better.'

Uncle Jalal had started out with a grocery, but by the time he brought Jack to Chicago, he had a restaurant and one of the first video shops in Little India. Jack worked in the grocery for a year or so and then agreed to marry his cousin, Nasreen, because he felt indebted to his uncle. 'He had it all figured out, like my old man, that what I needed was to be accountable and responsible and shit. The reason for coming to America, he thought, like every other Paki, was to make money.'

How could Jack resist? Just twenty years old and he hadn't ventured out of Little India more than twice a year. So Jack was married at the age of twenty-one; Nasreen was nineteen. Uncle Jalal bought them an apartment in an old brick block, on Rockwell, between a park and a cemetery, and Nasreen set about trying to please her new husband. Jack didn't mind having someone cook for him and massage his feet in the evenings but Nasreen was too sincere for his taste.

'She tried her best, you know, to be a good wife. Just like in the movies. I dug it at first but then her trying became too much.'

'Was she born in Chicago?'

'No, she left Pakistan when she was two, so she was an American chick for all that. But man, she was more Pakistani than the real ones. Even insisted on speaking Urdu with me in the house, like we were actually in Karachi not America.'

Jack hadn't come to America to speak Urdu. Within a year, communication was starting to break down. He was beginning to pick up the way black people on the streets spoke. He hardly ever came home. He had convinced Uncle

Jalal to lease him a green-and-white taxi, which he drove most days, fifteen hours straight.

'That's when I started to really understand America. Had people doing every damn thing in the backseat: snorting, shooting, basing, screwing, fighting, dealing. Every type of person rides Chicago taxis. Moonies and them Jehovah's Witnesses, never shutting up about the end of the world, and the little old lady going to the grocery store who was scared shitless that I would rob her. And chicken-lip businessmen in their fancy suits, flying around the country doing deals. Whores running from their pimps, kids running away from home. Asian tourists who gave you whatever you wanted 'cause they'd been told taxi drivers are murderers. Everybody doing everything.' Jack poured a second glass of Absolut.

What impressed him most was the variety of people in the city: blacks, Hispanics, Indians, Polacks, Italians, honkeys. They all had something to bitch about as Jack drove them around town, but they all seemed to co-exist all right with one another. His entire life in Pakistan, and in Little India, seemed to have been one-dimensional by comparison. Everyone a Muslim. Every night the same spicy, oily food. The same boring conversations about 'back home' and the endless bitching about Pakistani politics. Cricket, the only sport. Noor Jehan, the only singer. 'That's when I realized that what I wanted in life, more than anything, was to experience the difference. Variety! What variety do you see in a place like this? It's all the same. If there's anyone different, they call 'em "kafir" and run 'em out of town.'

A crack of thunder followed by a bolt of lightning made the lights flicker off for a second before sputtering back on: dim at first and then incredibly bright. The tape machine warbled but eventually stabilized.

'Had to make some money. Driving a taxi was for losers. The real bucks was in leasing.'

Afroz, who was resting one of her legs on his knee asked him to light a cigarette for her. He did, then pinching the filter in his fingers put it gently between her fabulous lips.

'I sub-leased my cab to another guy and then helped a Polish dude run a bunch of gypsies on the north side.'

'Gypsies? In Chicago?'

Jack laughed.

'Cabs with no licences. Illegal taxis. Guys just doing a bit of cash making on the side, you know. Now that was good money!'

'What did you do with all the money?'

'Hung out in bars, sharking pool most of the day.'

'What about Nasreen?'

Jack didn't care. He spent most nights in the bars downtown or at private parties, maybe crashing with a chick he'd picked up. Part of Nasreen's upbringing was not to complain and not to question her husband about his activities.

Jack moved out of their apartment and in with his first business partner. They maintained a good lifestyle until the city cracked down on gypsies and sub-letting. Jack was arrested. Being a first-time offender, he was let off lightly: his licence was suspended and he was placed on probation for half a year.

From sub-letting Jack moved into the fencing trade and a bit of shylocking with some Russian Jews over in Skokie. A lot of weekends Jack would deliver a van load of stereos, TVs, bikes, microwaves—just about anything that a man could lift out of a house with his bare arms—up to Milwaukee, or down to Memphis, or even out to the east coast a couple times. A run like that got him a couple hundred but nothing great. Shylocking was good from time to time but more hassle than it was worth. If the client didn't pay it was Jack's rap and he was liable for the dough himself. He figured there were some months where whatever he made as a fence he lost to bad loan customers. Once or twice, he'd even had to resort to violence, which, as a rule, Jack didn't like.

On one of those January ice-cube days—clear and frozen—Jack was given a new Econoline van crammed with Japanese tape decks and turntables to deliver to a warehouse outside of Moline. No more than half a day's job for a payoff of six hundred bucks. As soon as Jack snapped at the bait he found himself caught on the hook. The warehouse was surrounded by cops within a minute of his pulling into the compound. The police found three kilo-bags of coke in one of the boxes, and for that—Jack claimed he knew nothing about it—he was sent to Cook County jail for two and a half years. But he was lucky. The Feds were starting to get ridiculous about sentencing and making the prison system run on small-time dope offenders. A year later, he would have done double the time for his foolishness.

Seventeen and a half months in prison shook Jack up. He tried to make amends with Nasreen, but her earnestness had changed to bitterness. There were no children and her reputation and status in the Pakistani community was crumbling under a constant undertow of whispers. In his first attempt to go straight, he agreed to manage Uncle Jalal's 'Star of Punjab' restaurant just off Devon.

'In the restaurant biz twelve-hour days are normal. On weekends, sixteen is nothing. And what do you get at the end except for crappy chicken masala and all the fucking papadams you can stand? Sixty, maybe seventy bucks pre-tax! Living at that level, at that pace, was something I was not able to handle for more than three weeks.'

Jack stood up and paced the floor, acting out the arguments he'd had with Uncle Jalal.

'"Boy," he'd tell me, "for twenty-two years I have built my

businesses up and I have given you my only daughter as your wife. Why? To destroy everything I have made?" I did feel kinda bad. He had rescued me from my old man and Pakistan after all. But shit! I hadn't asked for Nasreen to marry. He forced her on me. Plus, I didn't love money like him and my old man. His business empire meant nothing to me. Was that my future? Restaurant owner? Video shop manager? Maybe he thought that was why I'd been brought to America. But fuck it, the America around Little India was not the America I'd travelled all that way to be a part of. I had wanted to escape from this hellhole, not settle down in a mini-version of it.'

Jack moved towards the table and took a big sip of vodka. Afroz leaned forward and turned the volume up on the tape player. 'Listen to this, Jack.' Asha was singing: 'Dil cheez kya hai/aap meri jaan lijiye'. 'It's from *Umrao Jan*. Have you seen it?' Afroz hummed the tune and sang along softly.

Jack had seen the movie. Several times. But he wasn't in the mood for love songs right then. He flapped his arm about, dispelling the smoke that hung in the room. He wanted to finish telling her about his life in America. Now that he'd begun he felt like he had to tell her everything.

'I moved to New York, figurin' that was far away enough from Little India. Drove taxi for a week but the city was too wild, and sub-leasing was impossible. The rackets controlled everything in New York. So, did a bit of dope dealing and pool-sharking. Things were just like back home 'cept for one thing: I got me a gun. A .38.'

Afroz sucked in her breath, gasping. Her eyes were wide.

'Because in all my chosen lines of business, I would have been a fool not to.'

Within a few months he was sent to prison again on concealed weapon, stolen car and aggravated assault charges. 'It was a set-up, Rose. Sure, I carried a piece but I didn't know the car was hot and nobody ever accused me of assaulting anyone. Not at that stage. But who was goin' to believe a little shit like me, right? So they gave me six and a half years in Sing Sing.'

'Sing Sing. What a lovely sounding name,' she said without any feeling.

'Well, it ain't no lovely place, believe me. New York State Prison. On the Hudson River, full of degenerates and rats.'

'Daddy was in jail in the 70s but he never talked about it, other than to say he had felt like an animal.'

She knew her father's prison years had probably been very different from Jack's. Even still, she sensed there was something in Jack's experience that could help her understand her father's.

'Tell me about it.'

Jack was skeptical. 'You sure?'

Though she tried to disguise it, Jack knew Afroz was apprehensive about what she would hear next.

She hesitated for a moment then nodded quickly, 'I want to know what it was like.'

'Fuck. I need another drink.'

The Absolut bottle was nearly empty after he refilled his glass.

'I could not imagine that a place like it existed on earth. Cook County Jail was a pissy little slumber party compared to Sing Sing.'

Mixed in with his bitterness Afroz detected a dirty piece of pride.

'It wasn't like a city within a city, more like ghettos within a city. And just like outside, where there are white ghettos, black ghettos and Latino ghettos, there were ghettos on the inside. Everyone stuck to their own 'hoods. Once in a while, the dealers and traders did business across groups, but generally it was an apartheid world. At meals the 'Brothers' sat together, the rednecks by themselves, and the 'tinos all in a group. That's when I realized, if I was to survive I'd have to find my way into one of these groups.'

Jack stood up on the bed, his legs sinking into the mattress, directly beneath the fan. He tried to dry off his soaked shirt but it made no difference. So he went on as the fan whirred.

'Eventually found a place with the Black Gangtsa Disciples. But had to pay a price first.'

'Pay money to join a bunch of gangsters?'

'Oh, there be plenty of money around...plenty of everything...but no, wasn't money I had to pay with. The BGDs, the Aryan fucking Brotherhood, the Latino gangs like Nuestra Familia, every single one...none of them was going to offer you protection if you weren't ready to prove your loyalty. It's the price and it's the law. '

Jack told her he was 'lame' when he got to Sing Sing, that he didn't fit in with anybody; too dark for the Aryans, too Anglo for the Hispanic crowd and so on. 'People were starting to move in on my ass, callin' me pretty boy and making me pay double rates for my smokes.' His only defence had been to act like a cornered rat, and at the first hint of trouble to start shouting and swearing at his attackers, acting tougher than he felt. 'I put on a big act. Swaggering and telling everyone to "Fuck out of my way." But I knew better than anybody that my ass was gonna crash and burn. I needed protection and belonging real soon.'

Within two weeks, the Black Gangsta Disciples said they'd been watching Jack, and he found out later, already protecting him. They liked his "Fuck You" attitude and thought they could benefit from it, so they offered him a place at their table. 'The BGDs were the first friends I'd ever known.' They never cut him down, always defended him and never cramped his space or style. 'Loyalty is love in my book, Rose. You don't fuck wit your friends. And the brothers in Sing Sing, they were my real family. I'd found them, at last.'

Jack's brown eyes were swirling and alert. Like a deer after a long run. He was no longer in jail but Afroz could see that he was still a prisoner. She understood that he'd been re-born in Sing Sing. At the point of furthest distance from everything and everyone he had been running from, Jack had at last found a sense of belonging and peace with the Black Gangsta Disciples. He had at last been able to shed his Pakistani skin and sever all that tied him to his culture and roots. At that moment, Jack appeared to her like an animal that had gnawed off its own leg after being caught in a hunter's trap. He thought he was free but in fact, he was just crippled.

Listening to Jack validated Afroz's own decision to return to Pakistan. She had felt dislocated and rootless in England. Especially after the accident. But unlike Jack, who seemed to want to sever all connection with home, Afroz didn't want to be drifting forever in a foreign land.

Her father had slowly fallen apart the longer he'd lived in exile. England had emasculated him, turned him into a nobody. Afroz had decided early on in her life that that was a price she herself would never pay. Better to be in your homeland than living a miserable life in someone else's.

Afroz saw Jack as the worst sort of by-product of migration. Someone so destroyed, he was frightening. But beneath his swagger and naive boasting of life as an American con, in the bundle of contradictions and bluster that paced her room, poking his cigarette and jive talking, Afroz also saw something tender. Someone with whom she might have a real connection.

'What price did you pay for their protection?'

She moved towards him but he didn't seem interested in talking about it any more. He slid down on to his haunches in a corner.

She sat next to him and gently nudged his cheek. 'Tell me, Jack. I want to know everything.'

'It was easy. Too easy.' Jack put out his cigarette and jumped up. 'Just like that,' he said, making a quick back and forth motion with his hand. 'In and out.' He made a clicking sound. 'In the shower...we're walking by and I just lean forward...and in and out, just keep walking. No more than two seconds. The dude collapsed right there... a big fat asshole with a swastika tatooed on his red neck.'

The fan's mechanical whir filled the silence for a moment.

'You killed him?'

'Paid the price...'

'Why?' Afroz's voice trembled. She pulled her knees tightly to her chest, hugging herself.

'Had to be done. Loyalty. I had no feelings, bad or good for the dude...just slipped in the knife. In and out.'

Afroz shook her head but couldn't say anything. For several seconds she rocked back and forth. Then she stood up glaring at Jack before running out onto the roof. The wind whipped the rain about and stung his cheeks and feet. He found her hugging herself and crying. 'You killed someone for no reason, Jack. How could you?'

He tried to put his arm around her but she moved further away. 'I had to do it, see. If I hadn't then someone else would have done it to me. They would have beaten me and let me die like a dog. It's the way of life in the House, Rose. No mercy.'

'You chose that life, Jack. Don't blame the system. You could have stayed with Nasreen in Chicago. You could have, should have, stayed here and never gone to America. What have you accomplished there? You chose to be a criminal.'

How could he explain to her that he had never felt in control of his life? Could she understand that there was always something else pushing him, that he didn't understand or have power over? Destiny. Fate. Kismat.

How could she understand that, man? You don't even understand it yourself.

He sat alone on the bed listening to Ghulam Ali singing his favourite ghazal. Afroz had been in the shower for ages. She hadn't spoken to him for over an hour. The rain and wind had turned the night cold. He smoked cigarette after cigarette to keep warm. Eventually, Afroz came out wearing a denim shirt over an old pair of men's track pants. Her hair reached down to her waist. Jack stood up to make room for her beside him but she got under the covers, and holding her knees close to herself said, 'Was there anyone else, Jack?' Her voice was shaking.

'I'm not a killer, Rosie. Just that once...cause I had to.'

'Would you do it again?'

'Kill? No way.' He looked right into her green eyes, 'Believe me.'

A silence hung between them, separating them. The music stopped and the machine clicked off. Jack took this as a signal to leave.

'What happened after Sing Sing?' She was leaning back against some pillows. Her arms were folded and her expression was stony. Jack looked at her incredulously. 'I want to hear everything,' she said.

He let go of a deep sigh and looked her in the eyes to make sure she meant it. She held his gaze but he saw the shiver pass through her.

'One thing I picked up inside was a nose for coke. Ever done cocaine?'

'Of course not.'

Jack said he'd used it a lot inside, that some of the guards were the suppliers. Nose candy was a way to make the time pass a bit quicker. When he was paroled after doing four and a half years of his sentence, he swore that he'd never go back to prison, no matter what. That he'd go straight.

'Only problem being,' Jack said, 'my nose needed candy every day and I had to find a way to make it pay.'

Calls were made to Nasreen and Uncle Jalal. All in all he collected five thousand dollars, which he consumed in the form of booze or coke. 'It's the most fantastic feeling in the universe. Was a time after Sing Sing, when I moved back to Chi-town that I worshipped coke. It was like God. But I don't go near the stuff now.'

He asked Afroz if she knew what it meant to die. She shook her head furiously. 'Sorry, Rosie, I'm talking about dying, not killing.'

Back in Chicago, a year or so after Sing Sing, he was riding the bus down Randolph, when right in front of the Daley Center he felt his left arm go numb and his chest get cold. He started to panic. He pushed himself off the bus but before he could move more than six feet he collapsed. He woke up in Cook County hospital with doctors and nurses all over him.

'Everybody be asking me this, that and the other thing and I'm not knowing where I am and if I'm dead or alive cause I can't feel my arms or anything. I was scared shitless. Like when the old man used to whip me with his belt.'

Jack was informed that he'd had a cardiac arrest. Did he do cocaine?

'I looked around for cops and then said, "Yeah."'

Jack was informed that he was lucky to be alive and that he should stop using the stuff immediately if he wanted to avoid another incident. The hospital gave him three group sessions with other snow fiends and sent him home with a book called, 'The Coke User's Bible: How to Quit your Habit and Regain Control of Your Life.'

'I haven't had a gram since. Ten years without a snort.'

Afroz didn't blink but she wasn't looking at Jack. She sat rigid too, absolutely still. Jack hit the tape machine and Ghulam Ali's voice began to fill the room. Jack slumped down on the floor against the bed.

In this desert there was once a city
what has become of it
desolation

This mad heart of mine
why have you stopped beating
desolation

The ghazal played through. Neither Afroz nor Jack spoke. The tape machine clicked off and snapped the silence. Jack stood up and stepped towards Afroz. Her face was expressionless and hard. She refused to look at him. 'Main gira hua insaan hun, Afroz. I'm a fallen man. I can't get up.'

Without thinking, she put her arms around him and pulled him down on to the bed, as if he was a naughty boy who'd run away and come home with muddy shoes and torn trousers.

Jack bawled in her arms amidst great convulsions. He clung to Afroz but dared not look at her. 'I don't know how to get up, Rosie.'

Afroz pulled off his jacket. Then she pulled the covers over them both and gave Jack a kiss on his eyes and his forehead, but he couldn't stop sobbing.

'Oh, Jack King,' Afroz said quietly, 'I think I love you.'

Afroz held Jack for a long while. She got up to turn off the light and lock the door. When she got into bed again Jack was awake.

'No one's kissed me for years. Will you do it again?'

She did and he moved in closer, wanting his head to be right next to her lips. Then he looked up at her and kissed her neck. She smiled and said it felt nice, so he kissed her lips. She grabbed him by the neck and pulled him on top of her. They moved as if they had been waiting for this cue. He unbuttoned her shirt and kissed her breasts, while she helped him undo his trousers. She sighed as he entered her. It felt like they were both caught inside a giant wave. The whole world turned warm and fluid, without constraint or fear, and as he moved with Afroz he was baptized into a place and time he had not imagined before. He opened his eyes and even though it was dark, they both smiled at each other and kissed again.

18

Dear Mr Gill,

I thank you for your earlier communications on the subject of the recent award of the Jaguar distributorship in Pakistan, and in particular to your telephone call of last Thursday evening. If your allegations are proven to be correct, Jaguar Cars most certainly will not be in a position to honour its award of the exclusive rights to distribute Jaguar vehicles and products in Pakistan to Shah Enterprises Ltd.

Your allegations with respect to the Shah family's involvement in the illicit trade of narcotics is most distressing. Certainly, Jaguar Cars cannot be associated with such unlawful activities. I am asked by the Executive Director and the entire Board of Jaguar to express our heartfelt gratitude for alerting us to Mr Shah's links with the drugs trade. Our legal advisory team has agreed with your recommendation to suspend the announcement of the award to Shah Enterprises Ltd, until such time as your own investigation into this matter is complete.

Yours sincerely,
Padraig Jameson
Jaguar Cars Ltd
Dubai
United Arab Emirates

Director General Mushtaq Gill read the letter a second time. So well written, so to the point. He folded it in half, dropping it into the desk drawer, and called his brother Razaq. He ran his tongue over his teeth to remove the obstinate remnants of breakfast while he waited. 'It's ours. Jaguar has suspended announcement until our "investigation" is complete.' Mushtaq giggled quietly to his sibling. 'That sisterfucker doesn't even know he's under investigation.' He instructed his brother to meet him at the coffee shop at the Marriot Hotel in an hour. 'An earthquake of massive proportions is about to hit Ali Hassan.'

Gill hung up and then placed another call, this time to Assistant Sub-inspector Noor Aslam.

Cream puffs and pound cake sat untouched between the two men. Aslam's stomach still ached from the last meeting. The news the old spy Khan had delivered, that a deal had been agreed with Mr King for thirty thousand dollars, had made his normally steely stomach queasy with joy. Aslam had always wanted to see the Taj Mahal, and Thailand, where on the beaches, he had heard, the ladies wore nothing but sunshine!

Khan Sahib had promised to deliver the money within an hour of Mr King handing the dollars over to Yahya. The Assistant Sub-inspector watched the geriatric spy rub his bald head. He allowed himself to be poked by feelings of contemptuous pity. Aslam knew that Khan Sahib harboured resentful feelings towards him for being an ASI, but obviously the old man was not cut out to be a top-notch operative. For one thing, he was too honest. He was offering to hand over thirty thousand American dollars to Aslam to hand over to Director General Gill. Blunderous! How could Khan Sahib know that ASI Aslam had already notified Director General Gill of Mr King's intention to purchase heroin, and that he had put in a formal request for a ten thousand dollar operational advance? The money which had arrived by NIA courier that morning was to be used as bait to catch the 'King fish' then returned to HQ. But in smuggling cases such advances had a regular habit of disappearing and HQ normally only recovered a tiny percentage. No one ever complained except the accountants. Aslam permitted himself a self-congratulatory smirk.

At last, with a little heart, Aslam delicately lifted a pastry with green and pink icing towards his mouth. As he chomped, Khan Sahib asked the question the ASI had been waiting for.

'Yahya will require some advance, sir, to purchase a token amount of powder as a sample for Mr King.'

Aslam snorted rather urgently, then swallowed hard, before saying, 'HQ has allocated five thousand dollars for such purposes. To be repaid in full, of course.'

Khan Sahib nodded, though, he—as surely as his sweet-toothed superior—had no intention of returning even a rupee of any advance. Blame was an easy thing to avoid in a city as chaotic as Peshawar, in an operation involving shady foreign smugglers.

Aslam had two more cream puffs and drank an entire pot of sugary milk tea as the old spy stroked his beard, and related how pleased Mr King was with Yahya.

'How much did you promise him for his help, Khan?' Aslam asked.

'Same, sir. Five hundred rupees, sir.'

'Good, good…' Aslam replied distantly. He was lost in his daydream of golden beaches and lovely ladies. His pudgy fingers swatted the crumbs from his dark blue tie.

'Mr King will return from Islamabad on Saturday, sir,' Khan Sahib was saying. 'Operation Kingpin is set to proceed.'

'What time will you return with the advance from HQ?'

Khan Sahib suggested a breakfast meeting at the Galaxy, as usual, on Sunday morning. Less than forty-eight hours from now. The ASI grunted his assent, miffed that he would have to rise uncommonly early. Khan Sahib slowly shuffled out into the street. Aslam readied himself as well, but a solitary pastry lay on the plate like a neglected orphan, its one creamy eye woefully staring him down.

'God!' he exclaimed as he took a bite and the cream dribbled down to add another stain to his only necktie. Glancing around to see if anyone was watching, he scooped the cream up with his forefinger and put it into his mouth. How wonderful. Life is a pastry, thought ASI Aslam as he waddled out of the Galaxy Hotel.

The Mongolian hot-pot was the specialty of the Pearl Dragon—a newly opened eatery in Islamabad. The restaurant was embedded like the guns of Navarone into the side of the brushy foothills that guarded the northern rim of the capital. On a clear day, from a table next to the bay window, you could view Islamabad in all its leafy glory, and watch the waters of Rawal Lake sparkle on the far horizon.

But today Andy had no stomach for anything; his mood was as flat as the Islamabad skyline. The colourless, foggy view below complemented the drabness he had felt ever since Jack had mentioned the kidnapping. The only good thing about the heavy feeling was that it kept his panic, anchored deep in the pit of his gut, in check.

He lit another cigarette—the hovering waiter had emptied his ashtray twice already—and surveyed the city gloomily. Jack King might be cut out for this sort of operation but not Gunnar Andersen. Why didn't he just bow out? Because where else was he going to get the chance to make a hundred grand? Because he could see his weasley kid brother Erik driving his black Lexus convertible and hear his father heaping praise on the runt for 'doing something with his life'.

Because he was scared about what that stubby little volcano Jack might do if he did bow out.

But where was Jack? They'd agreed to meet for an early lunch to finalize the plan. He was seven minutes late already.

Andy's green tea tasted like dishwater. Wisps of smoky mist, like bits of cotton blowing in the wind, drifted over the tops of trees into the bay window and disintegrated. He shared their fragility and lethargy. A white Land Cruiser pulled into the parking lot and out jumped Jack. With one hand in his black jeans, Rayban aviators, sparkling brass buttons on his blazer and his shiny black Florsheims, he walked with the swagger of a tycoon. Now he was making some joke with the cute Chinese girl at the front desk. Why was it that the lower Andy sunk the happier Jack became? Probably got laid. Andy snubbed out his cigarette bitterly.

'My man!' Jack beamed and swung his blazer onto the back of the chair opposite Andy.

'You're late,' Andy said with a fresh unlit cigarette moving up and down between his lips.

'You know what the queen of flowers is?'

'What?'

'The rose,' said Jack, grabbing the menu, not even looking at Andy.

'Whatever.'

'What you goin' to eat? They have chicken almond ding? Love that dish.' Jack flipped the pages of the red-and-black menu.

'I'm not feeling too hungry,' Andy was staring out the window again.

Jack looked over the top of the menu, giving Andy a McEnroe stare. 'Still feelin' scaredy, are we?'

Andy frowned.

'Be cool, man. What I tell you? Tomorrow we roll.'

'Just tell me the plan, Jack.' Andy's throat was raw from the incessant smoking of the last few days.

'You feel better with something in your stomach, dude.' Jack ordered a cashew chicken, special fried rice and a Coke. Andy shook his head at the waiter and poured some more tepid tea into the tiny porcelain cup. Jack reached for one of Andy's Winstons and began to explain how they would kidnap Ahmadzai's daughter.

That afternoon Andy would place a call to St Mary's Convent in Rawalpindi and introduce himself as a friend of Mr Ahmadzai's. He would explain to the Mother Superior that Mr Ahmadzai had asked him to take his daughter, Farah, to the mountains for her usual weekend away, as Mr Ahmadzai was going to be in Karachi on business.

'Usual weekend away?'

'That's right. Cousin Shahid ain't a journalist for no reason. Man, you should have seen him jump on the story when I told him Mr A's little secret.'

'What else do I have to do?'

'Take little Miss Farah to the Pines Hotel in Nathiagali. Keep her happy for the weekend. Take her on walks, buy her things, then bring her back to school on Monday morning. Simple as pie.'

'And what makes you think that the Mother Superior, or Holy Mother, or whoever is going to hand the kid over?' Andy was fiddling furiously with his rat-tail.

'Because you're going to have,' Jack was reaching into his blazer pocket, 'this letter.' Jack pushed the letter he had picked up, envelope and all, from the secretary's desk the day he'd visited Ahmadzai's office, towards Andy.

Andy studied it. 'This is just legal shit about some case. Nothing about me and his girl.'

'Give it to me,' Jack said in exasperation. He snatched the letter back from Andy. 'It's got the man's signature, daddy-o.' He stabbed at the letter. 'All we need.'

Andy pulled on his hair.

'You want to build your dad a little cabin up there in the mountains or you just want to dream about it?' Jack twisted around and put the letter back inside his blazer. 'I'm through with dreamin' my ass off. It's up to you, pardner, but I'm getting goddamn fed up with your whining. In or out. Your call, dude.'

'All the Mother Superior has to do is call Ahmadzai and find out that he's not authorized me to do anything of the sort. This is completely bogus, Jack.'

Jack was eating quietly and between mouthfuls said, 'I got his card.'

'So?'

'So?' Jack set the fork against the plate. 'So? So because...' Jack took a deep breath and swallowed a mouthful of rice and cashews. He drew out from his shirt pocket Ahmadzai's business card. 'See here, this number?'

Andy smiled sarcastically. The number was crossed out and another one was scrawled over it in blotchy ballpoint ink. 'You expect this will convince the nuns?'

'I'll be getting a new one printed this afternoon.'

'Whose number is this?'

Jack held up a pocket phone. 'My cousin Shahid's been real nice to me. Wants me to have all the help I need in getting set up in business.' Rice clung to his front teeth as he flashed a big smile.

'You're going to impersonate Ahmadzai?' His tone was dull and disbelieving.

'Only if I get the call. Mmm...this stuff ain't bad at all.' Jack popped the last cashew into his mouth.

For a long minute Andy stared at Jack. *What the hell am I doing?* He turned away and watched the tiny cars far below, moving like ants on the straight boulevards into the horizon, where unseen in the low hanging clouds lay Rawalpindi. Picking one tiny vehicle out, Andy watched it make progress up the highway: stopping, starting again, slowing down then speeding up, moving farther away into the dreary afternoon. Tomorrow he'd be driving down that very road. Straight into a fucking mess.

The coffee shop at the Marriott Hotel was full. The maître d' bowed slightly when he saw Afroz. 'Good afternoon, madam,' he said quietly. He led her to a small table separated by a splashing fountain from the rest of the lunchtime crowd. 'Alone today, Miss Afroz?'

'My uncle will be joining me soon. Just coffee for me, thank you.' The man moved away and Afroz quickly surveyed the atrium. Korean businessmen sat in small groups jabbering loudly, Arab labour recruiters smoked aggressively, assessing everyone that walked by, local politicos, decked out in immaculate shalwar-qameez and waistcoats, hovered around the buffet table, dipping copper ladles into the steaming trays.

And sitting at a table next to an elevated platform, where two stiff-backed musicians played a Bee Gees tune on a sitar and tabla, was Mushtaq Gill. Afroz saw him in profile. He was squinting at his companion, his brother Razaq, and nodding his head as if he were in a serious discussion. The Director General glanced, just for a moment towards Afroz, who instinctively, lifted the menu to cover her face. When she peeked over the top, Mushtaq Gill was staring right at her. He winked and gave a slight wave.

She smiled stiffly in reply and returned her attention to the menu.

Gill pushed his chair back and mumbled something to his brother who kept talking. Dropping his starchy napkin on the table, he shot a glance in Afroz's direction which said, here I come.

'Oh God,' muttered Afroz. She picked up her bag and

rummaged through it in the hope of finding protection among her lipsticks and perfume sprays.

'Hello, sweetie,' a deep male voice said. Afroz jumped in fright. The man was elegantly done out in a hand-tailored linen suit, a white silk shirt and a deep purple tie.

'Oh, thank God it's you,' she laughed and told the man to sit down. 'You came.'

'Of course, I came. Have I ever missed a chance to see the prettiest girl in Islamabad?'

Afroz squeezed the older man's hand and beamed. 'Don't you mean Pakistan?' She noticed that Gill had sat down again and turned his back to her and her uncle, Mr Inayatullah Ahmadzai.

'But I'm afraid I can't stay, Afroz. I'm off to Karachi for the weekend.'

Afroz didn't try to hide her disappointment. 'When are you back?'

'Saturday night. Late. I fly direct to Peshawar.' Ahmadzai adjusted his tie and prepared to leave.

'I've got news,' Afroz said. 'I need your advice.'

Ahmadzai put down his Gucci briefcase and leaned forward. 'What is it, beti?'

'No, I'll tell you next time. I want to tell you all about him from top to bottom. I'll be in Peshawar in a couple of weeks.'

Ahmadzai touched his niece's cheek tenderly. 'Okay, tell me all about him then. I'm glad you've found someone. It will do you good. ' He towered over her and smiled, then moved towards the front of the coffee shop.

'Wait,' Afroz called out. 'I'll walk you out.'

They passed the the Gill brothers' table who were deep in discussion. Mushtaq Gill was leaning forward, hunched over the table, balancing on the two front legs of the chair. As she passed him, Afroz gave the chair a slight nudge which sent the unsuspecting Director General crashing to the floor. 'So sorry, Director General sahib,' she said, but didn't stop. Her uncle was waiting for her at the front desk.

William moved slowly through the muddy, ravaged streets around Rawalpindi's main bus terminal at Pirwadahi. Grease monkeys hammered away on tin and iron vehicle frames. Sparks from welding guns punctuated the dark, wet day like mortar bursts. A pungent smell of burning rubber hung in the air. Punjabi disco songs blared from big speakers inside the terminus, and drivers repeatedly squelched the air horns of their soon-to-depart buses.

Jack instructed William to stop the car. He disappeared behind a bus and didn't return for fifteen minutes. When he did, he was agitated.

'Next stop, Raja Bazaar,' he said.

As the car slushed slowly through the clogged streets, Jack wondered where he was going to find a gun. Pirwadahi had been complete chaos. No one seemed to speak Urdu, let alone English. Within just a few minutes he knew it was a lost cause. Then he remembered that years ago, Kamran, the family cook, used to say that everything could be found in Raja Bazaar. But toy airplanes were one thing. Handguns quite another. He knew it was a long shot but time was running short. Twenty-five minutes later, William parked the jeep next to a pale mauve-and-blue cinema. Jack told William he'd be back.

'Okay, saab. I waitit.'

As soon as he stepped out, Jack was swallowed up by the mass of moving people. His Florsheim wingtips were soon caked with mud. 'Pigsty country,' he said as he passed a boy selling balloons and cheap plastic sunglasses. The boy held out a blue-and-red cellophane encased noise-maker. 'Get lost,' Jack snapped, as he pushed further into the crowd.

Where the hell am I going to get me a gun?

A crack of thunder announced a fresh downpour. Jack jumped under a tree next to a man who was raffishly dressed in a yellow-and-red striped jacket, tight white jeans and an old pair of sneakers. Jack watched the rain come down. Most people had found shelter in storefronts or teashops.

'Hashish!'

Jack turned towards the man in the loud jacket. 'Hashish,' he whispered again.

Jack didn't respond. The man refused to acknowledge him. Rain was pelting the streets. Visibility was no more than twenty metres.

'Ladies. Hashish,' the man's lips barely moved.

'Regular singing canary, ain't you,' Jack said staring right at the man.

'You want ladies? Young. Too sexy.' The man stared ahead.

Jack shook his head.

'Hashish. Ganja. Powder.'

The Canary side-stepped closer to Jack. 'What you want, mister? Whisky? You like boys?'

Jack was getting ready to bolt when he got an idea.

'What you like?' the man tried again, finally tossing a quick look in Jack's direction.

'Gun.'

It was all the Canary needed to hear. 'Come. Come.' He grabbed at Jack's sleeve. 'This way. Quickly.'

The man flitted and jumped from one semi-dry storefront to another; running quickly across the road, then ducking behind a taxi and finally up a cement staircase to a dark hallway where the exposed electric cables dangled dangerously low. 'One minute. Wait here.' Puffing, Jack leaned against a mildewy wall. The Canary moved down the hall, knocked on a door and waited, throwing furtive glances at Jack and indicating with his open hand that he should sit tight. He mumbled something low and indistinct before the door pulled open. 'Come, come,' he stage-whispered to Jack.

Inside, in a bare-walled room sat three men, one of whom was wearing the light blue shirt of a cop. Jack stopped cold. The other men laughed and indicated that Jack should sit down on a string bed. The Canary nodded at the cop and said, 'Friend. No problem, mister. What you like?'

Jack looked at the other two men. They were tall, well-built, middle-aged and unshaven. Both wore dhotis. One was lying on the bed, propped up on an elbow. Jack decided to leave. He shook his head at the Canary, 'Nothing, man.'

Sensing his anxiety, the Canary came closer, 'No problem, mister.' He turned towards the reclining man and said something in Punjabi. The cop stood up, put on his dark blue beret, checked himself in a mirror, mumbled a farewell and stepped out of the little room. Jack listened to his steel cleated boots clicking down the hall.

The Canary said, 'Good quality hashish. You like? Baluchi hash.'

With his heart thumping, Jack said, 'Pistol.'

The Canary said something to the others. One of them lobbed a key which the Canary took over to a cupboard built into the concrete wall.

'Holy shit, Batman,' Jack gasped. Inside, hanging like sides of beef were at least a dozen Kalashnikovs and M16s. The Canary pointed out an Uzi, nodding enthusiastically and grinning.

He unhooked one weapon and shoved it at Jack who fell backwards onto the charpai. 'Kalashnikov. Russian one. Original maal.'

'No thanks,' Jack coughed.

The room smelled of mutton curry, and sweaty feet. A pile of rubbish comprising scraps of bread, onion peels, greasy paper and dirty plates had been pushed into one corner. A neon tube light flickered intermittently.

'Pistol, dude,' Jack said, making one with his forefinger and thumb. 'Something small and light.'

One of the men shook his head. The Canary shrugged. Jack sighed. 'Okay, thanks.' He got up to leave.

'One minute, mister,' chirped the Canary. The three men huddled together. There was shaking of heads, twisting of fingers and scratching of balls. 'Ten minutes. You wait, okay?' Before Jack could respond, the Canary flew out of the room.

The two unshaven villagers stared blankly at Jack. Jack stared at his hands and tried not to think of the cop. Ten minutes passed. Fifteen. Twenty minutes turned to twenty-five and then to thirty. The two village men talked among themselves. The Canary finally returned forty-five minutes later, cradling a soiled cloth bundle in his arm. One of the villagers latched the door behind him as the Canary dropped the bundle into Jack's lap. He undid the cloth, exposing a well-used snub-nosed pistol with a laminated wood grip. Even in the dim light it seemed to be shine. The Canary stepped back. Jack picked up the gun, a Beretta Tomcat, pointed it at the wall, cocked it and pulled the trigger. A nice and tight solid sounding click. He put it into his blazer pocket: easy fit. He pulled it out, tossed it to his left hand, then back to the right, bouncing it to get a comfortable grip. 'How much you want?'

'Dollars? Rupees?'

'American.'

'Five hundred,' said the Canary but Jack could detect hesitation.

'Who you trying to kid? One of these be no more than three hundred where I come from.'

'Four fifty. Last price.'

'Get real!' Jack said. He put the gun down on the bed.

'Okay. Tell me last price?'

'Told you, man. Three hundred dolleros. Take or leave it.'

The Canary looked at the two men. They whispered together and shrugged a few times. Then at last the Canary said, 'Okay. Give me money.' His small palms opened and shut anxiously a few times.

19

The meeting with Sister Teresa at St Mary's Convent had nearly not taken place. All the way from the guest house to the other side of Rawalpindi, a trip of nearly an hour, Andy had had to calm himself by breathing deep and keeping the image of a completed mountain cabin firmly in his mind's eye. Several times he pulled out the forged business card and letter of authorization for reassurance, but instead, they only mocked him. Mr Ahmadzai was identified on the card as an 'Advocat'.

He was met at the gate of the Convent by a nun named Sister Dorothy. She led him through several halls, up and down staircases until they reached a cavernous room dominated by a large rosewood desk on the far wall. Andy was asked to wait. Jesus looked down at him, exposing his bleeding, wounded heart. The Pope's picture, Andy noted, was larger and had a more elaborate frame. Lowering his eyes, he begged silent forgiveness for the sin he was about to commit.

Sister Teresa swept in and without introduction sat herself down behind the desk and pressed an unseen button, sending a loud ring echoing down the empty hall. Sister Dorothy quietly stepped forward. Sister Teresa commanded her to bring Farah Ahmadzai at once.

Andy cursed Jack with well-chosen but unspoken epithets.

'Mr Ahmadzai has called me just now,' Sister Teresa said. The announcement made Andy jump slightly. His heart banged like a steel spoon against a griddle.

'He did?'

'Yes, from the sky,' Sister Teresa said. 'He informed me he was in the airplane flying to Karachi.'

As far as Andy knew, Ahmadzai had left for Karachi the previous night. Had he delayed his trip? Did he know what Jack and he were up to? 'Oh God,' he moaned.

'Sorry?' Sister Teresa leaned forward.

Andy looked at her face. It wasn't kindly or soft. Her nose was too big and she had jowls like a man. His panic increased. He gazed into the woman's eyes. In a millisecond he decided to confess everything. 'Sister,' he began. 'I am afraid that I must—'

'Yes, he has called but it was quite difficult to make out his voice. At first I did not recognize him. He sounded like an American. But he told me he was in the airplane and there was "atmospheric distortion."' Sister Teresa was not entirely convinced.

Andy tried to smile as a way of reassuring the nun but the telephone on Sister Teresa's desk suddenly jangled.

The breakfast meeting with the American Congressional delegation had been hell. They were demanding that Pakistan stop meddling in Kashmir. Aid would be cut back even further if this wasn't immediate, they reminded the local delegation. Basically, what they wanted was for Pakistan to bend over and take it in the rear from India. All for what? A few hundred million dollars in aid? But the Prime Minister was desperate to have the sanctions lifted and he had personally requested Rahman, Khan and Ahmadzai Ltd to ensure that this happened.

Karachi was a simmering cesspool of heat and angst this time of year. The taxi drivers were terrorists and the police, extortionists. As soon as he arrived, Inayatullah Ahmadzai had made his way straight to the Avari Hotel. Safely in his icy air-conditioned room he cracked open a hip flask of Black Dog Scotch and let the liquor slowly melt the morning's tension away. After the Americans, more meetings had followed: with the military Corps Commander, who wanted advice on the order the Prime Minister had issued to arrest over two hundred 'anti-national elements' a week before the Assembly elections and with the French Consul, who needed his recommendations on how to hurry the paperwork through the courts so that a Parisian woman accused of smuggling thirteen kilos of hashish could deliver her baby in a French prison.

There would be two more consultations later in the afternoon but now, just before lunch, Inayatullah Ahmadzai knew that nothing would relieve his stress more than hearing her sweet giggly voice. He took off his shoes and loosened his tie as he flopped back on the king-sized bed and hit the remote control.

CNN flickered on but he immediately hit 'mute' and began to dial a number on the hotel phone. As he waited for someone to answer, he watched his favourite newsreader Cindy Pereira blink incessantly at the camera, as if her contact lenses didn't quite fit. She silently mouthed the day's events. The screen switched to a crumpled mess of train carriages and smoke. The dateline was somewhere in the southern United States.

'Hello,' he said. 'Is that you, Sister Teresa?'

'Ah, you've called again.'

'Again?' Ahmadzai hesitated.

'Yes. Just one hour back, Mr Ahmadzai. Your voice was not clear.'

'I was in a meeting one hour ago,' the lawyer replied. He sat up in surprise. 'This is the first moment's rest I've had since...' He tossed the remote control onto an armchair and as it landed the 'mute' button clicked off. Cindy Pereira was shouting at the world beyond the screen now. 'What more can you tell us, Bill, about the investigation that is underway into the causes of this terrible accident?'

Ahmadzai shouted into the phone, 'Excuse me, Sister, one moment please.' He put the phone down and stretched across the bed to retrieve the remote control. At full spread he only managed to push it to the floor. 'Damn!' he huffed.

'And so it appears that the captain of the train disregarded the signal, is that right, Bill?' Cindy was blinking furiously at a studio screen where Bill could be seen nodding gravely, as fire crews swarmed out of focus behind him.

Ahmadzai brushed the hair from his face, crawling on his hands and knees to grab the remote. Cindy and Bill were silent once again.

Ahmadzai stood up, let out a sigh of relief and strode back to the phone.

'Hello, Sister? I'm so sorry for that but there was some problem with the television. Please forgive me,' he sat down on the edge of the bed.

'Atmospheric distortion again, no doubt,' Sister Teresa replied thinking she was being helpful.

'Sorry? No, there is no distortion here...unless you mean the TV. I'm afraid I'm not following you, Sister.' He caressed his temples. Then he cursed the horribleness of the day, right from breakfast to this conversation. 'Is it possible to speak with Farah, Sister? My departure was unexpected and I didn't have time to inform her.'

'Yes, why not. I have already sent for her. One moment, Mr Ahmadzai.' Sister Teresa set the phone down and looked at Andy who had been listening to the conversation with paralysing horror. 'Would you like to talk with Mr Ahmadzai while I fetch Sister Dorothy?'

Andy didn't get up. He stared ahead at Sister Teresa

who was now coming around her giant desk towards him. He gave a quick supplicatory glance to Christ and the Holy Father as a cold wave of nausea churned upwards from his pelvis. 'What's wrong with you, Mr Andersen,' Sister Teresa whispered loudly. 'It is rude to keep such a man waiting. Go on. I'll be back in just a jiffy.'

Ahmadzai continued to massage his temples, wondering what Sister Teresa had been talking about. He hadn't called the Convent for three days. Why had she summoned Farah to her office? Atmospheric distortion? He waited, holding the silent telephone, trying to make sense of the nun's conversation.

Andy stared at the phone as if it were a deadly snake. Better to ignore it and get the hell out of there. He slowly turned his head to the left, stood up and started to inch towards the door. Before he had taken more than two steps, he heard the sounds of several people making their way towards the office. 'Oh my God,' Andy whimpered. 'Damn you, Jack! Why the hell did I believe a thing you said?' His recurring nightmare—of being led away in shackles to some dim, ratty prison cell by smirking policemen—snapped into his mind. He moved back to the chair, closed his eyes and waited for the inevitable.

The door opened and Sister Teresa, Sister Dorothy and a young girl in a school uniform entered the office. The girl dropped Sister Dorothy's hand and raced to pick up the phone. 'Daddy Daddy!' she squealed as she made herself comfortable in Sister Teresa's big stiff-backed chair. 'Where are you, Daddy?'

The two nuns beamed at the young girl as she spoke

exuberantly to her father. Andy's expression was rigid and his face, he was sure, looked grey. He didn't acknowledge the Sisters, staring zombie-like at Farah. She giggled and then her voice became serious as she told her father of her homework and then she laughed again. In a few minutes she said, 'Accha, Daddy. Cheerio.' She dropped the phone on Sister Teresa's desk with a thud. Sister Teresa moved quickly to pick it up but Ahmadzai had hung up.

'You must always let me speak to your father after you have finished, Farah,' the nun scolded. 'I wanted to confirm your programme for this weekend with him. And now see! You should tell him I wanted to speak with him.'

'What programme, Sister?' The young girl was off the chair and curious. 'Tell me please. What programme?'

Sister Dorothy came to stand next to the big desk and took the girl by the hand again. 'Mr Andersen, here is Farah. Go on, Farah, give your hand to Mr Andersen. He has come to collect you and take you to Nathiagali for the weekend. Don't be shy. He is your father's good friend.'

A flush of prickly warmth flushed through Andy's body and out through his hair. His ears were hot. The knotted feeling in his stomach eased slightly. But he still couldn't move.

'Mr Andersen,' Sister Teresa called out from behind her desk. 'Are you not feeling well?'

Andy shook his head and muttered, 'I'm fine.' He smiled at the young girl who instantly sucked in her lower lip and turned away.

'Silly girl. What is wrong with you, now? Say hello,' Sister Teresa boomed.

'Good morning sir,' the little girl managed to say, but only just. She put her hand over her mouth to stop sniggering. She didn't know what to make of the man's thin rat-tail.

The little girl's good spirits influenced Andy's own mood.

He wanted to shout and punch his fist in the air and scream, 'I did it!' but instead, reached forward and took the girl's hand. 'Hello Farah. We'll have a good time this weekend, won't we?'

Farah was staring at the floor, avoiding Andy's unfamiliar face.

'Right, Farah. You have everything for the weekend?' Sister Dorothy then addressed Andy. 'Remember you must return her to us by five p.m. on Monday. Our gates close at that time.'

Sister Dorothy led them back to the front gate where the taxi was waiting. Andy waved to the Sister and gave Farah's ponytail a tug. She stifled a giggle and jumped in the back seat. When they had driven about fifteen minutes, Farah said, 'Is there a VCR in Nathiagali, Mr Andersen? Can we watch Riverdance. It's my favourite film.'

'If there isn't, I'll buy one,' Andy said winking at her again. And he meant it. With a hundred thousand dollars coming his way, he could buy whatever she wanted.

Early in the morning they were still awake, talking. The rain had stopped but a gale was shaking the windows and whistling through the cracks. Every few minutes, bursts of rain would spit against the glass panes, hard as gravel.

Afroz leaned back on the pillows and made no attempt to cover her breasts. 'If you're a fallen man it's because of that place. America.' Jack was sitting facing her, his wiry body barely covered with a sheet. They shared a cigarette. 'This is where you belong, Jack. Not there.'

He watched her smoke. She was not wearing lipstick but her lips still managed to glisten in the dim light. There was no other place he wanted to be but here, with the woman he loved.

'Can't Rosie. Ain't much for me in America, that's true, but there's absolutely nothing here.'

'How you can say that? You've been in jail and you became an addict. You went there to find life and freedom but you became a murderer.' Afroz gave an involuntary shudder.

'I've rejected this place and it's rejected me, too.'

'Start again, Jack. Nothing is written in stone.'

He shook his head. He knew the answer to this one. He'd been telling himself for years to start over. He'd started over so many times, he'd lost sight of the road. 'I'm too tired, Rose. I've forgotten what it's like to live like a Pakistani, all normal and by the book. I just can't.'

'Why can't you?'

'I've always taken the downhill road. The one that doesn't take much trying. The road you're on, that's too much for me.'

'You're not an American, you know that. It's all your pretending that makes things hard for you.'

'It's too late, Rosie.'

'What's to hold on to?'

He didn't have an answer.

'If I ain't American, what the hell am I?'

'Is being Pakistani so awful?'

The softness evaporated from his voice. 'I'd rather die,' he muttered.

She pulled him close but he remained tense.

'You know what I think, Jack? You know what you're afraid of?'

He didn't move.

'Love,' Afroz whispered. 'Mohabbat. That's all you need.'

He tried to smile.

'You know, love isn't so scary, especially compared to what you've been through.' She moved his head onto a pillow and came closer. With her hand tickling his thigh she began to kiss his neck, lips, eyes and forehead. She covered them with a sheet, straddling atop him, as he gently raised his hips again and again. Her cigarette, resting in an overflowing ashtray on the floor, eventually burned itself out.

20

Jack was pumped. It was one o' clock on Sunday morning. He drained another can of San Miguel and settled back in the rattan armchair in front of the large window looking out into the garden. He'd been drinking vodka and beer since he'd reached Peshawar around dusk. He wasn't drunk but he felt light, like a butterfly—flitting just above Andy's marble floors. He looked at the clock every few minutes, waiting for it to strike one-thirty, when William was to give a quick honk as a signal. Every light in the house was off; total darkness. It helped him focus on the next couple of hours.

The first shipment would be in Chicago by August, Labour Day weekend, for sure. What Rosie had said was true. He knew things wouldn't stay cool for too long in this sort of gig. That's why he figured he'd need just three, maybe four shipments to make his fortune. Stay active in the game for a year, two at the most. Then he'd shut the pipeline down and think about going straight.

The reason he had never succeeded in the straight life before was there had been no incentive. Manage an Indian restaurant? Get real. Stay married to Nasreen? Yeah right. Even the idea of the superette up in Coon Rapids hadn't turned his crank hard or long enough. Maybe Rose was the missing incentive. The woman who would help him leave the streets at last. He sat by the window listening to the trees rustling in the wind.

He took a final swig of his drink and looked at the clock.

1:31. Where was William? He tapped the bulging pockets of his black leather jacket. Cigarettes. Switchblade. Ski-mask. Beretta. When he heard the soft bleep of the horn outside, he jumped up and said, 'Let's go, daddy-o.'

In the gali called Wali Lane, at number 33/12, Sher Jan was spooning powder from a big plastic bag into three small sachets torn from today's newspaper. One of the packets would be enough to put a man out for three hours, but this was a special occasion. Yahya had said they were going to make at least one hundred thousand each! Such a big amount of money deserved a large dose of poison. And with three packets he'd prove to Khan Sahib that the idea was a good one.

Yahya stuck his head into the room. 'Sheru,' he whispered. Sher Jan looked up. The cousins winked at each other and laughed. 'Tomorrow we are kings!'

ASI Noor Aslam had been asleep for hours. Next to him on a sagging charpai was a messy collection of travel brochures. Happy couples running down the white beach hand in hand, laughing and splashing in the bluest water he'd ever seen.

Thailand. Let us enchant you this year.

He snored softly in rhythm to the rise and fall of his rotund belly.

The only one sleeping in Khan Sahib's cramped rented rooms was his wife. The old spy got up just after midnight—after tossing in his bed for what seemed like hours. 'Have you glass in your bed?' his wife asked irritably. No, there was no glass in his bed but his mind felt as if it were being cut into strips. Would Yahya and Sher Jan get to Ahmadzai's place on time to waylay King? What if they arrived too late? As

Khan paced the narrow veranda of his third-floor apartment he watched the dark shadows of the night dogs pawing through the mounds of rubbish below. He became more and more oppressed with thoughts of all the ways that Yahya and Sher Jan could bungle the job. Six more hours till first light, when he was to meet Yahya at the tea shop near the railway station. It seemed like an eternity.

The drive from Andy's house on Gulmohar Lane to Ahmadzai's place in Hayatabad, where the nouveaux-riche of Peshawar society had their palatial houses, took no more than fifteen minutes. At the police checkpoint they offered the sleepy men cigarettes and were waved through.

William pulled into Street 54. The streetlights were few and dim. They did nothing to guide the way. With the engine cut off, the jeep rolled forward slowly until it stopped fifteen metres from Ahmadzai's house. The two men sat in silence. No rain, no wind. But that could change any minute. From where they sat Jack could see Ahmadzai's house clearly. He had scoped it out twice, earlier in the evening. The white marble facade almost glowed in the blackness. A light was on in a rear upstairs window—the man was working late. Jack preferred it that way 'cause you never know what stupidity a man who is disoriented and woken from sleep is capable of.

The front gate was slightly open; just six inches or so. What did that mean? Jack watched to see if anyone would come in or out but after a few minutes, said to William, 'You see me go over the wall, that's your signal to go up to the gate and start talking to the chowkidar. Right?'

William wasn't happy with what Mr King had been telling him this evening but he was an employee, and so replied obediently, 'Right, saab.'

Jack shut the car door silently as he hopped out. In his

black ski cap, black jacket and dark jeans, he was nearly invisible. He dashed barefoot across the road and onto the grass. It was wet but warm under his feet. Before he knew it, he had reached the side wall of the Ahmadzai's compound. He caught his breath and wished he could light a smoke. The open front gate bothered him. But it also encouraged him. Maybe the chowkidar had wandered off to another house to have a chat with some other guard.

Jack crept towards the front gate but a few metres away, he stopped dead in his tracks. Someone was whispering frantically. 'Sheru, Sheru,' was all Jack understood. The voice sounded familiar but he couldn't place it; instinctively, Jack pulled back into the shadows. He'd wait for a few minutes. By this time he figured the voice was that of the chowkidar who was probably talking to a guard who had visited him. But why were they whispering so desperately?

Yahya had been keeping watch by the gate, when he saw the headlights of the jeep turn into the street and then go off. Mr King had arrived.

At 1:10 Sher Jan and Yahya had walked up to Ahmadzai's gate and knocked. When the gate opened a crack, they began talking like they were refugees who'd just come down from the mountains. They said they were lost and asked for directions. The chowkidar opened up wider and told them to come in for a second and have some tea. The tea was already made and sitting in a battered blue enamel teapot, simmering on a small coal stove. Yahya distracted the guard by telling him in a frenzied tone the story of how they had been forced to leave their village three days ago after some mujahids had stormed through and set every house and vehicle on fire. As he explained to the wide-eyed guard how they had been separated from their families, Sher Jan opened one of his packets of powder and poured the contents into the guard's cup. Within five minutes of taking a sip the man's eyes started to close; he said he felt sick. Sher Jan smiled at Yahya. They laid him on his charpai and headed towards the house.

As Sher Jan went in, Yahya hung back to make sure the guard didn't wake up, and that no one else stuck their nose into the affair. After Sher Jan's powder had worked so quickly on the chowkidar, Yahya felt confident that his cousin would have no problem with the man inside. 'Once he's out, give me a signal and we'll take the money. Hurry now. Mr King will be here soon.' Sher Jan winked and disappeared inside with a bright blue sports bag they had bought that afternoon to carry away their fortune.

It had been more than half an hour now. Yahya was sure Mr King would be coming any moment. The jeep, as far as he could see, was still there. He hadn't seen anyone get out of it, but felt certain that Mr King was around. He'd already decided that he'd shoot Mr King if he had to; he'd use the guard's Kalashnikov. But he wanted to have the money in his bag before any shooting started.

The chowkidar was still out but every once in a while he seemed to have a small fit, shaking and groaning. It made Yahya nervous but more than that, he could sense Mr King's silent presence. He whispered again, louder than before, 'Sheru!' The house was completely silent, though, he thought he'd heard some low voices before.

Yahya looked at his watch. Ten minutes to two. Where was Mr King? He looked over at the guard. His mouth was open and his tongue slightly out, like a dog in the heat. There was still no sign of his cousin, so Yahya decided to step outside to take a leak and use the opportunity to find out what Mr King was up to.

As he stuck his head out and edged along the concrete boundary wall, Yahya thought: what if that is not Mr King's jeep? What if Khan reported this to the police? But why? The greedy old man wants the money more than we do. But if it isn't the police, why is King so quiet? Yahya was getting more worried by the moment but kept inching along the wall, deeper into the shadow. A lop-sided moon appeared for a moment between the dark clouds, then ducked away again. For a second, he hesitated because he thought he heard a noise from back inside the house. What if the guard had woken? At last, he felt the corner of the wall. Getting a good grip around the edge, he turned the corner in a quick movement and gasped, as he felt something sharp bite his chest.

Jack recognized Yahya, his heroin dealer. He had no idea who Sheru was, but when he saw Yahya inching along the wall, he knew that there'd have to be some bullshit before the night was over. Without thinking, he pulled out his switchblade from an inner pocket. The same one he'd carried since his first month in Sing Sing. The one he had killed the greasy Aryan redneck with.

It was a four-and-a-half-inch blade. Jack's fingers opened and closed around the ivory handle a few times and with his other hand he got ready to pull Yahya in towards him so he couldn't move. For a quick moment, he thought of Afroz, but he blinked and shook it off. He hadn't planned on this. What choice did he have?

He could hear Yahya breathing heavily on the other side of the wall. Jack held his own breath and as soon as he saw the man's hand come around the corner he braced himself, grabbing Yahya's neck. It went stiff as he stuck the blade deep into him. The Pathan tried to resist, but Jack could already feel the wet ooze on his fingers. For a second, Yahya stared at Jack before falling to his knees with a slight wheeze. The giant rolled over onto his stomach, as if he thought he could plug the hole where he was losing blood. Panting, Jack put the knife back into his pocket and made his way towards the gate, now wide open.

He saw the chowkidar lying on the string cot and wondered why the man didn't go inside. The rain was starting to come down again and he would catch a cold. What if he woke up while Jack was inside with Ahmadzai? He stepped closer to have a look. The man was barely breathing. One eye was half-open but the other was closed completely and his tongue was hanging out. Jack concluded that he was not about to cause any trouble. He walked casually towards the wide-open kitchen door. The light was on, just like Khan had said it would be. Jack's feet were cold. Inside, he wiped each foot on his pants and had a look around. A fridge droned loudly then shuddered off. Jack moved towards the dining room. The light was still on upstairs and he could hear someone talking. Was Ahmadzai on the phone? He made his way quickly but cautiously towards the light. Out of the dining room and into a large living room with baroque furniture, just like Nanima's. At the bottom of the stairs Jack could clearly hear Ahmadzai's voice. He was agitated, speaking in Pashto. Jack smiled, pulled on the ski mask and took to the stairs, two at a time. When he got to the top, he heard Ahmadzai shouting.

The door to Ahmadzai's office was open but Jack could only see shadows. Moving towards the voices, he pulled out the Beretta, clipped the safety off and put it back in his pocket. Seeing a shadow move, like it was coming towards him, he slipped into the nearest room. It was a bedroom that smelled faintly of mothballs. Cracking the door slightly, Jack listened. Ahmadzai was yelling again. Then there was an answer, equally gruff and loud. There was something familiar about that voice, too.

Suddenly, as Jack pressed his ear to the door, it fell into place. Yahya's desperate whispers for Sheru. Sher Jan, that screwball thug who wanted to poison Ahmadzai. The guard downstairs, out like a log. So Yahya and Sher Jan were in on this together. But what was their angle? Yahya didn't need money, not if he was who he said he was, with connections in Bulgaria and Antwerp. Maybe they had their own beef with Ahmadzai. But that didn't add up. Maybe Yahya wasn't who he said he was. Maybe he was just another photocopy of Sher Jan. A small-time loser looking for the big payout. But Khan Sahib? The old man had insisted that Yahya was one of the country's top smack kings. Why would he lie about Yahya? Unless he didn't know himself? But Khan had provided all the other information as well. About the house, the entrances, the guard, who was where at what time. Khan Sahib knew a lot. Surely, he had to know whether Yahya was who he said he was.

Ahmadzai was really going for it now, screaming at the top of his voice. Sher Jan was silent. There was a scuffle. Jack heard a chair, or maybe a small table falling over. Then he heard some more shouting. This time, it was Sher Jan. Jack listened intently, but couldn't take his mind off Khan. He was too old to be pulling horseshit like this. What was in it for him? Why was an old man with no interest in heroin working with these two jerks?

'It's a set-up,' Jack muttered in the darkness as he heard glass smashing inside. 'They're trying to kill the poor man.'

Then the last piece of the puzzle fell into place.

They were trying to set him up to take the rap.

'Well, fuck that shit,' Jack said as he came out of the bedroom. In an instant, he decided he'd have to go in and save Ahmadzai from this asshole. He pulled out the Beretta, checked his grip a couple times, then stepped towards the office. He heard a loud groan and the sound of a body falling to the floor. He'd done it. Sher Jan had killed Ahmadzai. And he was coming out of the office now. Jack pressed himself against the wall in the dark. As soon as the man stepped out of the office, he closed his eyes and squeezed the trigger twice, and then a third time. The shots sounded like thunder. When he opened his eyes, he saw, lying at his feet, holding a sword, Mr Ahmadzai—in his chequered bathrobe and slippers. Blood seeping from his chest. Deader than Elvis.

With Ahmadzai dead—the man had not even had time to comprehend who it was that shot him—Jack peered into the office. Sher Jan lay crumpled in a pool of sticky blood. In their struggle, Ahmadzai had grabbed an old ornamental scimitar—the second of the pair still hung on the wall—and split Sher Jan's head almost in two. The dead man breathed his last, smiling up at the ceiling as if he had just recalled a joke. A foot away, near his right hand, was another pool of liquid: an overturned bottle of Coca Cola.

A pall descended around the place. Jack's ears still rang from the gunshots. Leaning against Ahmadzai's desk, he slowly processed that two men were dead, and a third was bleeding outside in the rain. 'What the hell?' Jack sighed as his shoulders slumped and his knees weakened. How did all this happen? His right hand still gripped the Beretta. The cute little snub-nose seemed ugly all of a sudden.

He studied Sher Jan for a moment, thinking what to do next. The idea of running—getting the hell out of this train wreck—was quickly moving to the top of the jumbled hierarchy of his thoughts. Still clutching the gun, Jack crawled towards the dead Sher Jan. Carefully avoiding the blood which was sinking into the ornate silk paisleys of the Kashmiri carpet, Jack extricated the pistol from his hand and fixed Sher Jan's lifeless fingers around the butt. He then wrapped one hand in his ski mask and the other in a hankie protruding from Ahmadzai's satin bathrobe and dragged the dead lawyer back behind his desk so it would appear as if Sher Jan had shot Ahmadzai at nearly the exact moment his own head was being swung at.

Jack moved to the window and with his back pressed against the wall, craned his neck to look outside. A few lights had come on further down the street but there were no voices or ringing alarms. He took a final look at the dead men, shook his head then ran downstairs and out of the kitchen door. The chowkidar was still out cold, but William, perturbed by what he had heard, was waiting at the gate with a twisted look on his face, wringing his hands.

'I hear shootit, saab.' It was both an accusation and a question. Jack put his arm around the driver and said yes, someone had been shot but that he had arrived too late to stop it.

21

All Andy could say was, 'Shit.'

Jack was calling from Peshawar and his voice trembled slightly as he told him about Yahya and Sher Jan and how Ahmadzai came bursting out of the office. Farah was sleeping. Andy had promised to take her horseback riding in the morning. How could he do that when her father was dead? Who was going to break the news? 'Shit. Shit. Shit. Are you sure you killed him, Jack?'

'Is the Pope a fuckin' Italian?'

'Not exactly.'

'Well, fuck. Yes, the man's dead,' Jack said dully.

The telephone line buzzed and crackled as both men considered the situation confronting them.

'You can't stay there. Not in my place. That would be the stupidest thing you could do. The police will be there any second.' Andy was whispering loudly into the phone.

'Chill, my man.' Jack was trying to control his shakes.

'Have you lost your mind, Jack?'

'Told you, Mr A—he was fighting with Sher Jan. Cops'll think they killed each other,' Jack said. 'No one will know we were involved.'

'You, Jack. You were involved, not me. I was in bed, here. Babysitting Farah.' There was a pause, then Andy moaned, 'Oh God, help me.'

'Better get your ass down here, pardner.'

'What about the girl? I can't just leave her here.'

'Bring her too. We got to think of a new plan.'

'Don't say "we", Jack. I had nothing to do with what went down.'

Jack was repeating the whole episode again, from the moment he arrived with William to when the shots went off, hoping that the story might have a different ending the second time around.

'But you got the money, right?'

'Fuck you saying, man? The man be dead. I had no time to say howdy, let alone have him sign the papers.'

Andy's body turned to ice. He'd got himself involved in nothing more than a murder. He was already busting out a plan he'd packed away in a corner of his mind, just in case something like this happened. While Jack had been spending his days in Islamabad with Afroz and forging documents, Andy hadn't been sitting idle. He'd made a tentative booking on the British Airways flight to London. As soon as Farah was awake he'd take her back to the safety of Sister Dorothy. With Ahmadzai dead, the most important thing now—besides getting out of the country—was making sure the little girl got home safely. After handing the girl back he'd find a dumpy hotel in the heart of the old town, lie low till Tuesday, praying all the way. His heart bounced like a yo-yo. 'I gotta go to bed, Jack,' he mumbled. 'Gotta lie down.'

A few drops of Drambuie dripped into Jack's glass. The only thing left to drink at Andy's place was a bottle of Haigs but Jack hated Scotch. As he sipped the sweet liqueur, he remembered his father's drinking parties. Laughing. Clinking glasses. 'Give me more whisky, yaar! Oh, yaar. Hey, yaar!' Ali Hassan could drink and laugh even when he'd just belted his son. The actions—beating and drinking whisky—were separate and distinct. He acted like they were carried out by two different people. But Jack knew it was the same person and he hated everything about him. He'd drink his own piss before he touched Scotch.

He lit a cigarette and picked up an old issue of *Time* magazine. The pictures of world events meant nothing but he flipped back and forth as if he was searching for a particular story.

There was a tapping on the front door. It was 3:24 a.m. He padded across the room, took a deep breath, and pulled it open. William was hugging himself against the early morning chill. 'Excuse me, saab. I cannot sleepit, saab. Too much thinking thinking.'

Jack invited him in and offered to make him a cup of tea. 'No thanks, saab,' said William. He gingerly set himself down in the rattan armchair as if he was afraid it might collapse with the slightest pressure. He stared at the floor. Jack lit another cigarette.

'You killit Mr Ahmadzai?'

Jack sighed. 'Ahmadzai is dead, yes. He was killed, but I don't know by whom. I told you there was someone else there in his office when I arrived.'

William nodded but wasn't convinced. 'Maybe they arrest me, saab. Chargeit me.'

'Why you? Relax, Willie, my man.'

'Relaxit is impossible, saab.' He looked at his hands and then into Jack's face. 'I tellit you before. I am Christian, saab. Ahmadzai, very powerful man. Makeit trouble for my peoples, saab.'

'Listen, William. Who knows you were there, eh? No one. Except me. Of all the people in the world, you think they going to pin this on you?'

The driver was nervously pressing his hands together. 'Police see me, sir. And you. Remember? At checkpoint at Hayatabad Chowk you giveit them cigarettes, saab.'

Jack had forgotten about that. He gulped in an attempt to swallow the panic that was shooting up his skinny legs.

'Listen, Willie, don't worry. I'm in control. They can't arrest you because they have no evidence, see?' He patted the driver's knees and tried to comfort him. William sat for a few minutes then stood up and said, 'Okay, saab. I sleepit now. I pray to Jesus, God's Son to protectit me. You also, King saab.'

When William left, Jack turned on the tape machine real low and tried to sleep. Fuck, those cops!

Jack fished his Casio watch with the broken rubber strap from his pocket. Ten a.m. For a moment he was lost in a post-nap haze, not sure what day it was or why he'd fallen asleep on the couch with muddy pants on. Afroz passed through his consciousness, leaving behind the smell of her soft, pale flesh. He smiled and turned his head to follow her, but she evaporated—pretty lipstick, nail polish and all. William was leaning forward with the same expression he'd worn since Jack had shot Ahmadzai. The panicked certainty of a man going down for the count. The driver's pained gaze pulled back the curtains of Jack's memory. Everything came back in horrible precision: Sher Jan's sliced head, his idiotic smile, Ahmadzai collapsing and a leather slipper popping off his foot. The bottle of Coke. Like a scene from a really bad Indian movie.

'We go now, King saab. Police lookit us any time.'

A sickening ball of dread, like a lump of cold oatmeal laced with poison, moved through Jack's stomach to the back of his teeth and settled in his abdomen.

'Sure thing, Willie,' Jack said. He stood up, pressed his black trousers with his sweaty palms and said, 'Got to piss. Then we leave.'

William jumped from the chair and ran outside to start the jeep.

In the bathroom, Jack splashed water on his face, struggling to keep his balance. He leaned against the sink, breathing twice and deep. His insides seemed to be working themselves up towards his throat. He held his head over the toilet but nothing came up.

'Get a grip, daddy-o.'

As soon as he opened the door to the jeep, William released the clutch and the jeep sped forward.

The streets of Peshawar were flowing canals of muck. The early joy people had felt towards the monsoon had turned into irritation, which was what Khan Sahib was feeling as he made his way to the Galaxy Hotel for his meeting with Aslam. As soon as he sat down at the small corner table Noor Aslam leaned forward in excitement, 'Where is it? Show me.'

'What, sir?' Khan knew what the man wanted but what could he say? He had no idea where 'it' was.

'What?' Aslam squeaked in a loud whisper. He shot furtive glances around the coffee shop. 'You ask what?' He looked out of the window and then towards the door. 'The money,' he hissed.

Khan had been asking himself the very same thing since 4:30 in the morning, when he had arrived at the tea shop opposite the railway station. He hadn't been able to sleep and his wife finally told him to leave the house if he wanted to stomp around like a mad bull. By 6:30 the ugly, one-eyed bastard had still not shown, so Khan ate a plate of greasy poories and waited. 7. 7:30. 8 o'clock. At last, at 8:15 he returned home to change.

Earlier, Khan had spoken to a broker about buying a plot in Nowshera where he intended to build a shop. With the rest of his fifty thousand dollars he'd buy a truck. There was a second-hand one available for cheap. Transport was a good investment in border areas. But where was that mule Yahya?

Khan removed his felt hat and gave the thinning hair on his dome a gentle massage. Then twirling the hat in his hands he placed it back on his head. 'Yahya has arranged to meet me this evening.' It was a hope as much as it was a lie.

'You told me he was meeting you this morning. With the money! Islamabad will want to know what is happening!' Aslam was apoplectic. His dark blue cream-stained tie seemed to be choking him.

Khan opened his mouth to speak when a waiter stepped forward to tell Aslam that there was a phone call for him at the front desk. Aslam moaned and looked first at the waiter, then pleadingly at Khan Sahib. Harrumphing, he finally lifted himself from the chair and waddled away.

Khan watched his boss turning pale on the phone. Aslam pulled his tie and tugged his pants up over his protruding mound of flesh. His knees sagged when he returned and deposited himself on his chair. Khan had decided what to say next. He opened his mouth to speak but Aslam cut him off, 'Ahmadzai is dead. Shot three times in the chest. Your Sher Jan is decapitated in his office.'

Khan could only whisper, 'What about the money?'

'Stop at number 126, Willie.' Jack said.

William hadn't stopped once on the way back from Peshawar. Neither had he been in the mood for conversation.

He jammed the brakes. 'Okay, saab, I seeit you tomorrow.' He hit the accelerator and left Jack under a tree with soggy, dripping branches.

Jack had decided he would surprise her when she got back from work. But when he got up to the roof he noticed that her front door was open. 'Rosie?'

There was no answer. He moved towards the bedroom when she burst out of the bathroom in tears. 'Oh Jack, thank God you're here.' She buried her face in his chest.

'Hey, what's happening?' He moved her to the cushions that lined the bare walls and they sat down. 'Rose, what's going on?'

She wiped the tears from her face with her dupatta. 'Someone's killed my uncle,' she said. 'They shot him last night, Jack. I can't believe it.'

'What? Who shot him?'

'Last night in Peshawar. Ayaz, my cousin, his son, just called from Lahore. The police just notified him. Someone broke into his house last night, drugged the chowkidar and killed my uncle. They say he killed someone, too. Oh, I don't know…' she bawled.

'Who's your uncle, Rose?' He lifted her face towards his. 'Look here.' She was too distraught to see the panic darkening his eyes.

'Uncle Inayatullah. The one I stay with…when I go to Peshawar. Mummy's eldest brother. Oh, Jack, why would they kill him? Do you know?'

He pulled her close again and said nothing. Her body shook and her tears soaked his shirt.

Jack's felt his own body go rigid. A shiver momentarily tickled his spine but then he went numb. 'Sssh, Rosie…' he whispered.

22

With the absence of anything resembling a neck, it seemed as if Razaq Gill's head was a wooden block hammered on to a larger, thicker block of wood.

He sat with his left leg crossed over his right, and his arms stretched out along the back of an orange velour sofa. He was in the living room of his house, which he shared with his brother and both their families. In front of him, on the mahogany coffee table, stood a bottle of Dimple and a plastic ice bucket. Across him sat his younger brother Mushtaq, done out in his black NIA uniform with red trim.

'No need to worry for Jaguar,' Mushtaq was saying, speaking as if they were sitting miles across from each other. 'The distribution rights will drop into our hands.' As Afroz Gul's nightie will fall from her body, he added to himself.

Razaq pondered his tumbler of Scotch, watching the solitary cube of ice slowly melt away. 'I wish I shared your confidence,' he sighed. 'Jaguar still refuses to make an announcement.'

'With the latest development, Jaguar will have no option but to award us the rights,' bellowed Mushtaq. He was enjoying keeping the news from his brother.

'Development?'

'Dear brother,' Mushtaq said, taking a sip of his drink, 'Inayatullah was murdered last night.'

'The fancy lawyer?'

'None other.'

Razaq put a finger into his drink and twirled it around. 'So?'

'And who is the guilty party?' Mushtaq was beaming.

'You are the investigator.'

'Mr Jack King.'

'Who?'

'I'm sorry, I should use his real name,' Musthaq paused and cocked his head sideways, 'Yaqub Ali Hassan Shah.'

Razaq's large head swung awkwardly to meet his brother's smiling face. 'That bastard's son?'

'None other. Ali Hassan and Shah Enterprises are finished for good. Dhamaka International has won!'

As soon as he had received the news of Ahmadzai's murder, Gill had set the wheels in motion: the Central Bank, Customs and Excise, and the Prime Minister's Office were all advised to freeze Shah Enterprises Ltd's assets pending a full investigation by the NIA into the alleged involvement of Ali Hassan Shah's son, Mr Yaqub Ali Shah, aka Jack King, in the murder of Mr Inayatullah Ahmadzai. Gill had used the word, 'accountability' a lot during these calls.

'Jaguar is ours, don't worry,' Mushtaq reassured his brother. 'Jaguar is peanuts. That which we have struggled for all these years is ours, Razaq bhai. When Ali Hassan is humiliated and imprisoned, the road will be open...' he made a grand movement with his open palm like a plane taking off, 'all the way to the PM's office. The Prime Minister will need a new adviser.'

'But are you sure that that boy is the murderer?'

'Even if he is not, he cannot escape now. Imagine! I was thinking a drugs case would cause embarrassment, but God is great, Razaq, don't I always say so? His gifts are much better than ever dreamed.'

Razaq Gill uncrossed his legs, and reached for the Scotch. Stirring his drink with a pinkie finger, he took his first big gulp. 'But unless we can prove it...that Ahmadzai was killed by this King...the Prime Minister will squash us, Mushtaq. Ali Hassan will not slip away quietly. What proof can you provide?'

'Proof always exists where the mind is imaginative and the will is sufficient. I know King was trying to extort money from Ahmadzai... for the brown sugar deal. I know, as well, he was to be at Ahmadzai's house on the night of the murder.' What I don't know, he said to himself, is why those other two donkeys were there.

Razaq screwed up his bristly eyebrows to indicate he did not follow.

'Sher Jan and Yahya. Two local badmaashes that Aslam uses now and then. One was posing as King's heroin dealer.'

'And the other one?'

'His head was nearly knocked off. He must have had a scuffle with Ahmadzai. The sword was found by his body.'

'So he's the killer, not King,' Razaq sighed.

'Sher Jan—the fool who lost his head—the papers are saying that he was Ahmadzai's servant who came to protect his master,' Mushtaq's eyes sparkled. 'Don't worry, Razaq bhai. This is the end of Ali Hassan Shah. I feel it in my teeth.' He adjusted his beret and started for the door.

'Where are you going? I've not yet told you about that Lebanani airhostess I met in Dubai! Kya cheez thi!'

'Later, Razaq. I have a house call to make.'

Afroz kept her head buried in Jack's chest for what seemed like an eternity. Since hearing the news in the morning her shock had slowly turned into a profound, agonizing sadness. Her head was so full of swirling emotions that it seemed it might spin off. She hugged Jack harder.

Eventually, she pushed herself onto her feet. 'I have to help Ayaz arrange the funeral. Auntie Beena can't make it back from London; her surgery is next week. This couldn't have come at a worse time for her. She'll have to be sedated when she gets the news.'

As she moved about the bedroom fidgeting, counting aloud the things she had to do before the funeral, Jack wandered into the kitchen and put on the kettle. He stared into the blue flame, still unable to comprehend what Afroz had said. Ahmadzai was Rose's uncle? No way, Jose. He felt like throwing up. Goddam Yahya.

Steam was shooting out of the kettle's aluminium spout, but Jack didn't turn off the stove. His head was thumping. *Got to tell the truth.*

You crazy, man? You going to prison.

No way, man! I love her but hell, no way I'm doing time! No fucking way.

Jack turned off the stove, hoping the commotion in his head would stop. He filled a mug with the tea and some sugar.

Afroz was at the dining table, her bag on the chair. She'd washed her face but her eyes were a deep red. Jack handed her the mug and kissed her forehead. His hand shook but Afroz didn't notice.

'Who would kill Uncle Inayatullah, Jack?'

Jack avoided her eyes. He stared at the ashtray overflowing with butts and matchsticks. 'All sorts of jerks in this country. Politics, probably. Maybe some shady deal gone wrong.'

'Not him!' she was adamant. 'Policy stuff and UN contracts and agreements. Memorandums of Understanding and things—this was what he did. He hated politics. The only political case he took was a blasphemy case in Gujranwala.'

Jack looked up. The case William had been talking about, where some poor Christian farmer was forced to sell his property to a greedy neighbour.

'He got a lot of publicity because of the trial but swore

he'd never do it again. He withdrew before the end of the trial.'

'Why?'

'Because the outcome was a foregone conclusion. The government wanted the Muslim man to win.'

'Why'd he do it in the first place?' Jack stood up and patted his pockets. 'Got a cigarette, Rosie?'

'The local businessman had friends in high places. Uncle was pressured to take the case as a favour to a Senator. They wanted someone with his visibility because they thought that would give their cause more credibility. He didn't want to, but in the end he relented. Soon, the media started calling him "Defender of Islam" and "Infidel Fighter" and he withdrew. Ayaz knows more about it than I do,' she pulled her hair back behind her ears. 'You don't think the government killed him, do you? They won the case in the end anyway.'

'Or maybe some Christian nut-o.' He looked away as soon as he spoke; he hadn't meant to say that.

'What do you mean?'

'Never can tell, Rosie.' He paused. Should he go on? 'William, Nanima's driver, he was telling me about the case, you know and how lots of his people are pretty pissed with him—your uncle—for what he did.'

'But he didn't do anything. He resigned from the case before it went to trial. Everyone knows that.'

'Just an idea. He's your uncle and if you say he wasn't involved in anything shady then you've got to look somewhere else.' Jack took a deep breath and leaned back in the chair. For the first time since she'd broken the news to him, he felt some relief. Maybe he didn't have to take this rap after all.

Someone knocked on the door.

A man in his mid-twenties, hiding behind large aviators and wearing a dark green polo shirt, stuck his head into the dining room.

Afroz jumped up, 'Ayaz! I can't believe it. It's terrible, just horrible.' She hugged her cousin and broke down again. Jack nodded at Ayaz and introduced himself but didn't get up. Ayaz said they would have to leave right away.

'Will you call me tomorrow?' She kissed Jack on the cheek and he gave her arm a squeeze. She walked out with her arm in Ayaz's. Jack put out his cigarette. He had never felt so unworthy of a kiss.

After a while, he walked out into the street. It was raining again. By the time he got out of the neighbourhood, he was wet through to his skin. But instead of hopping into a taxi, he turned left on Margalla Road. He would walk back to Nanima's place. There was a mess of things to think about. He needed time.

'We have met before,' Mushtaq Gill said. He'd been waiting in Nanima's sitting room for more than half an hour, while Jack finished his shower. There was rejoicing in his voice and a pitilessness in his smile.

Jack ignored the man's outstretched hand. 'Y'all come to punish me for being rambunctious wit you?' Jack flopped onto the sofa.

'Don't mention it, Mr King.' Mr Gill moved closer but didn't sit down. Another man in a black beret and a dark grey woollen shalwar-qameez stood quietly by the door, avoiding Jack's eyes. Across his shoulder was a holster with a pistol. Probably some sort of Glock. 'At parties some people drink too much and become foolish. Ha ha.' He did not seem amused.

Jack lit a cigarette and returned Gill's stare. The DG shifted his weight from one foot to the other and said, 'Mr King, I must ask you to surrender your passport.'

'Fuck that shit,' Jack blew the smoke directly into his face.

'I've got me a visa. Your consulate in Chicago issued it. Or don't you trust them?'

'Your visa is not in question. Please, may I have your passport?'

Jack noticed the man with the beret and gun move closer.

'What's wrong wit my passport? I'm an American, y'understand. Americano. *Amriki*.' He said the last word in an overly western accent. 'What's your jurisdiction over me?'

'Your nationality is one thing. But even Americans cannot escape Pakistani law, Mr King. Please, surrender your passport.' He extended his hand once again.

'Surrender my ass!' Jack was standing now, leaning into Gill's face. 'I'm not one of you. My passport is mine. Piss off.'

The man in the beret pulled out his pistol from its holster and levelled it at Jack. Jack didn't move. The three men stood frozen—gun pointed, hand extended, stock still. Eventually, Jack muttered, 'I'll be back.' The man with the Glock followed Jack upstairs. They returned in less than a minute.

'It's brand new, so don't get your curry fingers on the pages. I'll sue your brown little ass.' Jack slapped the passport into Gill's hand. 'So what's the deal here, sheriff? What law am I breaking other than being alive and using my brain? I know that's probably anti-Islamic.'

'Thank you, Mr King. I will keep your passport in a secure place until the case is concluded.' Gill flipped through it nonchalantly, but kept his eyes on Jack.

'What case you talking 'bout, pecker?'

'Tomorrow you will be receiving a chargesheet for the murder, on Sunday morning last, of Mr Inayatullah Ahmadzai, in his home in Hayatabad, Peshawar. Normally, you would be held in remand custody until the case is concluded, as this is a non-bailable offence. However, due to your family's prominent standing in Pakistan, you will be allowed to remain in Islamabad until the trial is concluded.' He drummed his fingers on the passport. 'That is why I need this. To ensure you do not abscond the country.' He turned towards the door. 'Khuda hafez, King sahib.'

Jack stared at the door. His grandmother called weakly from upstairs. 'Who is there, beta?'

'Nobody important, Nanima.' Jack snapped. 'Nobody at all.'

'Where you been, Shahid?'

After six attempts, Jack had finally got hold of his cousin. He ordered him to come over right away. 'Now!' he slammed the phone and knocked the ashtray to the floor.

Jack was trying to forget the image of Gill smirking at him. *How the hell did he know I was at Ahmadzai's place?*

He closed his eyes. His great escape had seemed so easy. How could it have gone so wrong? Jack thought back over previous screw-ups, like the gig that landed him in Pontiac. Someone had ratted on him then, too. *Someone's trying to make me the fall guy again.*

Every other time he'd been in this situation, he'd found himself behind bars. He glanced in the mirror hanging over the dresser and promised himself that if Mushtaq Gill was looking for someone to jail, it would most definitely not be Jack King.

When Shahid arrived Jack pulled him into the living room. 'Can you get me some booze, dude? Vodka, wine? Anything?'

'I've got a bottle of Teacher's in the car.' Jack was willing to drink Scotch tonight.

'What's up, Jack? Haven't seen much of you for the last week.' Shahid poured two big glasses of whisky and another two of water. Jack drank half the water then poured the whisky into the rest of the water and stirred it with his finger.

'Takin' care of business, man. Nothing heavy.'

'How is it going, then?' Shahid was curious about the urgency.

'Great. Real great, Shahid. A couple more meetings and everything will be tied up, just like a Christmas present, know what I mean?' He raised the glass to his mouth and chugged the Scotch like lemonade. It slipped down the corners of his mouth but Jack grimaced and said, 'Aaahh! Excellent. Real great.' He poured another one. Shahid watched his cousin silently.

'You sure, Jack? You sounded upset when you called.' Shahid noticed his cousin's hands were shaking.

'That muthafuckin' police captain, or whoever he is, just stole my passport.'

'Who are you talking about?'

'That fucker... you know I pushed him on his ass at that party.'

'Mushtaq Gill? He was here? What? Why did he take your passport?'

'Fuck do I know? Said I'm the man who killed that lawyer everyone is crying about. What's his name? In Peshawar?'

'Inayatullah Ahmadzai? Is he mad?' Shahid took a bigger sip of his drink. 'Did you kill him, Jack?'

'Fuck you, Shahid. Fuck you!'

'Sorry, Jack. But why would Gill accuse you?'

'Am I God Almighty, man? Do I look like the bloody prophet of the Bible that I'll figure out the mysteries of everything? I don't know, dude. If I did I wouldn't be talking to you now.'

'Why take your passport?'

'He says now I can't leave the country. Man, good thing he did too, because I tell you what, dude, I be ready to leave his shithole right now—tonight if he hadn't. Where's he get off telling me I killed some dickhead lawyer?' A third drink was poured. The bottle of Teacher's was half-empty.

'Ahmadzai is Nanima's lawyer.' Shahid was talking to himself. 'You were meeting him in Peshawar, right? That's what she told me.'

'So? Yeah, I met him in his office. So what? He wouldn't do what I asked so I said, "Screw you, buster, I'll do it on my own." Like I always done. I don't need no lawyer.'

'How's Afroz taking it?'

Jack jerked his head up but didn't say anything. 'Real bad, man. Not good.'

The cousins sat together drinking for a few minutes. They couldn't believe what was happening. Shahid smelt a dead fish. Gill was known as a desperate man who would do anything to get higher up in the bureaucracy. And, to fulfil his lust for Afroz. This was his little game of revenge. He'd make Jack grovel as payment for insulting him that night, but eventually return his passport: at the airport with a big stamp in it barring him from ever returning to Pakistan.

As for Jack, he couldn't get Afroz out of his mind. How was he going to explain this to her? She had to find out soon. Gill was already moving in for the kill. How did *he* find out so fast? Who ratted? Andy? Couldn't be. Khan Sahib? Maybe, but why? He knew about the shake down, but man, Sher Jan was lying right there. Obviously he'd been fighting with Ahmadzai. *Why blame me?*

'You got contacts in the paper business right? Find out what this fuckin' cop is after? He wants money? We'll have the old man pay him. Sure. Just find out what he's dickin' wit me for? Is it 'cause I pushed his ass to the floor?'

'Your father arrived back from Malaysia yesterday, Jack. What will he say?'

'Fuck do I care?'

'I'll make some calls and see what I can find out. Try to relax, Jack.'

23

The sky was grey and leaking like a cheesecloth. Andy stood leaning into a phone-booth at the Islamabad airport. It was early, not even 7 a.m., but he felt Jack should know. After the eighth or ninth ring he was going to hang up but Jack picked up and mumbled sleepily from the other end.

'It's me,' Andy said.

'Pardner!' There was a pause. 'What time is it?'

'I thought you should know, Farah's back in the Convent.'

'Sure.' Jack stifled a yawn.

A loud garbled squawk announced the last call for the British Airways flight to London on the PA system.

'What's all that noise? Where you calling from?'

Andy stared at his boarding pass. Seat 54A. Near the back, but a window seat at least. 'Listen, Jack.' His heart, which had been cantering ever since he'd met Jack, broke into a thumping gallop.

It had been a dumb idea from the beginning. What was he thinking? Building a cabin in the mountains? On heroin money? Standing here in the departure lounge Andy could see Jack's grand plan for what it was: a half-cocked, ridiculous two-bit scam. Who cared if little brother drove a Beemer? He was not going to spend the best years of his life in prison for murder.

'You there, pardner?' Jack asked. 'Come on over for breakfast. We gotta talk.'

'Are you in trouble?'

'Didn't say that. New situation, new plan. Simple. You know where Nanima lives. I'll be waiting.'

Andy winced. Could he just walk out on Jack now? For a long second he hesitated. At last he said, 'On my way, Jack.' He hung up and took a deep breath. Turning around, he strode quickly towards Departure Gate Number Two.

Khan Sahib was stalking back and forth on the veranda of Khyber Hospital's ICU ward. A string of wooden prayer beads dangled from his right hand. If anyone had bothered to look closely, they would have seen his lips moving rapidly, almost imperceptibly. Desperate supplication to the Creator, or vile curses for Yahya? Yahya, the doctor had said, would probably die. He'd lost too much blood. If he spoke it would only be with great difficulty. Khan didn't care. He just wanted to find out what happened at Ahmadzai's place. And where his fifty thousand dollars were.

As he paced back and forth, out of the corner of his eye he caught the headline of the early edition.

'Ahmadzai's Attacker Part of a Gang of Bandits:
Broke into Advocate's Home for Robbery Purposes.'

Have the police already discovered so much? *Oh Allah!*

Should he tell Aslam now while there was still a chance to pass the blame to Yahya? But if he did, Aslam would demand the ten thousand dollars deposit back in full. Yahya would be unwilling to tell him what had become of the money. But if he didn't tell Aslam then he could be facing arrest for Ahmadzai's murder. He knew they'd love to grab him and settle the paperwork quickly. Phat-a-phat.

He *had* to talk with Yahya and find out about the money. He'd promised his broker a deposit by the middle of the week. And Aslam would be making noises about returning the operational advance.

But Yahya wasn't able to speak. He wasn't even able to open his eyes when, an hour later, Khan was allowed in, by his bedside.

Mr King probably had all the money. This would mean a trip to Islamabad. The old spy left the hospital and made his way to the Galaxy Hotel where he found Aslam dozing with his jowly face, at a table littered with a thousand crumbs. Khan Sahib cleared his throat and tapped his superior's fleshy knee. Aslam awoke with a snort, immediately grabbing the knot of his tie. 'What is it?' he mumbled.

'Excuse me, sir. I must notify you that I will be making an urgent visit to Islamabad, at once.' His fingers squeezed the prayer beads madly.

'Where is the money?'

What answer could he give his boss, who did not know that Khan had sent Yahya to Ahmadzai's house and for what reason? If he was ever to make his wife happy, leave spy work behind and run his own shop, house and truck, Noor Aslam could not know about this side-job.

'Well?'

'Mr King is demanding that we deliver the sample to his house in Islamabad today. I must leave at once.'

Aslam blinked, uncertain what to say. The old man was up to something. He could feel it in his stomach. But then, after his extended breakfast of pastry he was not altogether sure whether it was Khan or the sugar that was beginning to trouble him. 'When will you return with—' he rubbed his fingers together as if he were counting notes.

'I will establish contact as soon as I arrive, sir.' Khan didn't wait for the man's approval and headed out the door. Aslam watched him shuffle at a speed he'd never seen before.

Nanima had refused to come out of her room for two days after she learned about Ahmadzai's murder. When Jack brought up the issue of the Zam Zam Trust, she pulled her ears and begged God's forgiveness.

'In this situation, I will have to seek advice from your father, Yaqub beta. I am an old woman who never understood money or business. Mr Ahmadzai was a good man. What animal would kill him?'

The mention of his father sent an involuntary shiver down his spine. 'Why ask him? I will be happy to manage the Fund. Write a letter to Mr Ahmadzai's law firm explaining that I am now in charge of Zam Zam and I'll take the burden from you.'

'Beta, it is not good to talk of such things before a man is buried.' She touched her ears again and muttered 'tobah' as she sent a quick glance towards heaven. She said that she would not discuss the subject until the forty days of mourning had passed. 'It is only right to honour the dead.'

DG Gill and his posse crowded the front entrance of the house like a pack of hungry dogs. One of the officers, a lanky man with a beard and no moustache, began to read the chargesheet: illegal breaking into Ahmadzai's house; attempted murder of the chowkidar; attempted murder of Mr Yahya, an innocent passerby; murder of Sher Jan, domestic servant of Mr Ahmadzai; murder of Mr Inayatuallah Ahmadzai, Advocate High Court. The skinny man pulled out another paper from a manila folder and read a second set of charges. These accused Mr Yaqub Ali Hassan Shah aka Mr Jack King and his father, Mr Ali Hassan Shah, president of Shah Enterprises Ltd and special adviser to the Prime Minister of the Islamic Republic of Pakistan, of conspiring to purchase and transport illicit narcotics for international distribution and profit.

The man finished and took one exaggerated goose-step back. In an officious voice tinged with glee, DG Gill said, 'You are advised, Mr King, not to leave Islamabad until the courts have pronounced their judgment in these matters. Your passport remains impounded and any attempt to procure or use another passport, Pakistani or otherwise, will be considered an intention by you to abscond the country and evade justice.'

After informing Jack that he would be jailed if he tried to abscond, and that his father, also in serious trouble, would be of no assistance, Gill ran his tongue over his teeth, cleaning them in anticipation of a good feed. Then he turned on his heel and with his gang falling in behind him, left Jack at the breakfast table where he had been buttering his toast and waiting for Andy.

Where *was* Andy? He should have been here an hour ago. Had he freaked out and confessed all to Gill? He recalled the panic in Andy's voice, and how nervous he'd been at the Chinese restaurant that day. Jack glanced at the big Seiko clock on the wall. 8:45 a.m.

He remembered all the background noise when Andy had called. Where could he have been, that early in the morning? He stared at the clock's seconds hand lurching around the dial. 8:48 a.m. He kept staring at the clock for sometime when it dawned on him. Loudspeakers? The dude was calling from the airport! He recalled Andy's last words: *I'm on my way*. He slammed his fist onto the table.

Breakfast time was over. Now that he was on his own again, he'd have to move quick.

'You'd think I was a regular Charlie Manson,' Jack said.

He was at the offices of the *Capital Crescent* newspaper in Aabpaara, in a new multi-storeyed complex with lots of windows. Shahid's desk was cluttered with clippings, and several computers and phones. Large gilt letters on the door, in both Urdu and English, informed the world that the large office belonged to the Editor-in-Chief. Though the building was new, the muggy air smelled of ink and cardboard. One floor below, the loud clanging of a heavy iron press sent tremors upwards, occasionally rattling Shahid's windows.

Shahid didn't know who Charlie Manson was. He was busy making corrections with a red ballpoint on a smudgy rough copy of the evening edition. He ignored his cousin.

'Gill's making me take the rap for two murders,' Jack yelled. 'And two attempted murders, man. Who the hell is this asshole?'

Shahid didn't look up from his task. 'His family owns half of Bahawalpur district. His brother Razaq owns and runs Dhamaka International, which got where it is on CIA dollars during the Afghan war. Together, the brothers have had a running battle with your father—our family, for the last twenty years. The Gills hate us because your father has all the politicians in his pocket. That new law to lift the tariffs on the import of next-generation fibre optics? That's Ali Hassan's work.'

'Didn't ax for a news bulletin on the old man,' Jack snapped. 'So he hates my old man, maybe we can be friends one day but right now, he's lookin' to hang my ass out to dry. Hey!' He slapped an open palm on the desk, making Shahid jump. 'Listen up!'

Shahid stuck his pen into his ear, twirling it slowly. He could see the panic eating up his cool American cousin. He needed a shave. Shahid pulled the pen out and answered Jack's unasked question. 'Your only hope, Jack, is to get your father's help. The Prime Minister listens to him and Gill can't fight the Prime Minister.' Shahid paused. 'There's no other way. With those chargesheets you're a dead man.'

Jack's eyes narrowed and his lips turned white. 'I'll die in hell before I beg for his help.' Shahid went back to his article.

Jack stared at his cousin. 'How many people read this rag?'

'Not many, a few thousand, if we have a good banner.' The editorial policy was to try to be as sensational as possible to increase visibility. Last year the *Capital Crescent* had been mentioned in *Newsweek* as one among 'a new generation of Asian magazines'.

Jack had been struggling with the outline of a new plan. He hadn't put all of it together yet, and he was wary of its true implications. But the printing press's muffled violence was working on his resolve. Each time, with every metallic shudder and slight shake of the window, Jack became certain that it was the only way out.

Last night, in semi-sleep, Jack imagined himself being led away into a Pakistani prison. He smelled the rancid aroma of Afghans and tasted the cold grease in the plate of food in his lap. Prison in America was slow death. In Pakistan, he knew he would die within a month.

Pointing the finger at William Masih didn't seem right but then neither did the idea of spending the rest of his life behind bars for murders he didn't commit. Hadn't William himself told Jack that Ahmadzai was a bad man? *Isn't that a motive?* Jack wished the damn thudding would stop for a second.

William had said he didn't like Ahmadzai. That was pretty serious shit in this country.

'Shahid, listen to me,' Jack pulled his cousin's arm. 'What's this Blasphemy Bill about? Rosie was telling me that Ahmadzai was involved.'

'It's something the mullahs and religious parties forced

on the government last year. To protect the name of the Prophet and Islam. Anyone who says anything against either of them can be brought up on the charge of insulting the Faith.' Shahid clapped his hand and shouted at a young boy walking by the office to bring two Cokes. 'It's a joke, really, but Afroz is right. Ahmadzai was involved in the first case last year but in the end, denounced the Bill as nothing more than a legalized rip-off of the minorities. We had some good headlines in those days.'

'So you say, Islam sucks or Mohammad was a fraud and they put your ass in jail?'

'If you say that they'd stone you as soon as the words left your lips. No, this Bill, why the minorities hate it is because you don't have to actually say anything against the Prophet or Islam. If I have an opinion about Islam and you disagree with me, you can accuse me of blasphemy because my interpretation is not the "right" one. Even if what you say isn't offensive, the Bill is helpful. A lot of civil cases, property and inheritance disputes are getting settled by this Bill. And no judge in this country is going to challenge the mullahs. And who really cares about the Hindus and Christians? They're sweepers, mostly. '

'And drivers.'

'Correct. No influence at all. The Blasphemy Bill is just a way for some greedy people to cover their crimes in the name of religion.' Shahid gave a short laugh. 'What else is new?'

'What if someone said that Ahmadzai was a bastard because he prosecuted that case last year. What if they said Ahmadzai was a bad man because of that?'

'Most Christians believe that but no one will say it. If they did they would be in court tomorrow.'

Jack grabbed one of the Cokes the young boy had planted on the table. 'You know William?'

'Nanima's driver?'

Jack nodded. 'He told me that he'd love to "killit" Ahmadzai for what he did to that Christian guy last year.'

Would Shahid catch the ball and run towards the end zone?

'When did he say that?' Shahid looked dubious.

'Coming back from Peshawar last week. He drove me to Ahmadzai's office and said he'd seen the man a bunch of times coming to visit Nanima.' Shahid nodded. 'Told me it was him who had prosecuted the case against that Christian guy and his son and that he would love to kill Ahmadzai for that.'

Come on, Shahid baby.

'You're sure?' Shahid stuck the pen in his ear again, sucking on the cold drink.

'Of course, I'm sure but just forget about it. William is a nice guy. He'd never do anything like that.'

'But Ahmadzai is dead,' Shahid finished his Coke and let go of a quiet burp.

Jack nodded, pretending he couldn't put two and two together. *Good boy, Shahid.*

'This is big news, Jack.'

'What is?' Jack's brow was furrowed.

'I see what's happened. Ahmadzai was killed in the early morning. Where were you then?'

'I was at Andy's, sleeping.'

'So William drives over to Ahmadzai's place, kills the guy and comes back. No one knows what's happened. You get blamed because Gill hates your father. This is serious, Jack.'

Touchdown!

'But Ahmadzai was shot. Where would Willie get a gun?' Jack was acting real dumb now.

'Shit! In this country, guns are cheaper than bread. I've got three at home, man. Everyone does.'

William Masih was feeling better. His wife had made a special hot beef curry with some of the tips Mr King had given him. After dinner he'd taken out the bottle of Johnny Walker Red from the old winter clothes trunk under the children's bed. Carefully pouring himself a generous drink, he downed the entire glass in less than five minutes. Normally, he would have nursed it over an hour or so, allowing it to slowly work its magic, but it had been a stressful three days.

His wife was cleaning up the dishes and the children were already asleep. William sat in front of the TV, which was off. There was enough action going on in his head. Everyone was talking about Ahmadzai's murder. Aloysius and Andrew had come round last night to talk about it. They all had their ideas about who had done it and why. William had kept quiet. He told his friends he'd been in Lahore with Mr King. Andrew, who liked to act tougher than he really was, said that if he'd had the chance, he would have done it the other way round: chop off Ahmadzai's head, not shoot him.

William didn't offer any opinions and made an excuse about having to get up early to take Mr King to Murree in the morning. Aloysius made a face and said, 'This Mr King is making you work too hard. Hope he's not taking advantage of you.'

'Never,' William said. 'He's not like the rest. He cares about Christians. I'll do anything for him.'

'He's a good tipper too, I hear.' Andrew smirked. 'I've never known you to turn down a chance to pocket some cash.'

'Mr King is like a friend. Now leave me. I have to get some sleep.'

After his friends left William couldn't sleep. Just knowing that Jack had been in the house when Ahmadzai was killed made William feel guilty. And even if Jack was questioned, what did have to fear? His family was made of steel. No one would be able to harm him. But who would speak for William if the police got the idea that he was involved, even though he wasn't? He was the driver and an easy target.

William was contemplating having another glass of whisky when someone rapped loudly on the door. He jumped up and threw the Johnny Walker to his wife, who immediately disappeared into the other room with it. William pulled open the door to find three policemen standing close together under one big umbrella. The rain was light but steady. One of the cops had rolled up his trouser legs. Across the road, under a streetlight, William could make out a police jeep.

'You are William Masih, son of Munawar John Masih?' one of the cops said.

William nodded and glanced over his shoulder towards his wife. She had come back out of the bedroom. 'Go back. It is nothing,' William said to her. When she was gone he said, 'I am.'

'You are under arrest.' One of the cops stepped forward and began to fasten chains to William's ankles. He didn't resist. This was the nightmare he had been waiting for. Amidst his confusion he felt himself relax slightly; the worst was over. Just as the handcuffs were locked on to his wrists, William's wife came running out of the kitchen and gave a low wail. He looked at her and tried to reassure her with his eyes. 'Keep still, Gladys,' he said. 'You'll wake the children. Call Father Charles and tell him what has happened. Say a prayer for me.'

The cops gave him a yank and he stumbled into the rain.

The *Capital Crescent*'s banner headlines stood two inches high:

AHMADZAI MURDER: REVENGE OF CHRISTIANS

Nanima was scandalized. At the breakfast table she wondered how she could have been harbouring such a fanatic on her staff. The police must have mistaken his identity for another. Jack stayed silent.

Other more serious papers were analysing the murder in this new light. What had seemed like a murder motivated by greed was actually the fallout of a Bill that should never have been passed. This was the government's and Ahmadzai's own doing. Of course, William Masih needed to be prosecuted for his terrible crime but perhaps the Bill would now be seen as provocative and rescinded by Parliament.

Mushtaq Gill put the morning paper down to let a tremor of unease pass through him. His cup of tea shook in his agitated hand. It was not that things were moving too fast but that he was no longer orchestrating the developments. Someone else was meddling. Just when he had been preparing to announce publicly that Jack King and his father, Ali Hassan Shah, were international narcotic smugglers and murderers, and that the son's passport had been impounded while the father's business assets had been frozen, the papers was baying for the blood of some nobody Christian.

Razaq Gill, sitting across the table from his brother, picked up the paper and immediately scanned the business section for news of Jaguar's announcement. Nothing. He, too, put the paper down and pushed his breakfast—one boiled egg and two pieces of untoasted white bread—away.

The brothers sat in silence, unwilling to share their sinking feelings with each other until Razaq's watch beeped, reminding him that it was thirty minutes past the hour. He stood up to leave and said, 'What of Ali Hassan? Father is keeping very quiet.'

'He issued a statement last night denying all charges and

claiming he has had no contact with his son for more than two decades.'

'Really?'

'What did you expect him to say?' Mushtaq's reply was tinged with irritation.

Razaq shrugged and tore off a bit of bread.

'Wait until tomorrow's headlines. Everyone will forget this driver. Ali Hassan and his bastard can't escape so easily.'

The next morning's headlines were indeed shocking. But no one was more shocked than DG Mushtaq Gill, who scalded his tongue with his morning tea.

AHMADZAI CASE NEW TWIST: WILLIAM MASIH PAID TO KILL BY GOVERNMENT. NEW ARREST EXPOSES NIA INVOLVEMENT.

ISLAMABAD: Yesterday evening, Mr Jamshed Khan, a resident of Peshawar city, was arrested at Kohsar Market by Capital police after failing in his attempt to forcibly enter into the residence of Mr Yaqub Ali Hassan Shah, also known as Mr Jack King, in Islamabad's elite residential sector E7. Inside sources have confirmed that Mr Jamshed Khan is an employee of the National Intelligence Agency (NIA). It is alleged by sources that he was sent to Islamabad to murder Mr Jack King, youngest son of the adviser to the Prime Minister and wealthy business magnate, Mr Ali Hassan Shah.

This reporter has ascertained crucial information that exposes the government's hand in the murder of prominent lawyer Mr Inayatullah Ahmadzai, on Sunday last at his home in Hayatabad, Peshawar. It is now clear that the dead man found lying next to Mr Ahmadzai was none other than Mr Sher Jan—well known in the city of Peshawar as a police and intelligence informer. The arrest of Mr Khan last night proves that the NIA was in fact party to the scheme to deprive Mr Ahmadzai of his life. The arrested man has made a full confession of his devious scheme to implicate Mr Jack King, known to be the temporary employer of Mr William Masih, lately accused murderer of Mr Ahmadzai, in the murder of the same. It now appears that high powers in the establishment have conspired to bring the hard-won reputation of one of Pakistan's most prominent families into disrepute.

Burning questions cry out for answers. What is the interest of NIA in killing Mr Ahmadzai? Why did Mr Ali Hassan Shah only return to this country from a foreign visit on the day of the murder? What is the evidence of the role of Mr Shah's son, Mr Jack King, in the murder of Ahmadzai? Why is NIA trying to rub out the son of the influential adviser to the Prime Minister? Who is duped and who is the duper? Once again it appears we, the people of Pakistan, are treated like fools by our so-called 'leaders' and prominent citizens.

'Burning questions!' Gill threw the paper on the table. 'Such as how much was paid to the editor to remove my announcement from the front page? Hell with you, Jack King.'

24

He walked into Jack's room unannounced just like he used to all those years ago, when Jack was Little Yaqub. Jack instinctively jumped to his feet and felt his limbs shrinking. An uncomfortable heat flashed up from his groin to the nape of his neck. His fingers twitched.

For a few days things had been looking up. The newspapers, led by the *Capital Crescent*, had convinced most people that Ahmadzai had been murdered by either a vengeful William Masih, or the government. Most likely both parties had colluded in the 'dastardly deed'.

But after some initial silence, under American pressure, the Prime Minister had started to put some distance between himself and his Special Adviser. Ali Hassan Shah was feeling the heat. His businesses were suffering and the banks were not transferring his money out of the country. Shahid had told Jack that his father was blaming him.

He had laughed it off then but now Jack's knees sagged. He reached out to steady himself against the bedside table. Everything good that had happened in the past week evaporated instantly.

Father and son had not seen each other in twenty-five years. He hadn't changed, the old man. His restless, cold eyes darted here and there, surveying the scene for weakness and opportunity. His belly was as big as ever—the essential evidence of his success and status. A few strands of grey had escaped the jet-black dye he used to colour his hair. He was wearing an ill-fitting suit made of unfashionable brown cloth, and a white shirt with one button missing. He looked like a bull trussed up at a mela.

Ali Hassan lifted both his hands and adjusted his trousers. Little Yaqub instinctively took a step back.

Ali Hassan spoke in Urdu; he'd never been confident of his English. He knew Jack might have to struggle to follow but language was a weapon he enjoyed wielding. 'Is it not enough to live in filth in that country? Must you spread it here as well?'

Little Yaqub said nothing, he was watching the man's hands, readying himself for the belt that would come loose any second.

'We agreed you would never again cause me shame. Did we not agree or am I a liar?' He moved towards Little Yaqub who stepped further back. 'But here you are again…I cannot be free of your devilishness. Even in my old age you insist on destroying everything I have created.'

He slowly stalked his son around the room. Little Yaqub had one arm behind him, feeling for any furniture or the wall, too afraid to take his eyes off the old devil. 'Fifty years of sweat and effort nearly destroyed by this little mosquito spawn. Constantly biting and sucking my blood.' Lunging forward, he managed to grab Little Yaqub by the neck. 'Mosquitoes are for squashing, and God knows I would squash you in this very place at this very moment, but the eyes of the country are upon me. Imagine the headlines then, you little cunt! "Prime Minister's Adviser murders Criminal Son,"' he puffed, holding Little Yaqub by the throat. His breath was warm and sharp with Scotch. 'I will squash you. Don't doubt it. That is the only solution for a demon like you.'

Little Yaqub was pressed to the wall like a bug pinned to a schoolboy's beetle collection.

'Your country is over there, in America. Why have you

come here after all this time to infect me with your poison? You will leave Pakistan immediately, do you understand? You will break all contact with every member of this family here and in America.'

'My passport is gone. They impounded it,' Little Yaqub's voice squeaked; the old man's grip was tight.

'I'm taking care of that snake Gill and when I do, you will leave. As long as you are in this country, I will never rest.'

Little Yaqub pulled himself free and rubbed his neck. He heard himself shouting at the old man: 'Bastard! Donkey's cunt! You selfish devil! You have never cared for anyone. You only ever loved money. And power.' He imagined himself pushing his father to the ground and kicking him, his bare feet sinking deep into the old man's soft gut.

But he said nothing, alert and anxious for the next move.

The old man took another step towards his son and gave him a push that sent him crashing against the wall. 'You are dead to me.' Spittle, pink with supari, bubbled on Ali Hassan's lips. 'I am undoing the damage you have done in the past month.' Little Yaqub swiped the old man's hand away. 'You think it is such a simple thing to destroy me. You cannot destroy your family. Gill is a puppet to me. I control the puppet-master; Gill will pay for this nonsense. He's been waiting for years to destroy me and I am not surprised that he has used you—my devil's spawn—to make his move.'

Little Yaqub swallowed painfully. His insides frazzled with fear, hatred and self-pity. Somewhere between his groin and his gut he found some words and spat them out: 'Why should I give a rat's ass for this family?' he said in English. Then switching over to Urdu, 'Nanima and Uncle Jalal were the only ones who cared. What did I matter as long as your stacks of money grew taller? Except as a drum to be beaten when you did your victory dance?'

'I punished your misbehaviour in the proportion you deserved.'

'Because I didn't think your thoughts? I had dreams different from yours.'

'Dreams and schemes to dishonour this family and bring my works to nothing.'

'Working a corrupt system to make a fortune! Shit on your hard work.'

Ali Hassan slapped Yaqub but the boy showed no feeling. 'They say you have tried to defraud Nanima, your mother's own mother. And Ahmadzai.' He glowered at his son. 'To buy heroin? Thank God your mother did not survive to see this day.... And accusing others of corruption...what hypocrisy! My money bought proper businesses—hotels, cinemas, factories. Did I ever distribute narcotics or anything illegal?'

'You're lucky hatred isn't against the law. And violence.'

'Shut your mouth, kaminey!' He stepped away, struggling out of his suit coat. 'I used my mind to build my family, not destroy it.'

'You didn't even come to your wife's deathbed! I hate you and your daughters, too. Your brothers are piss afraid of you. Did you know that? Congratulations. It's a lovely family!'

'Success has a price.' The father widened his legs. 'But from the moment you cursed me with your birth you have been nothing but a failure. Becoming a big criminal is not a success. Did you know that? Are you proud of sitting in jail with those...nigger apes?'

'Fuckin' watch your fuckin' mouth.' Jack was no longer Little Yaqub. 'People you call monkeys got more heart than you ever will.' Jack shoved the old man and sent him tumbling backwards onto the bed. The door to the room was still open. The house was silent. Jack slid down the wall, his knees against his chest. He watched the old man wheeze and stare at the floor. There was something sad about his father, but only in a pitiful and revolting way. He had never felt any sympathy for him.

'From the day I was born you've hated me,' Jack couldn't help his eyes becoming warm and wet. 'What did I do?'

Without looking up, Ali Hassan replied, 'There is no end to your crimes. Your antics at Hallbourne made me a donkey in front of society and shamed the entire family. Now you've managed to label me a criminal. Do you wish me to join you in jail?' He could no longer control himself and stood up. 'The destiny of criminals is punishment. Don't complain to me about your misdeeds.' He punctuated the statement with a slimy gob of spit which hit Jack below his right eye.

Jack bit his lip and sobbed. 'I would have done anything for you. Why did you beat me then?'

The old man stared down at his son with an expression as cold as the full moon. Jack looked up, wiping the spit from his face. 'Piss on this family. I've had more love from murderers than from you.'

'You could have had all that is mine...but it's too late.' Ali Hassan was picking up his jacket.

'What would you leave me? Instead of sharing your money you've handed out violence to all of us. What lesson did you learn on that train?'

Ali Hassan hesitated.

'I hated you for disowning me but no more,' Jack continued. 'Whatever I have is mine. I made it without you. You treated me like a dog, you starved me of even a morsel of affection.'

But the old man wasn't listening. He slipped on his ugly brown jacket. Just like his entrance, his exit came without warning.

Jack kicked the door shut and shrieked as loud as he could, sliding face down on the floor. His body shook uncontrollably as he bellowed in anguish. For several long minutes, Nanima and the servants ceased their activities and waited for the rant to subside. Only when he had exhausted himself and lay panting like a wounded beast, did Nanima lift herself off her prayer mat and enter his room. She found him curled up in a corner with his face to the wall. Lifting the shawl from her shoulders she covered her grandson and wiped his brow with her dupatta.

'You are too tough, beta,' she whispered and as she closed the door.

She is with you, Yaqub. She loves you.

25

Afroz looked stunning in a mustard silk shalwar-qameez with gold filigree trim, and amber drop earrings. A deep blue ribbon held her hair back.

Jack hadn't seen her for ten days; his arms opened without thinking when a servant showed her into Jack's room. They hugged for a long while, and he kissed her forehead. She stifled her tears and whispered, 'It's been hell, Jack.'

Since she had left, they'd talked once on the telephone. She had been too upset with the funeral preparations and being back in the house where her uncle was murdered; she hadn't said much. Under the circumstances Jack didn't have much to say either. His virtual house arrest, Andy's disappearance, William's arrest, the back and forth headlines, Khan Sahib's arrest, and the old man's visit—there hadn't been a lot of love to feel.

But Afroz was ready to talk now, she had to talk. She described the funeral and how terrible it had been to have to bury her uncle when her auntie wasn't even able to return from England. Jack listened. He wanted her to talk all day and never stop because he knew when she finally did, it would be his turn. Afroz leaned towards him for reassurance; Jack hugged her, stroking her hair.

He couldn't break the news to her. At this point, if he told her the truth about what went down at Ahmadzai's, she'd be devastated. *And you're just a big pussy, daddy-o.*

'He was always special to me, Jack. He gave me a home

after my parents died. He treated me as his own child. He was my rock once Daddy was gone.'

What about Farah? Mr Niceguy Ahmadzai had his little secrets, Rosie. He was a philanderer, a hypocrite, just like the rest of them. Pushing minorities around to make a name for himself.

His silent accusations seemed to rise up of their own accord.

'He was generous, compassionate and honest. Though he had been offered all sorts of posts by several governments he had always refused, because he felt he could do more for the country as a lawyer. And even the blasphemy case, he withdrew when it became obvious what the real agenda was. He had so much integrity Jack. That's what is so sad, because this country has so few people like that left. It's not just me and Ayaz and Auntie, but the whole country has lost a rock.'

'He was a big lawyer,' Jack said. He could sense his mean side waking up. 'In my experience the only thing lawyers are good for are lying to get your ass out of jail.'

'Not Uncle Inayatullah.'

'He must have had a few shady deals going on. No one is as good as you make him sound.'

Rose pushed herself away from Jack. 'Why are you saying this?'

Jack reached his hand out and rubbed her cheek. 'I'm sorry, Rosie. It's just so much is being said about everyone these days. They say William is an Indian spy. You believe that? And the government was involved in killing your uncle. The papers implying he was a shady character. You know they even accused me of being involved. In the beginning before they arrested William, before they caught that old spy who was trying to kill me.'

'I heard about that. Why you, Jack?'

'Fuck if I know.' He shrugged but he couldn't look at her. His hands were fidgety. He pulled a bottle of wine out from under his bed. Bunty had come through with a case of Blue Nun. Jack had been working his way through it ever since the old man had shown up. He found an extra glass, rinsed it out in the bathroom and held it up to Afroz. She refused.

'You look tired.' His eyes were bloodshot and he hadn't shaved for a couple of days. His breath was starting to smell rancid. 'It's awfully dark in here, don't you think?' She was off the bed, pulling open the curtains. 'Jack, are you okay?'

'Just the hullabaloo, you know. My old man showed up the other day.' He paused then snapped, 'Prick.'

'What happened?'

'Same old shit. Told me I was a mosquito and he was going to squash me. He thinks I'm writing the headlines and accusing him of being a murderer. That's all Gill's doing, not me!' His voice shook angrily.

'I'm sorry Jack.' She patted the bed beside her and told him to come sit down. 'At least you two met again.'

'What good did it do? He doesn't listen and he talks with his fists. He's an asshole. He told me to leave and never come back to this country.' Jack turned towards her but didn't sit down. 'Thinks that's punishment!'

There was a silence as he swayed slightly from the drink and his agitation.

'You're not leaving are you? Not now?' Afroz didn't try to hide her disappointment.

'Damn tootin', Rosie. Came back to take care of business and check out what happens. I'm accused of killing people, and all...all this.' The wine slopped over the edge of his glass. 'The old man keeps fucking wit me. Even Nanima won't support me; says she can't be talking 'bout money for forty days after Ahm—' he hesitated, 'your uncle's...what happened.' He gave her a quick look. 'Why the hell should I stay? Tell me, Rose. Thought there might be something here, you know like you said, but no more. That's a wasted idea.' He took a big gulp. 'I'm outta here just as soon as I can be.'

'Do you really have to?'

'Old man says so. He been sending me out of his life for years. First to my room, then to boarding schools. Now to America. Again. Not that I want to stay. Nothing in this shithole of a country for me.'

Afroz moved towards where he had slumped into a chair. She gently massaged his neck and shoulders.

'What about us?'

'Why don't you come with me? Never understand why you love this country. Must be a temporary thing...your childhood and memories. I understand the shock you experienced wit the accident in England and all, but look at you, girl. You're no Pakistani kudi. You're a babe. A sophisticated lady. You belong over there, where they appreciate fine things and people like you. Here there ain't nothing but cheats and animals.'

Sunlight streamed into the room for a few minutes then disappeared. She wished he would hold her and longed for the day when they would make love again. The thought of him disappearing as well brought her to tears.

'Whaddaya say, Rosie? Come back to Chicago wit me.'

'I can't. Especially now.'

But maybe, she thought, one day you'll come back. Maybe one day you'll stop ranting against the world and let yourself be loved. Maybe.

She sat on his lap and touched her face to his. They hugged each other quietly, taking in each other's smell.

'Did you know William was going to kill him?'

Jack didn't want to talk to her about this yet. Framing William had been essential, a survival move. But the *Capital Crescent*'s latest articles, all lies about the angry avenging Christian murderer, were becoming too heavy to bear. Jack had promised himself, the next time Shahid came around, to tell him to lay off the William angle.

'No way. Willie told me that he thought your uncle was a bad man because of that case.' He made a sudden move and knocked an empty wine glass on to the floor.

'Take it easy, Jack.' Afroz grabbed his wrist. 'Do you have to drink so much? I like you better when you're not like this.'

'It's not that much, Rosie,' he snapped. He pulled away from her, put a cigarette to his lips and inhaled. 'Just you know... the old man. Freaked me out a bit.'

'Well, they say he has confessed,' she said. 'At least that's something, isn't it? It makes me feel better that the man who killed Uncle Inayatullah is in jail having confessed, awaiting punishment. I always imagined myself to be a gentle person, but at the moment I've got very bitter feelings. I want the man who killed my uncle to die himself.'

He wanted to steer away from this particular conversation, shooting a quick, worried look at Rosie. 'So, you're gonna stay here?'

'Yes. I need a place. Maybe, because there is no one left any more that I'm close to, Pakistan seems like my only surviving relative. If I went back to England I'd be all alone. I am not as good at that as you are.'

This was something he'd never understand, this idea of Rosie's. But he envied the fact that she knew she was home. He put his drink down and in a barely audible voice said, 'Prison or the street, two places seem to be the only home I know.'

Afroz looked at his bloodshot eyes, the bald head beaded with sweat and his bare feet, and wondered why she wanted to make a place with him. He was nothing like the man she imagined she would end up with. He was a wolf cub, playful but dangerous at the same time. But he made her heart beat faster. With so much death around her Jack's wild energy kept her connected to life.

After making love that first rainy night, Jack had broken

down and told her that he was a fallen man. Afroz knew then that she loved him. When he had fallen asleep next to her she had thought of her father in their row house in Parsonage Lane, outside Oxford. She knew that he felt he was a failure. He had been a big shot in Pakistan and now he was a shopkeeper, a trader selling newspapers and sandwiches and sweets; he had fallen so far. He couldn't see a way up, she heard him say once to Mummy, when they hadn't known she was listening. Afroz had wanted to tell her father that it didn't matter, that she loved him and that she wanted to help him. But she'd never done it. When he was killed her failure to help him made the loss all the more painful.

Now that Uncle Inayatullah was gone, her wounded heart was feeling more broken than ever. If Jack would just allow himself, she knew they could build something together. If he would let his guard down once and for all, she was certain their hearts could heal. Jack might find his mother again, and her father could, at last, feel her love.

26

'Try to appreciate the fact that Ali Hassan and Shah Enterprises Ltd are finished,' Mushtaq was saying. 'Within six months we'll put so much fire to Bangash's feet, he'll hand over his daughter with the franchise just for good measure.' Mushtaq Gill was trying to make his older brother Razaq feel better about the announcement by Jaguar Cars that its Pakistani distribution rights had been awarded to Bangash Motors, a small outfit based in Lahore that no one had ever heard of.

Razaq grunted, seeking consolation from a greasy kebab with bits of onion and green chilli poking through its burned skin. 'Have you talked with Ali Hassan?' he asked as he licked the salty grease from his fingers.

'He has called three times to make an appointment but I refuse to see him,' Mushtaq smiled. It was a source of pleasure that Ali Hassan Shah was desperate to see him.

'What does he want?' Razaq was scooping up the congealed fat from his plate with a tattered naan.

'To have me drop the case against him. He's told the Prime Minister that if I release his son's passport, he will ensure that he never returns to Pakistan.'

'That's it?'

'Oh, he said he would make a payment to Dhamaka International as well, as a sign of goodwill.'

Razaq looked up anxiously. 'How much?'

'The figure of ten million was mentioned.' Mushtaq clicked his teeth as if that sort of sum was nothing.

'Rupees? Does he think we are donkeys?'

'Dollars.'

'American dollars? Ten million? You agreed, surely!' His voice was trembling. Screw Jaguar. 'With ten million, we can begin developing that land near Simli. Hilton or Sheraton are looking for partners. When do we receive it? The money... come on!'

'I refused.' Mushtaq Gill sat up straight, pulled off his shoes and began massaging his feet.

'Have you gone mad?'

'That is why he called three times today. He is losing half a million per week with his bank accounts and assets frozen. Does he think he can buy us off with less than one quarter's earnings?'

'Why not? Ten million is ten million! American, no less.'

'Shah Enterprises is worth more than a hundred times that amount, dear brother. But what is money?'

'Everything!'

'Luxury hotels, even two or three, will mean nothing if Ali Hassan continues to make laws by whispering into the Prime Minister's ear.'

Mushtaq Gill had already decided that he would release Jack King's passport next week. Let the idiot cause trouble for the FBI in America. His house arrest had been the bait to get Ali Hassan snapping at the hook. And he was squirming like a Kaghan trout on the DG's line. 'Ten million American is a big amount Razu,' Mushtaq reassured his brother that he had not taken leave of his senses. 'Ali Hassan will deliver to us more, much more than ten million. Something of far greater value.'

'What?' Razaq pouted, picking his teeth with the fingernail of his pinkie.

Afroz Gul! Mushtaq Gill smiled as he thought of her full, lipsticked lips. How soft they would feel when he kissed them. And the perfume she wore! As beautiful as an entire bush of jasmine. He would insist she wear it all over her body! 'I have arranged to meet Ali Hassan tomorrow. I will demand twenty-five million be paid into Dhamaka's Bahrain account. If he refuses, I will order his arrest. There is no shortage of crimes to Ali Hassan's rise to power.'

'And Jack King?'

'I will order his deportation within forty-eight hours. But only on one condition will I release his passport.'

Razaq mouthed, 'Afroz.'

'Mine, for one week. He'll never refuse.'

'She is not Ali Hassan's daughter that he can make her stay with you.'

'No, but you see dear brother, Jack King is friendly with Afroz. What she sees in him is beyond me, but it's true. All interests are inter-linked, Razu. Ali Hassan wants his accounts unfrozen. He also wants his son out of the country. Ms Gul loves Mr King and will not want to see him enter jail. I control all the buttons. Ali Hassan knows this. He will find a way to fulfill my demand.' The Director General had crossed his legs and was rubbing the ball of his foot. He clicked his teeth in glee.

'But what if he refuses, Mushi?' Razaq wanted to make sure that twenty-five million didn't disappear like Jaguar and the ten million. 'Then what will you do? No randi is worth such a risk.'

'The Prime Minister will never listen to him until all charges have been dropped. And Jack King will want to avoid prison. Have you seen Adiala jail from the inside? Even after remodelling it would be impossible for a soft rabbit like him to survive in there for more than three months, before going mad or being murdered.' He stopped massaging his feet, wondering what Afroz's hair would feel like falling over his tired, scheming soles.

'I think you're right. Afroz Gul is but a randi and they are not going to endanger everything for a whore.'

Ali Hassan Shah sent a maroon BMW to Nanima's with instructions for Jack to come immediately to his office in the new Zardari industrial development zone, on the shores of Rawal Lake. Jack told the driver to take a flying leap, but changed his attitude when he saw the two giants waiting on the front veranda. Wearing white waistcoats, green shalwar-qameez, leather sandals and shoulder holsters, they pushed their way into the living room, grabbed Jack's arms and carried him out like a lightweight package.

'What do you want?' Jack snapped as soon as he was delivered to his father in his well-lit, spacious office on the top floor of a new glassy tower. On the drive over he had decided that he was not going to cringe any more. He threw himself into a chair in front of his father's huge desk. A few Persian silk carpets covered the floor but everything else was as Jack expected—tacky and cheap. A lurid colour photograph of the Victoria Falls hung on the wall next to a black and silver engraving of some blessing from the Koran. The most awful green and grey curtains. Even the desk was of cheap laminated wood and kitschy onyx objects, shaped like elephants, or camels crowded its top.

'I have made arrangements for you to return to Chicago day after tomorrow.'

'Told you, Gill has my passport.' Jack stared straight into his father's eyes. For a brief moment, Jack relished the idea of being stuck in Pakistan. The old man seemed nervous. Like he needed Jack for once. Jack could see beads of sweat forming on his upper lip.

'It will be returned at the airport. All charges will be dropped but you will be declared PNG. Persona non grata. Never to return to Pakistan. Understand?'

'Gill wanted to fry my balls and eat them for breakfast last week. Now he wants to see me go, just like that? Don't think so. What's up?'

'Police are the biggest criminals,' Ali Hassan was fidgeting with one of the onyx ele-camels. 'How can I say why he has changed his mind? You will be needing some money. You will have enough, but this is the last time you can expect anything from this family. Get prepared to leave.'

His father's offer—five hundred thousand in US dollars; hundred thousand in cash, the rest by wire transfer when he got back to Chicago—was completely unexpected. But with the agility of an experienced opportunist, Jack scooped it up without blinking. Now Nanima wouldn't have to find out what he'd been up to.

His father, sunk way down in a black leather armchair, didn't know what to do with his hands. They went behind his head for a second, then he folded them on the desk in front of him. He contemplated his son for a second, then grunted. 'There is one thing. Who is Afroz Gul?' He was fidgeting with the stone creatures again.

Jack sat up straight. 'Who wants to know?'

'She is sexy?' Ali Hassan spoke like a man who had no curiosity or interest in beauty or the feminine. He was assessing a product by its most obvious quality: This kerosene is pure? She is sexy?

'None of your damn business.'

'I don't care. Not in the least. Not in her sex. Not in her anything. A hole is a hole.'

Jack shot up from his chair, 'Fry in hell, old man.'

'You are friendly with her, I understand.' Ali Hassan was tracing a fat finger over his desk in an idle search for dust. 'Gill is jealous. He insists that your friend, Afroz, give him pleasure. It is the condition of you receiving your passport.'

'He can keep my passport.' The thought of the old letch putting his hands on Rosie turned his stomach.

'You cannot leave without it.'

'How 'bout a Pakistani one? Use your influence and get me one.'

'The days of my influence are severely diminished, thanks to our mutual friend, Gill sahib.' Ali Hassan leaned forward on the desk. 'Temporarily, of course.'

'The embassy will give me a new one. I'll tell 'em someone stole it, that's the truth, too.'

'Gill is my enemy but he's not a fool like you. Do you think he has not kept the Americans informed of your activities? Your government is always eager to make examples of criminals such as you. It will confirm their view that we Muslims are up to no good.'

Jack sank back into his chair, the weight of defeat settling on his shoulders.

'For one week, only.' Ali Hassan chuckled at his son's entrapment. 'Done?'

The very idea made Jack's skin crawl. But it was the only way to get out of this piss hole.

Ali Hassan, the born businessman, interpreted his son's silence as a ploy to drive a hard bargain. 'Seven lakhs. But you deliver the girl to Gill tomorrow. You leave the country the next day. Your money will be in Chicago within one week. Agree?'

For once, the numbers meant nothing to Jack. Someone was whispering in his head that he could make a killing here, but the stack of bills seemed less crisp and attractive when his father was desperate to get rid of him. 'Why not a million?' he mumbled.

The old man looked at his watch as if the final number would be found there. He sighed. Everyone was demanding millions these days. This morning Gill demanded twenty-five. The damage this affair had done to Shah Enterprises could only be calculated in the millions. And here, this shameful excuse of a son was making his grab as well. 'It will take some time. Within fifteen days I can arrange it but you guarantee to deliver the girl?'

The old man's sudden acquiescence hit Jack like a baseball in the nuts. He hadn't really expected a million dollars, just like that, on a friggin' plate. Something inside snapped him out of his stupor—a hundred thou was good, half a mill excellent. But a million! Now that was Big Time. *No need to get my hands dirty with this heroin shit.* Let the Zam Zam Trust make the pilgrimage happen for a few thousand poor folks. A week, after all, was only seven days. Nothing in the span of a lifetime. It would go by just like that, and she'd be ready to get the hell out of Pakistan by then, anyway. They'd start again in Chi-town. He'd go straight. With the Queen of Flowers by his side he'd be able to do it.

Jack rubbed his chin, looked up and gave a quick nod.

'Good boy!'

Later in the day, back at Nanima's, Jack lay in his bedroom. It was Thursday afternoon, not even 4:30 yet and he was already toasted. The day's events were swimming around in his head.

On Saturday evening, he was to catch the 9 p.m. flight to Karachi and by 2 a.m. he'd be on the flight to Chicago. Rose had left a message for him to call her about dinner but he hadn't yet. He'd need to be pretty tanked before he saw her and laid out the scenario.

It had seemed like a good idea at the time. A million big ones just for agreeing to get the hell out of... hell! Now, a few hours down the line, it seemed less brilliant.

For an hour or so his spirits had lifted dramatically, as he etched out a counter-scheme to Gill's. Explain the whole mess to Rosie—not the murder, not yet—book her a flight out of here, leave Gill hanging in the breeze, and meet the Queen of Flowers in London. But the euphoria soon evaporated as he remembered the million dollars would arrive in Chicago only after Gill's week of love with Afroz.

The idea of refusing the money still floated around in his mind but it was sinking fast. If he refused now, Gill would push through the temporarily forgotten charge of Ahmadzai's murder. The story was starting to die in the press already but it would take nothing for Gill to quietly arrest Jack and send him off to some festering provincial jail. The hairs on Jack's neck stood up at the prospect. He ripped the tab off the beer can and chugged deeply.

Afroz, the Queen of Flowers, was the love of his life. *But we're talking a cool million here. Or my ass disappearing into hell.* With a million, I going straight will be piece of cake, he thought. Party for six months, get it out of the system and then buy that superette up in Minnesota. Settle down. Sort of.

He got up to take a leak. It was 6 p.m. He'd call Rosie now. As he made his way to the toilet he stopped and gazed into the mirror. It was hard to face his own reflection.

The person staring back at him was scared and fading fast. His eyes were red and droopy; his cheeks were burning. *How many times you tried this before? Going straight is not your thing.*

A million bucks, dipshit! You gonna turn your back and walk away from that shit?

'Get real', he said out loud to his reflection.

...She'll probably like it.... You know she was having a good time with him when I came on the scene—talking and carrying on at that party. I'll never see her again anyhow so won't bother me.'

Jack could see his nasty face looking back. It was pathetic. He leaned up close, as if the reflection was saying something he couldn't quite hear. 'I can't, man,' Jack was telling it. 'I can't.'

Then he grabbed the bottle of Blue Nun and flung it into the mirror, splintering the ugly face into a million sparkly bits.

Why didn't she pick up? *Come on Rosie, pick up the damn phone.* He thought he'd give it twenty more seconds, but he wanted her to answer now because later might be too late.

'Hello?' The voice sounded anxious.

'Afroz? Where you been? It's me, Yaqub?'

'Yaqub?'

'Yeah, Yaqub. You know...me.'

'Jack? What's up? I thought you didn't get my message.'

'Nothing's up. Are you around tonight? Was thinking of coming by.'

'Sure, of course, Jac—I mean Yaqub. I think there's some gin and a little bit of cognac Ayaz left me, but I'm not really in the drinking mood. You can have it.'

'Whatever. Be there in fifteen. Don't go anywhere.'

They sat on the cushions on the floor in the living room. Jack hadn't touched his drink. He was too nervous about what he had to say and all the thoughts bumping into each other. They were sharing a cigarette and she was cuddling up to him.

They kissed lightly before Jack said, 'Rosie, we gotta talk. Some things got to be said.'

'Are you okay?' She grabbed his shaking hand. 'Why are you calling yourself Yaqub? What happened to Jack?' Her smile was mischievous but reassuring. His eyes were hollow.

'I like it better than Jack,' she purred.

'Rosie, what I'm gonna say is gonna be weird for you to hear. I know you gonna be upset but just let me say what I got to say and then say whatever you like, okay?'

'What is it?' she whispered. She wanted him to hurry up so they could make love.

'You know this stuff that's been happening lately,' Jack made sure he looked her in the eyes, 'your uncle and the police on my case and all.' She nodded. He noticed her lips quiver. 'Well, I been involved in it.'

'I know, you already told me that Gill accused you of those murders. Bastard!'

'That's right. And I told you I had nothing to do with them, right?' She nodded again. 'Well,' Jack pulled deeply on his cigarette, 'it's not true.'

'I know, Yaqub. I believe you. Gill is a bastard. Everyone hates him. He'd accuse his own mother to go one rung up the ladder.'

'I'm talking about your uncle. Him dying. It's not true that I wasn't involved. I didn't kill that Sher Jan dude, he just popped in and fucked it all up. If he hadn't been there none of this would have happened but he did.'

Afroz was stunned. But Jack knew that he'd have to keep going. 'I didn't kill Sher Jan but I shot your uncle by mistake. Just a reaction thing. I thought I was going to save him, because I heard him struggling with Sher Jan and then I heard someone yell and fall to the floor. I thought it was your uncle but it wasn't. But before I could tell, I pulled the trigger and he just collapsed. I didn't mean to, Rosie. Honest, I didn't. I didn't know who he was…that he was you know… like your dad to you. I'm sorry…'

Afroz screamed and ran into the other room, slamming the door shut. When Jack knocked on it tentatively, there was no response, except the faint sound of sobbing.

Jack picked up the phone and dialled a number. It was answered immediately by a gruff-sounding man. In Urdu,

Jack asked to speak to Director General Mushtaq Gill. A few seconds later Gill snapped, 'Ji. Who is speaking?'

'Me. Yaqub Ali Hassan Shah. I am at Nanima's house in E7. You know where it is. I want to confess to the murder of Ahmadzai.'

'Are you mad? Don't play jokes,' Gill shouted.

'This is no joke. I went to Ahmadzai's house to threaten him. To make him give me some money and shot him by mistake. But I killed him. I'll be waiting for you here.'

'What about her? Afroz?'

'She knows. I told her. She needs help, can you send someone to be with her?'

'So you refuse your father's offer? You deprive me of her again?'

'I am waiting, Mr Gill.'

'Don't be a fool, boy!' The Director General was desperate. 'I will jail you and you *will* die. What about your father? He cannot help you. Where is Afroz? Just one wee—'

Jack hung up.

The morning headlines read:

AMERICAN BUSINESSMAN SON OF ALI HASSAN SHAH CONFESSES TO AHMADZAI MURDER.
PRIME MINISTER DENOUNCES CLOSEST ADVISER.
MURDERER'S TRIAL TO BE GIVEN TOP PRIORITY.

Shahid came to see him in the lock-up on Saturday afternoon, and assured him that he would arrange for a lawyer to visit him in Adiala jail. He was to be kept there in remand until the trial. Shahid said that he couldn't believe it. That everything had turned out this way. But things could be worked out. 'Sure, a couple of years in prison, you'll have to do that, but if we get Raja Jhangvi to defend you, who knows Yaqub, you'll be back in America in no time.'

'I'll never go back, Shahid. What's the old man say?'

'His passport's been impounded, too. Gill is moving in for the kill. But you know your dad—he's a fighter. He'll survive and come out of it richer, somehow.'

'Did he say anything about me?

Shahid shook his head.

On Sunday morning around eleven, Jack was taken out of his cell, with chains on his legs and arms. It was time to go to Adiala. The lawyer Shahid had got hold of—Raja Jhangvi—said not to worry. 'I was the one who had brought down Bhutto single-handedly, so saving you will be no problem.' He laughed like an earthquake. Jack looked at the man's polyester suit and long sideburns and said, 'Whatever.' He didn't care. He just wanted to get to Adiala and begin getting to know the place.

With his legs and wrists bound together like a tin man, Jack was told to sit and wait for the cops to round up a vehicle.

He stared at his bare feet in chains, feeling their weight. Was he going to be locked up for the rest of his life? If Raja Jhangvi could at least get him out of these chains, that would be a kind of victory in itself.

'Jack.' Afroz was standing near the door of the thana. A cop made a coarse gesture with his hand and rudely asked what she wanted. She ignored him, and came and sat next to Jack.

'Afroz!' Jack was surprised. The Queen of Flowers was the last person he had expected.

'I wanted to see you before I leave, Jack.' She squeezed her hands together. He could tell she had been crying.

'Going back home, huh?'

'A friend in Birmingham has said I can stay as long as

I want. I leave tomorrow. Shahid told me you were being transferred to Adiala today, so I wanted to see you before that.'

'Just in time, Rosie. Any minute now, I'm a goner.' He smiled weakly.

She stared at him and pushed away a tear. 'Jack, I'll never be able to forgive you for what you did. I know I won't. I've tried to tell myself to pick up the pieces and move on, but I'm too weak. I can't.'

He wished he could hold her.

'But even though I can't forgive you, I know I'll always love you. That's what makes it so hard, Jack. I can't forget that.' She looked at him. 'Goodbye, Jack King.' Afroz leaned over to peck his cheek then darted outside into the cloudy day.

The monsoon was nearly over but it could still be chilly on overcast days like this. The pick-up had arrived and the cops were coming to get him. The floor was icy and his bare feet had gone completely numb. *Got to get me some socks*. He'd ask the lawyer to arrange it first thing.

Acknowledgements

I would like to thank Naresh Fernandes who gave me the opportunity to write for *Scroll.in* and to Kanishka Gupta who liked what he read and through whose efforts this book has seen the light of day. A big thanks to Kartikeya Jain from Speaking Tiger for his insight, persistence and calmness throughout the editing process. To those who read the manuscript and liked it, and even those who didn't, thanks for bothering. Honest criticism and heartfelt encouragement is what every writer craves and needs.

ALSO FROM SPEAKING TIGER

THE INVISIBLE MAN FROM SALEM

Christoffer Carlsson

'This unique Nordic thriller of enthralling suspense takes a sickening dive into the murky corners of Stockholm and its suburbs ... a new and inspiring example.' —*Le Figaro Magazine*

'An unnerving, unsettling, and intelligent crime novel.' —*Dagens Nyheter*

'Carlsson's *The Invisible Man from Salem* is something different in the current wave of Nordic crime: ambitious, idiosyncratic and dripping with noir atmosphere. [...] Leo Junker is a memorable creation.' —Barry Forshaw, author of *The Rough Guide to Crime Fiction*

In the final days of summer, a young woman is shot dead in her apartment. Three floors above, the blue lights of the police cars awaken disgraced ex-officer Leo Junker. Though suspended from the force, he can't stay away for long. Bluffing his way onto the crime scene, he examines the dead woman and sees that she is clasping a cheap necklace—a necklace he instantly recognizes.

As Leo sets out on a rogue investigation to catch the killer, a series of frightening connections emerge, linking the murder to his own troubled youth in Salem—a suburb of Stockholm where social and racial tensions run high—and forcing him to confront a long ago incident that changed his life forever.

Now, in backstreets, shadowed alleyways, and decaying suburbs ruled by Stockholm's criminal underground, the search for the young woman's killer—and the truth about Leo's past—begins.

ALSO FROM SPEAKING TIGER

KINGPIN: MADE IN SINGAPORE, DESTROYED IN DUBAI

Kavita Daswani

'[Kavita Daswani's] culture-clash dilemmas ring heartbreakingly true.' —*Entertainment Weekly*

Anil Raichand was once the kind of man you might see in the pages of your favourite society magazine—the handsome high-flying industrialist with the rich father, the Ferrari, the clubs, the cigars and the secret peccadilloes. At twenty-six he was society's most sought-after bachelor. Educated, charismatic and heir to his father's wealth, Anil decided he needed two things: to become a business tycoon in his own right by any means, and the perfect wife to help him get there. But, nearly fifty, Anil looks back at a devastated business empire, a pulverized marriage, an estranged daughter and embittered parents. He pushed himself to amass fabulous wealth but found everything crumbling around him. And now he is compelled to confront the cost of his ambition even as he desperately holds on to the memory of a woman he once turned his back on.

Unfolding over four decades—from Anil's boyhood in Singapore, his foray into the Bombay marriage market, falling in love with the wrong woman in Hong Kong, to his meteoric rise and fall in Dubai—Kingpin is a dazzling, high-octane story that will entertain and enlighten you.